Seasons of Love: Book 4

Christmas by Candlelight

A Cozy Collection of Christmas Themed Romances

By

* *

* * *

* * * *

LORI LEGER
KIM HORNSBY
TRISH F. LEGER
KAREN SUE BURNS
CARMINE VALENTINE

*

Seasons of Love: Book 4
Christmas by Candlelight
Compiled and arranged by:

 CAJUNFLAIR
PUBLISHING

ISBN-10:1940305047
ISBN-13:978-1-940305-04-2

ACKNOWLEDGMENTS

Cover art and interior formatting by
Lori Leger/Cajunflair Publishing
http://www.CajunflairPublishing.com

Edited by Karen Sue Burns and Lori Leger

Special thanks go out to Kim Hornsby, Trish F. Leger,
Karen Sue Burns and Carmine Valentine—
the lovely ladies who've embarked, once again, on this
journey with me. I appreciate your talents as writers, and I
value your friendships . . . each and every one of you.
Lori

TABLE OF CONTENTS

Lori Leger	BABY BLUES CHRISTMAS	1
Kim Hornsby	CHRISTMAS IN WHISTLER	77
Trish F. Leger	GIFT FROM THE HEART	165
Karen Sue Burns	A HEART AWAKENS	221
Carmine Valentine	ONE STEP OVER THE MISTLETOE LINE	297

Baby Blues Christmas

By Lori Leger

Chapter 1

November 1ˢᵗ

Cathryn Ferguson waited a full ten minutes before checking the EPT test stick. Her eyes squeezed tightly shut, she pushed open the door while whispering a silent prayer.

"Only positive thoughts," she murmured.

Cat opened her eyes, stared at the strip on the countertop, and released her breath with a hiss and a curse. he picked up the test strip to stare at the negative symbol before tossing it into the trash. She'd hoped to be pregnant by Christmas, but at this rate, that wouldn't happen.

It may never happen.

She cringed inwardly as Dr. Brown's words came to her after her surgery two weeks after her and Zach's wedding. "With endometriosis as severe as yours, Cathryn, it could take years and another surgery or two to get pregnant. And, there's the possibility that—well—it may never happen."

It was difficult to stay positive with that looming over her head.

A bluish-gray ball of fur wrapped itself around her legs as she walked out. She lifted her cat, a gift from her husband, Zachary, after she'd left Dallas to move back home to Lake Erin, Louisiana in March. The tom touched her face gently with one paw, as though trying to tell her he was there for her. She found it amazing that Chableu always seemed to know when she needed a little extra loving.

"You're my good, sweet, boy aren't you? Yes, you are," she crooned. Chableu rubbed his head under her chin and purred like there was no tomorrow.

She carried him to the open living room of the Acadian style home Zachary had built nearly six years earlier. She'd fallen in love with this place the moment she'd seen it, even as messy as it had been at the time. Cathryn smiled, remembering it as it was then, littered with empty beer bottles, tattered furniture, and everything covered in dog hair. A vast difference from the showcase home the two of them had created together. They'd filled the place with period pieces, memorabilia, and artifacts, such as hand tools and small farming implements from their Cajun ancestors' way of life. They also displayed their own collections of books and artwork.

As she sat with Chableu in one arm and her notebook computer in the other, she heard her husband's truck roll onto the drive.

She scooted from the sofa to meet him at the kitchen door. "What are you doing home?"

"I forgot something. Hey, did you hear that the electronics store got broken into?" He wrapped his arms around her waist and lifted her, giving her a big kiss.

She returned it willingly, taking it a step further by wrapping her legs around his hips. "Nope, I hadn't heard that. Did they steal a lot of stuff?"

"Nope, just did some damage to the building itself. Broke windows, spray painted all over the interior. Mm...damn that feels good."

Cat smiled as she massaged the back of his scalp, hoping to relieve his tension. She craved the touch of this man. Looking back on it, she wondered how she'd managed to miss the fact that she'd always been in love with him. It had taken twelve years being away from him, before she'd realized that the one thing missing in every relationship she'd ever had, was Zachary. No man had ever measured up to him, and no man ever would.

"Can you stay?" She started pulling at the snaps on his long sleeve western shirt.

"I hadn't planned on it. Just came by to pick up the suppliers agreement with the LeMaire's."

"And . . . " She opened his shirt and slipped her hands over his smooth skin, molding them to the shape of his chiseled abs. Zach didn't need a gym membership to stay in shape, not when he worked as hard as he did at their business, the only feed-store in town.

"They're ready to sign it."

"Great, is that for two years?"

"Nah, I gave it to them for one year. I figure they'll be so bowled over by the excellent services we offer, they won't want to leave me at the end of the year."

"Mm, and I can verify that you're the man when it comes to servicing." She nipped at his earlobe. "Can you stay?"

His low growl rumbled in her ear. "When you ask like that, how can I refuse?" He carried her to the master suite and dropped her on the bed they'd waited until their wedding night to christen. Since then it had endured a steady stream of lovemaking episodes, as did the couch, the recliner, the utility room, and even once on the front porch swing.

"Take your boots off, cowboy."

He grinned at her, his blue eyes sparkling with laughter. "Are you sure? I might get better traction with 'em on."

"You don't have a problem with traction, trust me Zach-attack." She helped him pull the boots off and giggled when he got on his knees and kissed her belly.

The shrill ring of the phone cut through the air.

He looked at her. "You want me to get that?"

"I know it's Mom. She's the only one who uses the landline anymore."

"Go ahead and answer it."

She lifted the phone from its cradle, smiling at the name flashing across the screen. "Hey my Mama, how are you this glorious day?"

"It surely is, isn't it? I'm fine, I only wanted to see if you were free for today. I feel like going to my favorite Mexican restaurant and thought I'd treat my two girls."

Cat checked the time. "Yeah, I guess I can make lunch, Mom. Cilantros at what time?" She giggled as Zach unzipped her jeans and started sliding them down her legs. "Stop, you're tickling me!" she hissed at her husband.

"What's that, Cat?" Ellen McDaniel asked.

"Nothing…what time?" She held her finger to her mouth when her husband unhooked the front clasp of her bra.

"How about an early lunch? Say 11:00?"

"Mm," Cat bit back a low growl as he buried his face between her breasts. "I can't make it for 11:00, Mom. 11:30 maybe, but if I'm a little late, start without me."

Zach lifted his head and grinned at his wife. "We're making you another grandbaby, Ms. Ellen!" he called out.

"Zachary! Shh!" Cat clamped a hand over the mouthpiece.

"Oooh! Well, I don't want to interrupt! In that case, we'll make it for noon, and if you don't show up, that's fine, too."

Cathryn laughed at her mother's comment. "See you there, Mom."

Zach took the phone from her and put it on the table. "You're mom's so freaking cool about her daughter having sex."

"She wants several grandbabies, bottom line, and will do anything to get that."

Zach buried his face between her breasts and gave a deep chuckle. "Well, then—let's see what we can do about giving her what she wants."

Cat inhaled the succulent aroma of beef fajitas as they sizzled on the cast iron grill. After a quick search, she slid in beside her mother at the round booth in the corner of the Mexican restaurant.

"Nice of you to join us today."

Kellie's smug comment reached her from the opposite side of the table.

"Don't fuss at your sister, Kellie. She and Zach were trying to make me a new grandbaby."

"Did you use the pregnancy test you bought yesterday?"

"Negative." Cat raised a hand at the devastated look her sister sent in her direction. "It's okay. We'll keep trying." Cat leaned over to lift her niece out of the infant carrier. "Don't you look gorgeous today, Princess Di!" She smiled as Diana squealed with delight at the sight of her. "Did you miss your favorite aunt, Pumpkin?"

"You're her only aunt, she has no choice," Kellie said, sounding a little sour.

Ellen gave her throat a delicate clearing. "For now, anyway."

Both Cathryn and her sister turned their attention to their mother.

Kellie voiced the question first. "What do you mean by that?"

Elaine beamed at her two daughters and placed her elbows on the table, lacing her fingers casually in front of her. "Oh, I don't know. Just making conversation, I guess."

Cat gasped as she caught sight of the diamond flashing on her mother's finger. "Oh. My. God! Doc Barton proposed?"

Ellen McDaniel lowered her hand so they could get a better view of the ring. She beamed at her daughters. "Last night, and isn't it gorgeous?"

"Very nice. Doc has good taste, but then we knew that when he started dating *you*." Cat leaned over to give her mom a hug. "Congratulations, Mom. I'm thrilled for both of you." She watched her mother's smile fade as she turned to her other daughter.

"Kellie? What's wrong, sweetie?"

Tight-lipped, Kellie stared at her mother. "You said *yes*?"

Ellen blinked before answering. "Well, sure I did. Why wouldn't I?"

"Because, you've only been seeing him a few months, that's why."

"I've known Gavin nearly my entire life, Kellie."

Kellie started packing her and the baby's things as though she were leaving. "That doesn't count if you weren't dating him. You always told us to get to know someone first."

"Oh honey, we *know* each other well enough, believe me."

Kellie stopped throwing things in her daughter's diaper bag long enough to aim a horrified look at her mother. "I can't believe you just said that to me. And I can't believe you'd forget about daddy so easily."

"Kellie Joanne, what are you saying? Are you trying to imply that I didn't love your father?"

"Sounds like it to me," Kellie snapped.

Cat stood, went around to the other side of the booth. "Kellie. Have you lost your mind? This has nothing to do with dad." She watched in horror as her sister sent their mother an accusatory glare.

"Well, that's perfectly obvious."

Torn between wanting to follow Kellie outside and stay in the restaurant with her devastated mother, Cat handed Diana to her sister and watched her storm to her car.

"Cat, I had no idea either of you felt this way."

She heard her mother's voice, wracked with pain, and knew she was hurt to the core at Kellie's words. "We don't. At least I don't, and the last time my sister and I discussed this, neither did she." She hugged her mother tightly. "Oh Mom, I'm so sorry. This should have been a wonderful moment for you, full of excited squeals, and smiles, and laughter. And instead it's traumatic and . . . *ruined* for you."

Ellen looked dazed as she turned her engagement ring nervously on her finger. "Maybe I should have spoken to you both first before accepting."

"What? No. Mom, no." Cathryn leaned to whisper harshly into her mother's ear. "We are adults. We have husbands, she has a child of her own. You raised us. There's no need for you to feel guilty about this. I won't let you."

She returned to the booth opposite her mother, suddenly angrier than ever at Kellie. "But we do need to find out what the hell's wrong with *your* daughter." She met her mother's confused look and lifted her chin. "I'm not sure I want to claim her as a sister anymore, not after that childish hissy fit."

Ellen dug in her purse until she pulled out a tissue to dab at her eyes. "Oh, honey, siblings aren't all that different from children of your own. You're pretty much stuck with them for life. It's not like you can divorce them, they're blood."

Cat covered her mother's hand with her own. "Mom, what were y'all talking about before I got here? Did she seem upset by anything?"

Ellen sat still for a while then shook her head. "No, she seemed a little preoccupied, but not exactly upset. But she was fine until you got here." She tapped one pale-peach polished nail on the table. "That's when her mood seemed to change all of a sudden."

Cat watched through the window as her sister's SUV pulled out of the parking lot. "I wonder what the hell is up with her. I'll go talk to her after lunch."

Ellen dabbed at her eyes again and fidgeted with her purse. "I can't eat a thing after this. You go on and order and I'll sit here and visit with you."

"It's no fun eating alone, Mom. I'll tell you what. Let's put this off until I find out what's up with baby sister, okay?

Try not to be too upset about this. She's just in one of her moods." Cat stood suddenly, as a thought came to her. "Oh, my gosh. I think I know what's wrong with her."

"Tell me."

Cathryn laughed and hugged her mom again. "Not until I have a chance to talk to her, but if I'm right, this has nothing to do with you marrying Doc Barton."

Cat knocked several times, and knowing Kellie wouldn't answer, opened the door and walked inside. She found her sister in Diana's beautifully decorated nursery, rocking her baby girl with a fury. She met Kellie's gaze, trying hard not to crack a grin at the steadily flowing trail of tears running down her sister's unusually pale cheeks.

Cathryn held up a finger. "I'll be right back." She backed out of the nursery, turning her back on Kellie's miserable glare at the last instant. After visiting the home's master bath for a restroom break, she re-entered the nursery, carrying a crucial piece of evidence.

She held up the oh-too-familiar plastic stick. "So, when's the due date, Sis?"

Kellie's face crumbled as she hung her head. "It's not supposed to happen this way."

"It's going to be fine, you'll see."

"Two children, no less than three years apart, but no more than five. I had a *plan*, Cat."

"Yeah, well. God didn't agree with your plan, obviously. And who are you to argue with God?" She leaned over to take the sleeping baby from her sister. "Go. Sit. Couch. Now."

Aunt Cat tucked Diana into her crib and patted her bottom until the baby slept soundly.

Tiptoeing out of the nursery, she stopped at the fridge just long enough to grab a bottle of wine her sister had chilling for emergencies—perhaps not one such as this, but an emergency nonetheless.

She met Kellie with half a glass of wine and a smile on her face. "Here, an ounce of wine just this once won't hurt that baby. You need to calm down. Come on, Kel. So, you'll get your two kids a little early. So, it throws your perfectly planned life off kilter for a while. What's the big deal? It's another baby to love."

Kellie's face crumpled. "It's a big deal, Cat. It's a very big deal. The doctor suspects . . . twins."

Cat's mouth dropped open as her sister burst into tears again. She realized that Kellie had probably planned to tell them at lunch. She also knew her sister well enough to know she was carrying her own feelings of guilt over this.

"Don't you dare go feeling bad because I'm not pregnant yet, do you hear me? I am absolutely thrilled for you and Bradley."

Kellie cried even harder.

"Does he know?"

"No. I don't know how to tell him."

"What do you mean you don't know how to tell him— wait—when's the due date, anyway?"

"M-M-May!" she sputtered.

"That's six months from now, and Diana is only four months old. That means that you and Bradley—" She stopped to do some calculating in her head, "—had sex before your six week check-up. No doubt, it was *his* brilliant idea to cheat a little when you weren't even completely healed, but the least he could have done was wear a condom. No way should he be upset about this, sis."

"That's just it, Cat. It wasn't his idea, it was mine. I practically seduced my own husband into having sex with me, and we *did* wear a condom. But the damn thing bro-oke," she blubbered. "Besides, I'm breast-feeding and I've always heard that you can't—"

"Myth! That's only a myth, Kellie. Breast-feeding does not keep you from getting pregnant." She sat on the couch next to her sister and pulled her close for a hug. "This is not the end of the world. You'll have help. Zach and I, and Mom and Doc Barton, we'll all help you. You'll see."

Kellie sniffed and wiped her eyes with the back of her hand. "You'll have to because Bradley's gonna lee-eave m-m-e," she said, hiccupping and crying.

Cathryn couldn't keep from laughing at that point. "No, he won't. Brad will not leave you. I bet he'll be a heck of a lot more excited about having these babies than you are."

"Of course he will. He doesn't have to carry them!"

"Uh-uh…you can't push that on him. You knew this could happen."

"I know. You see? You s-se-see how bitchy I am already? He's gonna l-l-leave meee!" she wailed. "Oh, God, I still had five pounds of first baby weight left to lose, and now . . . I'm gonna be a big, fat pregnant lady again. And, bitchy to boot. What man would want to come home to that?"

"This man would."

Cathryn turned to see Bradley standing at the door, carrying a huge bouquet of gorgeous pink, and pale yellow roses.

"I got three dozen for the three beautiful babies we'll have." He shrugged. "I got yellow for the twins because it's way too early to know the gender yet."

"But how did you . . . who told you?" Kellie said, as tears flowed steadily down her cheeks.

"Doc Barton called me. Your mom was upset about what happened at lunch and he figured it had something to do with this. He knew you said you had to work up the nerve to tell me." He set the roses on the end table beside her and knelt before his wife.

"Babe, how could you think I wouldn't be thrilled about this?" he said, kissing her swollen face.

"Be-c-cause we had a p-p-lan!" she stammered.

"No, sweetie. *You* had a plan. Me? I just wanted you as a wife and a house full of babies." He kissed her gently on the lips. "I'm feeling like the luckiest son of a gun on the face of the earth right now. I love you, sweet girl."

"Oh Brad . . ."

Cat backed out of the room and snuck out through the kitchen door. Although, she suspected she could have cartwheeled out of the room and no one would have noticed. With time on her hands, she headed for her husband's feed store business.

Zach Ferguson loaded a bag of chicken feed and two bags of oats onto the bed of a customer's pick up. He closed the gate and waved the driver off as Cat pulled up in her SUV. As soon as his beautiful wife stepped out of the car, he knew she had news for him. Judging by the smile she tried to pull off, but couldn't quite manage, he figured she was feeling torn about something.

"Hello, gorgeous, it sure is good to see you in the middle of my workday." He opened his arms and she walked into them, snuggling against his chest. He held her tightly, swaying with her in the cool November breeze. He kissed the top of her head, breathing in the scent of her. "What's wrong, babe?"

She gave his waist one last squeeze before lifting her face for a kiss he was only too glad to oblige her with.

"Nothing's really wrong, Zach. I'm just . . . I don't know, I'm happy, but sad at the same time."

He cocked his head. "I thought you were having lunch with Ms. Ellen and Kellie?"

"It kind of got busted up early. Kellie, well . . ." She sighed, covering her eyes. "It's a long story, but if you take me to lunch, I'll tell you. I'm starving."

"Sure I will. Let me tell Gus and then we can go."

Within two minutes, they were buckling up into Cat's vehicle. "You want to go back to Cilantro's?"

"No. Take me to The Regatta for some fried oysters instead." She stared out the window as Zach pulled onto the street. "My appetite is kind of ruined for Cilantro's."

"Spit it out, babe. What happened?"

"Mom called us there to show us her engagement ring from Doc Barton."

"That's great news, isn't it? Hell, you and I were expecting to hear that any day, weren't we?"

"Yes, but Kellie got upset, insinuated that was turning her back on dad or something. It was awful."

"What the hell? Is she insane?"

"Temporarily, it seems. Mom said she was fine until I mentioned something." She faced him, her eyes sad and brimming with tears. "We're not pregnant, yet."

He grabbed her hand, suddenly understanding why she was so upset. "Pee stick was negative, huh?"

She nodded.

"I tell you what, babe. From now on, you don't take anymore pregnancy tests unless I'm there with you. Deal?"

"Deal, but it's not just that, Zach. When I went to Kellie's, I found out why she was so upset. She's pregnant again."

"Ah, that explains."

"For twins."

"Oh, damn."

"Yeah."

"Wonder how Brad's gonna take that."

"He's ecstatic, apparently. My future step-dad called him when he found out how upset Kellie had been. Brad came in with a huge bouquet of flowers for her. They'll have three babies under a year old—"

"Kind of a good thing you're not pregnant right now, then, huh?" He'd rushed to cut off the comment he knew she had brewing—no doubt something negative about herself not being pregnant.

Her eyes widened as she gazed at him. "Why do you say that?"

"They're going to need all the help they can get when those babies get here. We wouldn't be able to help nearly as much if we had a newborn of our own."

"Are you saying we should stop *trying*?"

"No, definitely not. I'm just saying if it doesn't happen anytime soon, maybe that's not such a bad thing."

He pulled into The Regatta parking lot and turned off the ignition. Her next words floored him.

"I thought you wanted me to get pregnant right away."

He gazed into her hurt, furious brown eyes. "I do, Cat. Honestly, I do. What I don't want is for you to take it as a personal failure every damn time that stick shows a negative sign. We're in this together, pregnant or not. And besides, it's far too early in the game to start worrying that it hasn't happened yet. Don't you think?"

"But Kellie and mom both got pregnant as soon as they started trying. And now Kellie's pregnant with twins without even trying."

"I'm sure they did something to make it happen."

"The condom broke."

"Right. It was probably an old one from before they got married."

She huffed an exasperated sigh. "The point is, I've been off the pill forever, and we've been trying nonstop for three months."

He pulled her into his arms. "And it's been a hell of a chore, let me tell you. You're practically a slave driver when it comes to demanding that baby-making sex." She finally produced the grin he'd been trying to elicit.

"I should be pregnant by now, Zach. I want to make a beautiful baby with you."

"We'll make that baby, Cat-tastrophy. I promise, we will . . . or I'll die trying." He kissed her, groaning at the need he felt for his wife every time he laid his eyes on her. "Mm, doesn't sound like such a bad way to die, at that."

She looped her arms around his neck and kissed him back. "Not bad at all."

Chapter 2

Kellie wiped the steady stream of tears from her cheeks. "Three babies in ten months, Bradley. What are we going to do?"

Brad kissed his wife tenderly on the lips. "We're going to love them and we're going to deal with it together. Now come sit here with me and relax for a bit." He settled back against the arm of the couch and cradled her in his arms.

"The thing is we nearly drove each other crazy during the first pregnancy. Me with all my bitchiness and sharp tongue, and you with your internet researched facts on pregnancy." She turned in his arms to stare at him. "Do you have any idea how irritating you are?"

Brad's mouth twisted in a grin. "No, but from the tone of your voice, I'd guess I'm about to find out."

Kellie faced forward again and sighed. "Brad, you have to stop, seriously. You can't spend a day or two surfing the net and researching pregnancy and then tell a pregnant woman how she's feeling. Not without making me want to scratch your eyes right out of that thick skull of yours."

"Don't hold back, babe. Tell me how you *really* feel about it."

"It's true. We all know you're a natural *Mr. Know it All*. I let you get away with it most of the time, but you can't pull that stuff on a seriously hormonal woman and not expect to get some kind of return fire. You are far too intelligent for that."

Brad leaned over to breathe in the scent of his wife, some kind of perfume-scented shampoo that made him want to eat her up. "You think I'm intelligent?"

She cocked her head. "Please don't tell me that's all you got out of that statement."

His deep laughter resonated in the air. "No, I got it. Honest I did. No more researching."

"You can research all you want, just don't tell me you know what it feels like to be pregnant, because you can't possibly know. I mean, I'm pregnant for twins and I have no idea what to expect. Except that I'll probably get huge . . . and miserable." She leaned her head back against his chest. "And Lord, I honestly hope I'm not twice the bitchy, for your sake." She released a long, low sigh. "Poor Bradley." She covered her face suddenly and released a groan. "Poor mom, I have to call her."

"What happened? All Doc said was that you got really upset and left."

By the time Kellie had filled him in, Brad was handing his wife her phone. "Call her, now. Tell her you're thrilled for her, and then tell her about the pregnancy. She'll understand, but the longer you wait to call, the worse she'll feel." He rose from the couch and stood over her. "You call her and I'll run a bath for you. You need to relax and take a good long soak."

"But what if Di wakes up hungry while I'm in the tub?"

"It's called a bottle and formula. I think I can handle it. I also know how to change her diaper."

"What if it's a poopy one?"

He headed down the hallway to the bathroom. "I'll handle it, Kel." He shook his head, adding quietly. "I won't enjoy it, but I'll handle it."

Armed with wipes, baby powder, and a fresh diaper, Brad built up his courage and held his breath for a peek into his daughter's diaper. "Aw, man." He jerked the diaper back into place and stared down at the grinning baby girl. "Good God, how'd you get so much in there?"

Kellie splashed from the tub. "I know, right? She eats, she poops, it's the damnedest thing I've ever seen."

Brad turned his head to take a somewhat fresher breath of air. "Don't be a smart ass over there, or I'll bring her to you."

His wife's chuckle travelled from the bathroom. "Oh, no you don't. This was your brainstorm and I intend to take full advantage of it. The candles were a nice touch, by the way."

He smiled in spite of the putrid, pooh-filled aroma surrounding him. "You like that, huh?"

"Yup, a girl could get used to being pampered every once in a while."

"I intend to, but we may have to bring a couple of those scented candles in here once I'm finished cleaning Little Miss Stink-butt."

Brad smiled down at his daughter. "Daddy scored a point. What do you think about that?" He laughed as she kicked her feet and cooed at him, batting her long lashes. "Oh, my gosh, Di, you're a beauty, just like your mom. Am I going to be in a heap of trouble when you hit your teens, or what?" He took a shallow breath. "All righty then, let's do this thing." Using the same technique he'd seen Kellie use, he cleaned her up as best he could. "Gah, why does she always do that?" he gasped, thankful for the changing pad Kellie had insisted he place under her to protect their bedspread.

"She peed, huh."

"Before I could get the fresh one under her. I'm guessing it's her usual thing?"

"That's a ten-four, big daddy."

Brad smiled, recognizing that relaxed slur in his wife's tone, and he was glad to hear it. He put the finishing touches to his daughter and powdered her bottom before pulling the adjustable tabs across her waist. He rolled up the dirty diaper then wiped his hands with a fresh wipe before depositing them both in the diaper pail.

"Now! You smell like a prin*cess* again. How'd daddy do, baby girl? Would you give daddy a perfect 10?"

Diana squealed, grabbing for her father's mouth and catching his lower lip. He blew a raspberry on her belly and chuckled when she broke into an adorable laugh. He carried her into the bathroom and leaned over to kiss his wife. "Bye mom. I'm going to feed her now."

"You might want to wait and let me do that. .I've just started her on her first foods. They're all pureed and can get a little messy."

"I'm a petroleum engineer, sweetheart. I think I can manage to feed her without the world falling apart. Just tell me where to find the grub."

Kellie walked into the kitchen just in time to recognize the gleam of intent in her daughter's eyes.

"Ahhhh….Pbbbbbt."

Brad jumped back as a spray of pureed peaches splattered everything in its path. "Good God almighty."

Kellie chuckled from the opposite side of the kitchen. "Yeah, that's her new game—blowing raspberries with a mouthful of food when she's had enough. You should see what she does with the prunes."

"Well hell, maybe we should hold a canvas in front of her when she does it. I bet we could sell it as Baby Art, start a whole new trend to pay for her college education."

"The trick is being able to predict when she's going to do it."

Brad looked down at his previously white shirt. "All I need to do is wear the darn thing. She'll hit it, I guar-an-damn-tee it."

Kellie giggled as she placed a cup of water in the microwave for tea. "I'll bleach your shirt, don't worry."

He nodded as he wiped the carrots from his daughter's chubby cheeks. By the time Diana was clean enough to remove from her chair, Kellie had seated herself on the couch with a cup of hot tea. Brad sat beside her and propped Diana between them.

"What are you hoping to have, dad? Girls or boys?"

"Maybe they're fraternal twins and we can have one of each."

Kellie smiled. "Yeah, I hadn't thought of that."

"Stick with me, babe. I've got it all figured out."

"Of course you do." She smiled at him. "But I thought about something when I was in the tub. You remember how sick I got during the first pregnancy?"

He nodded. "Yep, you couldn't keep a thing down the first four months." His gaze clashed with his wife's and he sat up suddenly. "But, you're already three months. Maybe you'll get to skip that part this time."

"I think so. It's already a completely different pregnancy."

He placed his left arm around Kellie's shoulders while cuddling Diana securely between them. "Do you feel any differently now that it's out in the open?"

She leaned into her husband's shoulder while twirling her daughter's silken tufts of hair around her fingers. "I'm okay with it, now that I know you are. It helped to talk to mom about it. She forgave me for ruining our lunch, by the way."

"Of course she did. And I bet she's thrilled about the twins."

Kellie smiled at him. "She's ecstatic that the third generation twin tradition is alive and healthy in our family, and it's being upheld by one of *her* children. She can't wait until we find out for sure so she can spread it all over town."

"I thought it was a done deal."

"The ultrasound machine was down today. Dr. Brown did a pelvic exam and he says I'm definitely pregnant, and believes he heard two separate heartbeats. He called Doc Barton in for his opinion, and he said it's probably a second heartbeat, but they both agreed it could be an echo. We won't know for sure until we schedule an ultrasound."

Brad shifted Diana so he could lean forward to speak directly to his wife's belly. "Hey, are you listening in there? This is your dad talking, and I just want you to know, whether you're one baby or two, a boy or a girl, or one or two of each, you're already loved. So you don't need to be scared. You've got the best mom in the world and daddy's gonna do his best to take care of all of you." He finished his speech by pressing a gentle kiss to her belly. By the time he straightened beside his wife, she was sniffing and wiping her face.

"Oh, come on, there's no reason to cry."

She shook her head slowly. "I'm imprinting those words and that kiss on my brain so that every time I'm tempted to be angry with you for some silly reason, I can pull it up and remember how much I love you, instead."

"Sounds good to me. What do you say to that Princess

Di? You gonna help mommy remember that I'm 'da bomb' when she gets mad at me?"

Baby Diana cracked a big grin as a long string of drool fell onto her father's tan khakis.

Brad laughed and kissed his daughter on the top of her head before reaching for Kellie. "I think baby girl's got her dad's back." He leaned over to kiss his wife's forehead, then both eyes, and finally caressed her mouth gently with his own.

He pulled away several luscious moments later, leaving Kellie breathless and wanting him.

She cleared her throat and took the baby from him. "I think we need to play with this little one so hard that she goes to bed early." She passed one hand lazily through Brad's thick hair and smiled. "Yeah, I think daddy's getting very, very lucky tonight."

Chapter 3

Ellen approached the corner booth where her two daughters sat.

Cat looked up from the half-empty bowl of chips and salsa. "Hey, Mom."

"Hello, my loves! Christmas Eve." Ellen slid onto the circular bench seat next to Kellie and kissed her cheek. "Where's Di?"

"Bradley offered to keep her so I could have a peaceful dinner. There is something about the sound of a fork hitting a plate that wakes Diana from a sound sleep or makes her fussy. What about Christmas Eve?"

Ellen dipped her chip into a bowl of salsa, groaning in appreciation at the savory spiciness of the dip. "That was sweet of him to offer. Our wedding—we want to get married on Christmas Eve."

"Mom! We always have Christmas Eve at Brad's parents' place."

Ellen met her daughter's shocked gaze with one of total acceptance. "Oh honey, that's fine. Gavin and I are keeping it simple. You girls don't have to be there." She waved her finger at her two daughters.

"What?" Cat sat there holding a tortilla chip in her hand. "Why wouldn't we have to be there? You're the only parent we have."

"Because both of you are busy with your own lives. Doc Barton and I can travel anywhere. We're actually considering going to Las Vegas to tie the knot."

"You can't get married in Vegas," Kellie said.

"Sure I can. I've never been and I'd love to go. I told

you, we are free to do whatever we want, go wherever we want. Gavin has a partner now and he can take a couple of days off from his practice as well as the hospital. We'll be back by Christmas night. Neither of us feels like going through the hassle of wedding planning at our age."

Cat reached out for her mother's hand. "Mom, please don't do that. Get married here, with family around. I think you should let us plan your wedding. Drew and his wife could help. Donna owns her own plant nursery and I bet she could help us plan something small, but *tasteful* and really beautiful." She turned to Kellie. "It won't kill Brad's parents for you to spend Christmas Eve with us for a change— especially for this."

"I suppose you're right. God I hate having Christmas Eve over there, anyway. It's so boring. Could I invite his parents to the wedding?"

Ellen beamed at her daughters. "I think that would be a fabulous idea. That way we could *all* be together for Christmas Eve. Are you girls sure you don't mind doing it? I don't have a creative bone in my body, so there's no way *I* could plan something like that."

Cat clapped her hands. "Oh, I'm so excited! A Christmas Eve wedding . . . an evening wedding with lots of candles and poinsettias everywhere, it'll be so elegant." She turned to her mother. "Where? Are we talking church or residence?"

"Do you think we could have it at Doc's house on the lake?" Kellie chimed in. "That would be awesome. Oh God, now I have to go pee. Come with me Cat so we can talk in the restroom."

Ellen's smile followed her daughters until they turned the corner, though she heard their chatter all the way down the hall. She pulled out her cell phone and made a single call.

"Gavin? It's me. They took the bait and ran with it, just as I told you they would. Best thing for you and me to do is sit back and let them handle the entire thing. Christmas Eve, evening ceremony, only they're talking about using *your* place. Do we want that much headache, or should I convince Cat that a country wedding in a beautiful Acadian style home would be better?"

Chaos.

That was the only word Zachary could think of to describe the scene in his living room. An absolute reign of pure, unadulterated chaos.

There must have been two dozen poinsettia plants lined up along one wall, while another dozen Norfolk Island Pines, each somewhere between three and four foot tall, took up space in the middle of the floor. Cat, Kellie, and Donna Barton, Doc's daughter-in-law, sat there, painstakingly stringing them with tiny battery operated LED lights.

He leaned over to give his wife a quick kiss before waving at Kellie and Donna. "How are you ladies doing today?"

Donna smiled up at him. "I'm good, thanks, Zach."

"You feeling okay, Kellie?"

Kellie smiled. "I am. Did you hear the news?"

"If you're talking about the flower shop getting vandalized, yes I have. If not, I obviously haven't because I don't know what you're talking about."

She placed a hand on her belly. "It's not twins. We found out today. And the flower shop was vandalized?"

"Uh-huh, second business this month." He scratched his head, clueless on how to take the other news. "No twins. Hm . . . is that a good thing or not?"

She shrugged, looking a little solemn. "It is what it is, I guess. It's funny, but once the idea grew on us we were both over the moon about it, and now, we're not. We just have to get used to the idea of a single pregnancy again."

He nodded, remembering how excited Brad had been when he thought they were having twins. He couldn't help feeling somewhat sorry for the poor guy.

"Was there much damage to the flower shop, babe?"

He gave his wife a nod. "Yep, but just like the other place, nothing stolen."

After several moments of watching her skillfully wire tiny lights and delicate crystal ornaments onto a Norfolk pine, he shook his head and grunted. "Isn't that overkill?"

She turned to him. "Excuse me?"

"I see all this stuff y'all have going on and I'm pretty sure Ms. Ellen and Doc Barton would have been satisfied with a lot less."

She nodded. "What they would have been satisfied with was going to Vegas."

"Yeah," Kellie added. "There's no way in hell we were letting some dude in an Elvis costume marry them."

Zach snorted. "You don't actually think they'd have gone through with it, do you?"

"That was their plan all along."

He gave his head a slow shake. "No, babe. I think they knew if she told you that, you and Kellie would jump in to take over the planning. That's exactly what you did, isn't it?"

Cat glanced at her sister then back at Zach. "You really think so?"

He shrugged. "I think it's a possibility, but it doesn't really matter, because I'm sure it'll be very nice. Not exactly what I was expecting for my first Christmas as a married man, but I'm sure it'll be fine and we'll have plenty of other

Christmases." He grabbed an apple from a basket on the table on his way out of the room.

Cat stared after her husband. "Do you think he sounded a little upset about all this?"

"We did kind of take over your house with the preparations."

Cat glanced around the room at the major mess they'd created. Thanksgiving was the day after tomorrow and their place looked like a bombsite. Not exactly what *she'd* imagined for her and Zach's first Thanksgiving. She stood and stretched her back before reaching out a hand to her sister and Donna. "Come on, we're stopping all of this until after Thanksgiving. Zach's right, you know. This is overkill and at this rate, we'll drive ourselves crazy by Christmas Eve."

Kellie stretched her back and placed a hand over her baby bump. "I could use a break from all this, anyway. I need to get some baking done for Thursday." She took a step toward the door then stopped. "Do you think mom played us?"

Cat thought about how her mom had been going along so easily with all of their plans. She hadn't given one solitary opinion since they'd begun making plans. "You girls do whatever you think is best," was all she ever said. She found herself nodding as she began to recall bits and pieces of their conversations. "You know, I think my husband has hit the target at dead center on this one. I believe our mother played us like a set of kettle drums. Hm . . . "

Kellie's gaze narrowed on her sister. "What are you thinking, Cat? I totally recognize the evil scheming glaze over your eyes. I haven't seen that look since I hit you with a water balloon on Halloween night about thirteen years ago."

Cathryn's chuckle resonated throughout the room. "Damn straight. I got you back good, didn't I?"

"Yes you did, but that was downright cruel and unusual punishment—planting a trail of toilet paper on the back of my jeans the way you did. It took me all of junior high to live that down."

"Ah, but you learned not to do it again, didn't you, young grasshopper?"

Kellie laughed and gave her sister a nod. "Yes I did, oh, venerable master."

Cat picked up her phone and began dialing her mother's number. "Uh-huh, I think we need to teach our mother the same lesson."

Ellen and Gavin wove their way around The Regatta restaurant tables until they made it over to a long table looking over the water.

Doc Barton smiled at the three women already seated at the table. "I thought I'd treat you girls to lunch today. I've seen Donna and Kellie recently, but how are you doing, Cathryn?"

"Just fine," Cat said, sounding somewhat unenthusiastic.

Ellen hung her purse on the chair and stopped to contemplate the sour looks all three young women wore. "What's wrong? Has something happened?"

Kellie and Cathryn gazed up at her, both of their faces masked in frowns and troubled brows.

Cat bit her lower lip and finally answered. "Zachary and I had a huge argument this morning."

Donna looked sheepishly at her father-in-law. "Drew

and I did, too."

"Oh, no, over what?"

Donna and Cat exchanged glances. "It doesn't matter," Donna insisted.

Cat put on a brave face and continued. "What's important is that you and Mr. Gavin have the absolute perfect wedding."

"I just came from my OB appointment, Mom. Dr. Brown put me on bed rest for the duration of my pregnancy. Cat and Donna are going to have to shoulder the wedding planning without my help."

"Which I don't mind doing," Donna said.

Cat picked up her glass of iced tea. "I don't either. Zach will just have to get over it. I'll ask my publisher for another extension of my deadline." She sipped her tea and sighed. "Surely, they won't drop me. I've only missed one," she added, in a barely audible whisper.

Ellen exchanged an antsy look with Gavin before addressing the three women. "Are you all crazy? Kellie, you need to go home right now."

"I wanted one last meal not eaten in a bed for the next five months, Mom. Guess we'll stay home for Thanksgiving this year." She sighed and looked down to finger the corner of her napkin. "Y'all have fun without me."

"Ohhh . . ." Ellen could have burst into tears at the thought of not spending Thanksgiving with her daughter, but if it was good for the baby, she'd find some way to bring Thanksgiving to Kellie.

She turned to Cathryn and Donna. "What's going on with you two and your husbands?"

"Zach's majorly aggravated at the mess in the house. He'll get over it. I mean, we'll have plenty of other quiet Christmas Eve's at home."

Donna shrugged. "Drew says I'm spending too much

time away from him and the girls."

Ellen collapsed on the chair across from them. "You girls cannot handle this on your own. What can we do to simplify things?"

Cathryn shook her head adamantly. "No, you wanted it simple. We know you and Doc didn't want to mess with any of this. You just wanted to go to Vegas and get it over with by yourselves."

"True. But you have such a lovely ceremony planned, and you've gone to so much effort already. I'll hire someone to take over all the preparations so you girls can sit back and relax."

Cathryn and Donna exchanged looks again and both reached out to grab one of Ellen's hands.

"Absolutely not, Ms. Ellen." Donna squeezed her hand tightly. "We wanted you to have the wedding of *your* dreams, not ours, but we kind of took over."

Cathryn looked from her sister, to Donna, and then to Ellen. "Maybe it would have been better if you and Doc had the wedding *you* wanted, instead of the wedding *we* wanted for you. Maybe you two *should* go to Las Vegas on Christmas Eve, like you'd planned to do from the beginning."

Ellen sat back. All the lift from her previously floating-on-air-soul had completely depleted in the two or three minutes she'd been listening to her daughters.

"You and Zach are really arguing over my wedding?"

Cat bit down on her lower lip and lowered her head in her hands, unable or unwilling to face her.

"And you and Drew are doing the same?" Ellen asked Donna.

Donna nodded as she met Ellen's gaze.

"I'm so sorry. I do want this wedding. I just . . . I'm awful. I'm an awful, awful, deceitful person."

Kellie clasped her mother's hands in both of her own. "No, you aren't. You're the best mother in the world. I'd bet my daughter's college fund that you've never done a deceitful thing in your life."

"Don't say *that* for God's sake!" Ellen pulled her hands out from under Kellie's and wiped her damp forehead as she faced her fiancé. "Boy it's hot in here, suddenly."

"No, it isn't. Are you running a temperature?" Kellie reached out to feel her forehead.

"No." Ellen shook her hands. "I'm, I'm not . . . oh, I'm sick all right, sick with myself." She took a deep breath and released it slowly.

"We owe you girls a big apology," Gavin said.

"No, I owe you girls a big apology." Ellen sat up straight as Kellie's eyes grew wide. Cat's shoulders began to shake uncontrollably as she kept her face covered. "Cat, sweetie, don't cry. I'll explain everything to Zachary until you two are okay again. This is entirely my fault. It was my idea, and Gavin just went along with it."

Donna pinned her with a curious gaze. "What idea?"

"I knew if I mentioned going to Las Vegas, that you girls would plan a wedding for Gavin and me."

"I don't understand." Kellie's eyes grew even wider.

"We *never wanted* to get married in Vegas—and surely not if it meant being away from our families on Christmas Eve. I only said that so you two would plan something for us. Donna, I had no idea you'd be dragged into this so deeply."

"You tricked us, on purpose?"

Cat finally stemmed her tears enough to uncover her face and gaze at her mother, her eyes red-rimmed from crying. "Are you saying you manipulated us?"

Ellen hung her head, shamefully. "I'm not proud of it, but—yes—yes, I did."

"We did. I'm just as much to blame as Ellen." Gavin put his arm around his fiancée's shoulder. "I hope you kids can find it in your hearts to forgive us."

Gavin's support didn't make her feel any less guilty. Ellen closed her eyes and waited for the shameful accusations to start. What she heard was a quiet sniffling, then snorting, then full-blown guffaws of laughter bursting from the three women seated across from them.

She gazed at her girls, Cat wiping tears of laughter from her eyes and Kellie holding her sides as she giggled uncontrollably. Donna slapped her thigh as her own laughter bubbled forth.

"What the hell?"

Ellen barely heard Gavin's mumbled question.

"Wait until I tell Zach he was right. Oh God, he's going to love it." Cathryn used her drink napkin to wipe her eyes.

"Brad, too, I can't wait to tell Dr. Brown how I included him in this. He said if it was true, he planned to give you a piece of his mind, Doc Barton. Shame on you both." Her attempts at being serious dissolved into another bout of uncontrollable laughter.

Donna finally gained control of herself. "Oh, God, this has been the best day ever. I wish the two of you could see the looks on your faces."

Ellen's gaze landed on one daughter, then the other, then to her future step-daughter-in-law. "You knew?"

"I didn't suspect a thing until Zach said something about it. Then the puzzle pieces started falling into place."

"Yeah, like you saying, 'You girls just do whatever you want to do,'" Kellie snorted.

"And 'I'm sure Gavin and I will just love it, you're both so incredibly creative and talented'," Cathryn added in an exaggeratedly sappy voice.

"Dad kept telling me how much he appreciated me

pitching in to help," Donna said.

"Well, I did!" Gavin admitted.

Ellen tried to suppress the grin but couldn't. Soon, she too, burst into an uncontrollable fit of giggles. Gavin eventually joined in with a masculine chuckle as all four women wiped tears of laughter from their eyes.

Ellen gasped for breath. "Oh, I so had that coming to me. I admit it. It was a nice touch to invite Donna to this."

"We figured it was only fair that she be included since she's been designing all the floral arrangements and purchasing the poinsettias and pines at cost." Cat shook her head. "You know, Mom, all the two of you had to do was ask. We're more than happy to plan your wedding. We, all of us, just want the two of you to be happy again."

"Seriously, we both would have been satisfied with something much simpler. You girls have all gone out of your way, but let's cut back on the plans and keep it simple for everyone."

Donna shook her head. "Nope. The plans are already simple enough—forty of you and dad's closest family members and friends at his home along Lake Erin. It'll be a quick ceremony by our priest so anyone with plans can go home and the rest of us can party all night long."

"That's right, plans are made and we're sticking to them." Cathryn nodded at Donna and Kellie. "But, the three of us have decided to push it all aside until after Thanksgiving so we can enjoy ourselves."

Ellen beamed as Gavin pulled her closer into his arms. "Do you girls know how much we both love you?"

Kellie smiled. "I think we do."

Ellen wiped her eyes and grabbed the menu. "I'm starving. Let's order and then discuss Thanksgiving."

Cathryn grinned. "Ditto. The three of us are ready to talk turkey if you are."

Chapter 4

*Z*ach pulled into his regular spot behind the feed store and climbed out of his truck. Zeus, his massive eighty-pound Golden Retriever, followed him out and ran to the backdoor. His immediate series of deep barks and growls got his master's attention.

"Oh man, don't tell me," Zach whispered under his breath. All the local business owners were worried about the break-ins around town, and he prayed his place hadn't been added to the list. He approached the door, saw it had been jimmied open, and immediately pulled out his cell phone and called the local cops. Rather than wait for them, he pushed the door open with his elbow and stepped inside. "Son of a—" The rest of the curse died on his lips as he surveyed the damage to his store. By the time the cops arrived a few minutes later, he'd already approximated the damage to be well over ten grand.

"They were thorough as hell, that's for sure." The chief shook her head at the mess. "This makes the third businesses in less than month. Every time it's the same thing—hardly anything missing, but a lot of damage. Whoever it is, they are really starting to piss me off."

"Anyone being questioned as a person of interest?"

"Not a one." Sherry Jeansonne cursed under her breath. "I've been chief of police for nearly ten years. We've had the occasional problems with mild vandalism in the past, but nothing this serious. Every business they've hit is a mom and pop that's been around for twenty years or more—Doucet Electronics, Lakeside Flowers, and now this place. It's almost like they're trying to drive people out of business."

"Or maybe we've been chosen because our places don't have fancy alarm systems."

Sherry nodded. "You could be right. The other businesses have all added them since the break-ins. They've all used Stanley Home Security out of Jennings. Everyone says SHS has been beating the prices of the bigger companies by enough to make it worth looking into. Personally, I can't stand dealing with them since the son took over the family business. That guy's a real prick, but that's just my opinion."

"Which son?"

"I think his name's Jack."

Zach grunted and coughed, nearly choking when he heard the name. "It'll be a cold day in hell before I buy a security system or anything else from that asshole."

She shrugged her shoulders. "I know, he's a sleaze-ball. It's a real shame too, because his dad ran a top notch operation for years. His systems were reliable. Really, all you'd have to do is keep that dog of yours here during the night. That son of a gun would make anybody think twice about breaking and entering. What do you feed that thing?"

Zach sent the chief a smile as he reached out to scratch Zeus on the head. "Only the best, huh, Zeus? And plenty of it, but I don't think he could take being separated from me and Cat for that long. For as big as he is, he's as loveable as a puppy and spoiled rotten."

Zach straightened and shook his head. "Man, I hate to rely on an alarm system. My dad and gramps always said if you can't trust the people around you, you can't trust anybody."

"Yeah, that's a noble thought, but the problem is that we have an influx of people who are new to the area and don't have your history. I'm not saying it's any of them, of course, just that we don't know them well enough to be sure they're trustworthy." She glanced around the building, surveying the mess. "How soon can you get me a list and total amount of the damages?"

Zach ran his hand through his hair. "I have to wait for my insurance agent to get here. I can't start cleaning up until Bev sees this mess. I'm sure as I clean, I'll uncover even more, but I'll get it to you as soon as possible, maybe by tomorrow."

Cathryn stepped inside and covered her mouth as she gazed at the damages to her husband's family business. "Oh, Zach, this is awful."

He met her and pulled her into his arms for a hug. "I know, right? But damn, babe, thanks for coming to meet me. How'd you know I needed a hug from my girl?"

She drew her arms around his waist and squeezed, trying to give as much comfort as she got from having his arms wrapped around her. "I came to see if you need help cleaning up this mess."

"Nah, me and the guys will handle it." He pointed at the men who'd worked with his dad and now for him.

He pulled away and gave her the most heart-achingly sweet smile a man could give. Funny, but all she could think of was how badly she wanted a child with this man. "I'm so sorry, Zach."

He lifted one shoulder in a shrug. "We've got insurance, and for all the damage they did to the building, they didn't destroy or steal any of the merchandise. My business won't be interrupted at all. I'll board up the windows and use padlocks until I can make repairs. I'll have to replace both computers, the cash register, and my printer combo—sons a bitches poured paint all over everything."

"If you write down some model numbers I can help you with that."

"When? In the middle of baking pies and stuffing the turkey for tomorrow? No, you've got enough to do." Zach waved his hand around to encompass the mess. "All this can wait until after Thanksgiving."

"After Thanksgiving? You want to go shopping on Black Friday? It's only the busiest, most crowded shopping day of the entire year."

"I was thinking more like Saturday. I plan on spending the first half of Friday eating leftovers until my belly hurts, and then sleeping it off the rest of the day. That is, if I can get my wife to get lazy along with me."

Cat chuckled low in her throat at her husband's low-keyed plans, knowing, without a doubt, he wouldn't keep still for that long. "We'll see."

By the end of the day, Zach and company had the store cleaned of all broken glass, and the windows boarded up. He'd finished placing the padlock on the back door when a black Cadillac SUV pulled up next to his truck. A man, possibly in his mid-forties, emerged from the vehicle and approached him, wearing a smile to go along with his casual business attire.

Zach was in no mood to do anything other than go home to his wife, mustered his manners and tipped his New Orleans Saints cap at the man. "What can I do for you?"

The man extended his hand and smiled too widely for comfort in Zach's current state of mind.

"I'm Jack Stanley from Stanley Home Security, just up the highway in Jennings."

Zach pulled back the hand he'd started to offer, and paused to study the man. The Jack Stanley that Zach remembered would be about thirty, and this guy looked a good fifteen years older. But yeah, it was him, all right. He had a much fuller face, a huge paunch, and about a quarter of the hair he had ten years ago. This jerk was the same sleaze ball he'd gladly give his left nut to have a go at in a back alley—again. "Zach Ferguson," he said.

"I hear your place was broken into last night."

"Oh, yeah? News travels fast. Who told you?"

"I spoke to Chief Jeansonne this morning. It's the third time in less than a month that something like this has happened in Lake Erin."

"That's what I hear."

The man whipped a business card out of his shirt pocket as quick as a psychic moonlighting as a magician. "Sounds like you may need a security system."

"I don't know about that." Zach refused to reach for it, and the pushy S-O-B reached over and dropped it in his shirt pocket.

"Seriously?" The man pointed to the padlock and the splintered wood around the door's edge. "That's not what I see."

"Well, you doing what you do, you'll see what you want to see, won't you?" He reached for the business card in his pocket and tore it in two before dropping it into a trash bin by the back door.

Jack Stanley laughed jovially considering the insult he'd just received. He jumped back as Zeus ran out from under the truck. "Jesus, that's a big dog!"

"Zeus, heel." Zach nodded as the dog sat obediently to his left side. "He's not quite a year, still got some growing to do. His dad pushed ninety pounds, easy."

"It must cost you a fortune to feed that son of a bitch."

"No, not really."

"Oh, sure, sure, you own a feed store. I bet you cut a deal with the suppliers every now and then. They give you a couple of hundred pounds off the top when nobody's looking?"

Zach sent the man an icy glare, then shook his head in disgust. "Nah, but I did cut a deal with the people in my neighborhood. They send all their pushy door-to-door salesman to my place and Zeus takes care of 'em for everyone. We never have to deal with *those* sons of bitches again." He pointed at the NO SOLICITATION sign tacked above the doorway. "*I'll* decide if and when I need a security system."

Jack's face turned a mottled shade of crimson, then he turned and headed back to his car.

Because he could, Zach snapped his fingers and pointed. By the time Jack reached the door of his Cadillac, Zeus was *there* to safeguard against any efforts by the scumbag to make a last second sales pitch. Normally, the animal would have stood and looked threatening without actually *being* a threat. For some reason, it didn't happen quite that way.

More than an hour later, Zach drug himself through the back door of his and Cat's home. The delectable aroma of pecan and spicy pumpkin pies would have made his mouth water at any other time. Tonight, it only made his stomach turn.

Cat walked from the laundry room, carrying a stack of folded bath towels. "Hey babe, I've been calling your phone. I was beginning to wonder if you were spending the night there." She stopped as he turned to face her. "What happened?"

"It's Zeus—"

"No! Did he get hit? Oh, God."

Zach went to his wife, trying to calm her. "No, he's all right, but . . . he's in jail. A salesman came by, trying to push a security system on me and I turned him down." Still fighting off his own shock, Zach described how Zeus had gone ape-shit-crazy—growling, barking and snapping as soon as the man had opened the door of his SUV. "I called him off as quickly as I could, but not soon enough to keep him from scaring the crap outta that guy."

"That doesn't make any sense. Zeus is a sweet-heart, a big, sweet, bear of a dog!"

Zach pulled his softhearted wife into his arms. "I know, but I could tell that guy was a slime-ball as soon as stepped out of his fancy black Cadillac. Even before I knew who he was."

"Who?"

Zach, took a deep breath, knowing his wife deserved to know. "His name is Jack Stanley, from Stanley Home Security in Jennings." He waited to see if the info would garner any reaction.

Cat frowned, then shook her head. "I don't think I know him. I wonder what set Zeus off."

"My guess is that he's as good a judge of character as his master."

She shrugged. "Either that, or he acted on the signals you were giving him. Poor Zeus. Where are they keeping him, and for how long? What's going to happen to him?"

"He's at the pound in Jennings. I don't know for how long, and I have no idea what will happen. But I doubt it'll be anytime soon." Zach felt sick even admitting it, but he couldn't make himself lie to give Cat false hope.

"I want to go break him out, poor baby—having to

spend Thanksgiving in jail." Cat groaned. "Did he actually bite the guy; you know, break the skin?"

"He nipped him. He wouldn't have done it if the jerk hadn't kicked him. When he did, Zeus caught the hem of his pants, and that's when it happened." He ran a hand through his hair and released a long, exhausted sigh. "I need a hot shower . . . and I don't want to talk about this for the rest of the night. I have too damned much on my mind right now."

Around midnight, Zach finally remembered what had been nagging at him. Unable to sleep, he climbed out of the warm bed he shared with his wife and made his way to the kitchen. The aroma of fresh, homemade bread teased and tantalized his senses, making his stomach growl. He poured himself a glass of cold milk and pilfered the largest bread roll on the covered baking sheet before seating himself at the snack bar. After he'd wolfed down the roll and was half-way through the glass of milk, he snatched the magnetic notepad from the fridge and started jotting down his thoughts. By the time Zach crawled back under the covers at 2 a.m., he had come up with a solid plan of action to get his dog back, among other things.

"There he is." Cat jumped out of the truck before it rolled to a stop. She ran to the large exterior enclosure where Zeus sat, half-in and half-out of a large doghouse in the back corner, covered and well protected from the elements. The huge animal ran to the fence, wagging his tail furiously at the sight of his family.

"Hey boy, are they treating you okay here?" Cat kneeled at the fence separating her from their beloved pet. She sniffled and wiped her eyes as Zeus whined and licked her hand through the galvanized wire enclosure. Zach knelt beside her.

"They better be or I'll be kicking ass and taking names," he growled.

Cat stood suddenly and faced her husband. "We'll get him back, won't we? I mean, you don't think they'd, you know?"

Zach pulled her close for a hug. "Sure we will. It's only his first offense and he barely broke the skin." He leaned over and stuck his fingers through the fence. "Don't worry boy, you'll be home soon, I guarantee it." He pulled his hand back to answer his buzzing cell phone.

"Hello."

"Mr. Ferguson, this is Jack Stanley."

"Well, speak of the devil, Mr. Stanley…" He smiled as Cat emitted a low snarl. "You are not real popular with my wife and me right now."

"I was wondering if I could offer you a proposition."

"A proposition, huh? I apologize if I gave you the wrong impression on our first meeting, but I don't swing that direction." He withheld a laugh as Cat snorted her approval of his jibe.

"You're hilarious, but no, this has to do with your dog, Mr. Ferguson. That animal is a menace and someone needs to deal with him."

"My dog? I hardly think the little scratch Zeus gave you is reason enough to worry about him being a menace. It's just that he senses people who aren't worth a damn." Zach squeezed Cat's hand, enjoying sparing with this asshole.

"You'd be more worried if you knew how many people in high places I know, Mr. Ferguson. With one phone call I can have that dog of yours put to sleep. But I'm willing to drop all charges against you and your dog if you promise to purchase a security system from my company."

"Now why would I trust a dog hater and a blackmailer

to protect my place of business?"

"Because you love your dog, and you want to keep your business and your home intact."

Zach stamped a boot on the ground, imagining it was Stanley's head. "Are you threatening me?"

"Absolutely not! I'm only trying to protect you from the unexpected."

"Yeah, whatever asshole."

"What's your problem, Ferguson? Even before this dog incident you've acted like an ass to me."

Zach watched his wife spoiling Zeus with choice scraps from their feast. If only he could tell this jerk the real reason he'd never get his business. "Any farmer worth his salt knows better than to let a fox near the hen house. You come anywhere near mine, you'll see the rooster guarding it has mighty big spurs and he knows how to use them. And I'm not talking about my dog."

He ended the call without waiting for a reply and made a few calls of his own, the last being to Chief Sherry Jeansonne, asking for a meeting.

Once he hung up and explained to Cathryn about Jack Stanley's thinly veiled threat, he couldn't persuade her to leave Zeus's side.

"I'm staying right here until we bring him home." She pulled out her phone. "I'm calling mom, and Doc Barton, too. Judge Baker is standing up as best man for the wedding." After a brief conversation, she slipped the phone back into her coat pocket. "They'll be here in fifteen minutes and Doc's calling the Judge. You go on back to Lake Erin and talk to Chief Jeansonne."

He shook his head, adamant about not leaving her alone. "As soon as the reinforcements arrive, I'll go. Not a second before then."

Ten minutes later, after the arrival of her mom and Doc

Barton, Cathryn gave him a kiss and pushed him toward the parking lot. "Would you stop wasting time? I'll be fine here."

Finally relenting, he walked toward his truck and turned back to her. "I love you, babe. Under no circumstances do you stay here alone."

"I love you too, and I promise; I won't be alone. Now go."

Zach sat in Sherry Jeansonne's office with the owners of the two other vandalized businesses. Not surprisingly, Jack Stanley had paid each of them a visit by the end of the same day the incidents had occurred.

The chief leaned back in her chair, and folded her hands across her lap. "I'm wondering how he knew about each of the break-ins so quickly."

Bob, the owner of Doucet's Electronics, stopped pacing long enough to face her. "He told me you'd called him that same morning."

Chief Jeansonne frowned. "I didn't call him."

Genevive Bertrand from Lakeside Flowers spoke up. "He told me the same thing. That he'd spoken to you that morning, Sherry."

The chief straightened in her chair. "I did speak to him, but only after he called me. After each incident, he called, saying he'd heard your places had been broken into and asked if it was true."

"He led me to believe you'd called him to inform him, almost as though he was using you as a reference." Genevive shook her head. "I'd never have used his company if I'd known you didn't have anything to do with sending him to see me."

Bob scratched his beard. "That's exactly the impression I got. What the hell does this mean, Sherry?"

Zach cleared his throat. "He's trying to blackmail me, insinuating he'll have my dog put down if I don't buy a security system from him."

Genevive gasped. "Zeus? He's nothing but a big ole baby. For his size, he's a sweet dog."

"He's never given me any trouble," Bob added. "You've been by my place with him dozens of times."

"I know that, but he took an intense disliking to this guy. I thought maybe he sensed the tension between us, but then last night I remembered something that had been bothering me." He twirled his cap in his hands, trying to gather his thoughts.

The chief leaned forward. "Go ahead, Zach. Anything would be helpful at this point."

"Zeus started growling and barking as soon as we got to the back door of the feed store yesterday morning. He didn't have a problem with Stanley at first. But once he opened the door to his Cadillac all hell broke loose." He looked pointedly at the chief. "What if he recognized the scent from the inside of his car as the same as in the store?"

Sherry placed her hands flat on her desk. "You're thinking he had something to do with it? Like maybe he broke in and did the damage, to make you all want a security system?"

Zach laughed and shook his head. "No way would that slimy piece of crap get his hands dirty like that. I bet he hired someone to do it for him. Maybe the person he hired was in his SUV at some point."

The chief laced her fingers together and seemed to contemplate this scenario. "Let me make some phone calls. I want to follow up on something I heard during an arrest last night. If what I heard is true, it might be the one thing that ties all this together." She stood and opened her door. "I'll let you know if it pans out."

Zach let the others exit first, then stopped in front of the chief. "Is there anything you can possibly do about releasing Zeus? He's wearing his tags and I keep him up to date on all his shots. Cat is so worried about Jack's threat, she's afraid to leave him alone at the pound."

Chief Jeansonne nodded and reached for her phone. "I'll call Jimmy and see what I can do."

True to her word, Sherry vouched for Zeus's easy-going temperament, and Zach returned to the pound in time for his dog's release. The massive animal bounded up to the couple, tail wagging, and whining with excitement.

Jimmy, the dog-catcher, laughed at his reaction. "You've got yourself a good dog. Great with people—I can't figure out what the heck he's doing here."

"I hear you. He's just a massive, spoiled baby, aren't you Zeus?" Cathryn buried her face in the dog's scruff as he reacted with absolute joy. "And believe me, I was not a dog person until I met this big guy." She turned to her husband. "Let's take him home."

Chapter 5

C athryn contained her laughter as her husband tried, and failed miserably, to sneak in the house without her knowledge. Poor Zach had no idea there wasn't a hiding place in the world safe enough to stop a curious woman from finding her Christmas gift. Fortunately for him, she adored being surprised. She gave him enough time to tuck it away before letting him know she was there.

She leaned against the door-jamb holding her favorite coffee mug. "I thought I heard you come in. What's up?"

Zach grabbed a set of clothes from the built-in shelves. "I need to hit the shower, sweetie. I'm filthy."

She tried, but couldn't keep the smile from her face. "I won't dig. You know I love surprises."

His left eyebrow rose suspiciously. "I don't know what you're talking about."

Amused laughter filled the room. "Yeah, right." She turned to head out the door. "It always amazes me how fast Christmas sneaks up on me. At first, it seems as though it'll never get here, then before you know it, it's over." She called back over her shoulder. "I've got a pot of homemade soup simmering, so hurry up and shower."

Cat set two trays holding bowls of soup on the cocktail table in front of the leather couch. She added saltine crackers and a bottle of Louisiana Hot Sauce for her husband, and programmed the flat screen TV to the Saints and Seahawks game. She added silverware, napkins, and a beer for Zach, and a glass of white wine for herself. As soon as she settled in the center of the couch, Zach walked in, looking warm and comfortable in faded jeans and a flannel shirt, both worn soft with wear.

He sniffed the air. "I'm starved, and damn but that soup smells good. What's in it?"

"Everything but the kitchen sink; just the way mom taught me to make it." She handed him the beer and patted the seat next to her. "I thought we'd skip the dining room tonight and watch the game while we eat. Okay with you?"

He scooted in beside her and put his arm around her shoulders for a hug and swift kiss on the mouth. "Could you be any more perfect than you already are?"

"I could try but it'd be a waste of time."

He smiled as he balanced a tray on his lap. "As usual, you've outdone yourself. How the hell did I get so lucky?" He dipped into the soup and took a big bite. "Seasoning is great."

She shook her head before laughing. "He says as he reaches for the hot sauce."

Zach paused, his gaze landing on hers. "It's seasoned perfectly for normal people. We all know I'm hotter than the average male." He lifted his finger to stop her reply. "Don't even think about denying that. If I wasn't, would I have kept you from marrying anyone else in the twelve years you were gone from this place?"

She closed her mouth with an abrupt snap. "How can one man be so full of himself?"

"Babe, the only thing I'm full of is my love for you." He liberally doused hot sauce in the bowl and took another bite. "Mm, but soon my belly will be full."

She snorted, accepting a tabasco flavored kiss. "I can think of something you're full of."

With full bellies, and drowsy from a long day of hard work, they'd both nearly fallen asleep when Zach's cell phone buzzed near the end of the third quarter.

Cat groaned at being uprooted from her current position of snuggling in her husband's arms. "Dang, it's almost ten o'clock. Who the heck is calling this late?" She reached for her husband's phone on the opposite end table. Glancing at the screen, she stiffened at the sight of *Lake Erin PD* flashing. She handed him the phone and braced herself, knowing in her gut, the news wouldn't be good.

Zach's truck skidded onto the back lot of the feed store as the fire department doused the last of the most noteworthy flames licking at the back siding of the building. He and Cat jumped out and met at the front bumper. Cat slipped her hand into Zach's as Sherry Jeansonne walked over to them.

"Zach, Cathryn, I'm sure sorry about this." Sherry shook her head, and muttered a low curse. "I thought for sure this crap was over with. We threw that S-O-B, Stanley in jail for suspicion of insurance fraud and embezzlement this morning. That high priced lawyer his daddy hired got him out of that with a slap on the butt-cheek."

Zach watched sixty years of the business his grandfather and father had nurtured, wither under the drenching from the fire truck's hoses. "Just in time for a little revenge."

Cat latched onto his arm. "Do you really think Stanley had something to do with it?"

He nodded slowly, trusting his gut on this one. "I sure do, and I don't think he'd hesitate to—" He stopped, remembering something Jack had said over the phone. The comment had only pissed him off at the time, but now it caused his gut to twist and sour. "Damn it!"

Chief Jeansonne turned to him. "What's wrong?"

"This is a diversion."

"What do you mean?"

"He tried to blackmail me over the phone and said I should take his security system because I loved my dog, and wanted to keep my business, and my home, intact." He spun and headed back to his truck. "I've got to get home."

Sherry pulled out her phone. "I'll call the Sheriff's Department to get over there, just in case you're right about this."

Zach jerked open his truck door and turned to face his wife. "I want you to stay here, Cat."

She slipped behind him and scooted into the driver's side. "Yeah? You can't always have it your way, cowboy. Now get in the damn truck."

"Cathr—"

"We left both Zeus and Chableu in the house."

He knew better than to argue with her, especially with her brown eyes sparking with fury. Without another word, he slid in and shoved her over.

Sherriff's Deputy, Wayne Babineaux, an old classmate of his, pulled into their driveway just after Zach's truck slid to a stop. The couple piled out of the truck simultaneously, calling for the man to follow them to the house. They heard the scuffle as soon as they got to the jimmied door.

Deputy Babineaux pushed his way in first, his gun drawn. "Are you armed?" he asked the man, pinned to the floor by two huge paws, while Zeus growled and snarled, inches from his face.

"If I was, do you think this son of a bitch would be slobbering all over me?"

"Zach, can you call him off?"

"Yep."

Several moments passed before the Deputy spoke again. "Zach?"

"What? You asked if I could, not if I would." He relented at Wayne's glare. "Damn, Wayne. You're still as much fun as a wet blanket. The son of a bitch just set fire to my family business, and I'm sure he's here to burn down my house. I'm not feeling the love from him, so why should I do him any favors?"

"He set fire to your business?"

"Didn't Chief Jeansonne tell your department when she called?"

Wayne shook his head. "I got a call from JD Security about a possible break-in. Looks like he tripped the silent alarm." He scratched at his chin. "As well as the not so silent alarm."

"Get him off me!"

"Hold it down, asshole. You're in no position to demand anything." Wayne turned to Zach. "Call him off."

Zach gave Wayne a reluctant nod, as he slapped at his upper thigh, and whistled. Zeus immediately stopped snarling and trotted over to his master, but turned to keep a wary eye on the intruder inside his territory.

"You have a silent alarm?" Jack sent Zachary an accusatory glare.

Zach nodded. "Nothing against your father's system and installment procedures, but the fact that you're involved is a definite red flag. How does your dad feel about his low-life, drug-head, thug of a son ruining, in a few short years, the business he worked his entire life to build?"

Jack gave him an evil grin. "About like you felt when you saw your store burn to the ground."

"Oh, but it didn't. Some kid saw the glow during his evening jog. Turns out, he was a volunteer firefighter so he knew just who to call and what to do until the rest of his buddies got there." He leaned over to sneer at Jack. "Even at arson you're a failure."

Jack turned defiant. "I don't believe that for a second. You're just saying that to get me riled up, but it won't work."

Zach straightened and gave him a "makes no difference to me what you believe" grin and a shrug. "By the time we got there, it was out already. Of course, I'll have water damages, but that's what insurance is for, right? I'll be up and running in a week."

The corners of Jack's mouth turned down in an ugly snarl. "One of these days, I'll give you just what you deserve."

Cathryn froze, her entire body tense. *Those words, spoken in that voice.* Suddenly it came to her, and she knew why the sight of this man caused her skin to crawl. Just as suddenly, she wanted to let him know he had no control over her, as he had all those years ago. Cat slipped her hand through her husband's arm. The look on Stanley's face had panic written all over it, making her wonder if he knew already. She gave Zach's hand a comforting pat and faced the man she'd allowed to chase her from her home for twelve years.

"Zachary already has what he deserves. And now, after nearly thirteen years, you'll finally get what you deserve too."

The man's brow creased with a frown. "Have we met before? You look vaguely familiar to me."

"Not formally, but then again, I'm guessing you didn't introduce yourself to any of the girls you attacked and attempted to rape while you were at LSU." She lifted her chin and smiled. "To tell you the truth, if I hadn't heard you speak, heard you say those exact words, I may never have recognized you. You look twenty-five years older than you did then." She smiled as he puffed up, seemingly affronted at her insult. "The fact that you don't recognize me tells me I must have been one of many."

"I've never seen you before in my life."

"Sure you have." She leaned forward and cocked her head slightly. "I'm the one that got away." She saw it then. A faint spark of recognition, of remembrance. Maybe he didn't know how big of an effort it had taken her to get away from him. How she'd had to summon every ounce of strength she possessed to free one arm and scratch his face. She'd used those precious seconds he'd been screaming like a little girl to run like hell.

She shook her head, letting him see the truth—that she would never be afraid of a sad little man like him.

"Don't you worry, now that I *know* your identity and what you do in your spare time, I'll be sure it's splashed all over every news network in the country. You're finished."

Zach hadn't taken his eyes off his wife during her speech to the man he'd known attacked her twelve years ago. He'd never forget the night she'd come to him, her jaw bruised where Jack had hit her, crying, pleading with him not to tell anyone. His heart swelled with pride at the strength she possessed now, the courage it took to step forth and admit something like that. To face her attacker. He could honestly say he'd never loved Cathryn more than he had at this very moment. Her confession convinced him to do the same.

He turned to the man still lying on the floor. "Now that Cat knows who you are, I guess I should also come clean. That beating you got behind the Chimes bar about two months after you attacked my wife? That was me. I heard you couldn't get out of bed for a week after that." He smiled down at the slug lying on the floor.

Stanley's eyes widened with panic. "You both have me confused with someone else."

Zach shook his head. "I'm not finished. That beating you got a couple of years after that behind the Circle Top in Gardiner?" The laughter rumbled deep in his chest as Jack winced at the mention. "Me again. You followed that girl outside, after she'd told you to get lost. You remember, don't you? By the time I got out back you had slapped her and had already ripped off her shirt."

"That wasn't me, and if you tell anyone it was I'll sue you for defamation of character."

Zach shook his head. "You have no character. You didn't learn after one beating so I figured I'd try to beat some sense into you again. I swear to God, I wanted to kill you that night. It took all I had to stop at breaking your hand and beating the crap out of you. I heard you were in bed for two weeks that time."

"She wanted it," Jack snarled. "So did your wi—"

Zach stepped forward to crush Jack's fingers under his boot. "You finish that comment and I'll break your other hand." He glanced at the deputy, recognized the look on his face for what it was—unhidden disgust for the man on the floor. "If Wayne would agree to escort my wife out of here for about ten minutes, I'd be glad to repeat the performance, maybe up that recuperation period to a month this time. Or better yet, give you a permanent limp."

Jack's face transformed from shock, trailed by a look of deep-seated anger, then pain, and finally, a well-warranted fear seeped into his features. He met the deputy's accusatory glare. "They're both lying, and I'll sue you for everything you have if you allow him to lay one finger on me."

Wayne shook his head, his brow furrowed with anger. "I've known Zach all my life. As far as I know, they're good people and I can't think of a single reason not to believe them. To tell you the truth, I'm finding it real difficult not to have a crack at you myself, but I'll do my job. Besides, you as much as admitted it just now." He chuckled as he shook his head. "Yes sir, the boys at Louisiana State Penitentiary are gonna adore you. I hear those guys at Angola love the newbies. Now get up so I can take you to jail where you belong." He grabbed Stanley's shoulder and jerked him to his feet.

When they were finally alone again, Cathryn drew a hot bath in the large soaking tub and convinced him to join her.

Within minutes, he was luxuriating in the hot water, with his wife relaxing in his arms.

She sunk lower in the tub, resting her back against his broad chest. "Mm, we need to do this more often."

He laced his fingers through hers and smiled. "You're right again."

"Zach?"

"Hmm?" He braced himself.

"Why didn't you tell me?"

It didn't do a bit of good to ask, "Tell you what?" It could be one of two questions: Why didn't you tell me you knew Jack Stanley tried to rape me? Or, why didn't you tell me that you'd beat him up?

The answer to both was the same.

"I didn't want you to relive it any more than you already had to," He said.

She re-laced her fingers through his and squeezed them

tightly, but remained silent.

"I tried like hell to convince you to go to the cops twelve and a half years ago, but you wouldn't. If you'd known who it was, would it have made a difference?"

"Knowing it was a rich kid with a father who always got him out of trouble, and had money to pay big time lawyers to run my family's name through the mud?" She took several seconds before shaking her head. "Probably not. I was better off not knowing. But how did you know it was him when I didn't even know?"

"That was nothing more than a lucky break. You remember my friend, Jeremy?"

"Jeremy, who should have been our best man, but was killed in a car accident?"

"The same. We'd gone to the rodeo in Jennings and ended up sitting two rows above Jack and a group of guys all drunk and causing trouble. Eventually, security threw them all out. Zach passed his hand over her arm, silky with hot water.

"Jeremy pointed to Jack, said he'd drank a couple of beers with that asshole across from the LSU campus one night after the LSU and Auburn Tiger Bowl. He said the guy left, and then came back in looking like he got in a fight with six-legged cat. Started bragging about how this chick tried to say she didn't want it but he proved her wrong—"

"—You know that's bullshit, right?" Cat said.

"Sure I know. Jeremy said they all figured it was a load of bull, but said he regretted not reporting it, anyway." He stopped there, took a deep breath, and released it slowly. "How arrogant does a son of a bitch have to be to brag about claiming to rape a girl?"

"I can't believe you remember that much about the night. I tried to forget everything about it."

He pulled her close, burying his face in the crook of her

neck. "I remembered, so you wouldn't have to."

She slid her hand along the length of his arm and cuddled close to him. "I know, and I love you for that, Zachary."

"I know you do, but I've loved you longer." He enjoyed reminding her that she'd made him wait twelve long years before realizing she couldn't live without him.

"I've wondered lately, knowing how you felt, how you could have been so patient with me. Now I understand."

"Cat, maybe I shouldn't ask this, but how long have you known he was the guy?"

She stopped the slow sensual rubbing of her hand along his arm. He held his breath, waiting for her to answer.

"I just figured it out tonight."

"How?"

"It was his comment to you. 'One of these days, I'm gonna give you what you deserve.' As soon as I heard it, I knew it was him. He told me the same thing when I told him to get out of my face inside the bar before . . . before it happened. I've always suspected he slipped something in my drink, but I couldn't prove a thing. Besides, I'd disobeyed mom, snuck off to an LSU game with friends who took me to a bar. It didn't matter that I was only drinking cokes. I'd already broken so many rules that I felt as though I did deserve it, in a way."

Zach's growl vibrated deep in his chest. "I hope you know what a load of crap that is."

She smiled and moved her hand to his thigh, began rubbing in a slow, circular motion. "I know now, but I was young and stupid back then. I don't mind telling you that episode set me back a bit."

Zach sucked in his breath with a long, low hiss. "Uh yeah, like twelve years." He could tell by her laughter that she knew exactly what she was doing to him. Knew her hand on the inside of his thigh was a sure way to get a reaction from him.

"But I've had therapy, and the fact that I called him out is proof of its success. Ten years ago, I wouldn't have been able to do that, I can promise you that."

"I'm proud of you. You know, as awful as that night was for you, because of it, I always had hope for you and me."

"Why?"

"Because I was the one you came to. You said I was the only person you would ever confide something like that to. You didn't even tell your parents or your sister."

She shifted around to face him and he smiled into the gorgeous brown eyes he hoped she'd pass on to their children one day.

"That's right, I only told my best friend, whom I knew would take it to his grave if I asked him to. And I've always loved you for that."

"I love you so much it hurts."

"I love you too, Zachary."

"No, really . . . " He slipped his hand behind her hip to adjust himself. "I'm so, ah . . .damn, that hurts."

She laughed as she wiggled against him. "Must you turn everything into sex, sex, sex?"

"I wasn't implying I wanted sex, I was only stating a fact. I mean, come on. We're in a tub together; naked, and you're all up against me and rubbing my leg. Of course things are gonna happen."

She turned around and straddled him, then kissed him long and hard. "Well, that's a lucky break for me then, isn't it?"

Chapter 6

Zach held tightly to his wife's hand while he gripped the bathroom doorknob in the other. "Are you ready?"

She nodded, her eyes bright with excitement and her face flushed. "Let's do it!"

He took a deep breath and pushed the door open to view the two pregnancy test sticks his wife had used to test for pregnancy. Cathryn drew her breath in a loud gasp, obviously knowing better what to look for than he did. "What am I looking at he—" That's when he saw it—the big bright plus sign that said they were pregnant. Check that—*two* big bright plus signs.

Zach wasted no time in sweeping his wife off her feet to carry her back to their bedroom.

"What are you planning?" she said, her beautiful smile reaching far and wide to the sparkle in her sexy, brown eyes.

He dropped her gently on the bed and leered mischievously at her. "To celebrate." He lifted her shirt and lowered himself to cover her tummy in kisses.

She giggled. "I think it's actually a little lower than that. It's not in my stomach."

He reached for the zipper of her jeans and gave her the one sided dimpled grin she claimed she could never resist. "I can remedy that—right damn now."

She smiled as he slipped off her jeans, never breaking eye contact with her. "Just how long is the celebration going to last? Cause you know, I asked Mom and Mr. Gavin to come over in a few minutes so we could tell them in case it was good news."

"Uh uh. While you were in the bathroom earlier, I called and cancelled our little visit. Told them we'd be busy."

She beamed up at him. "Oh yeah? Busy doing what?"

"I told you already—Celebrating. All. Night. Long."

Candlelight illuminated every corner of Gavin Barton's living room, filling it with a lovely, soft glow. Delicate crystal ornaments from the boughs of several decorative pines, glistened and sparkled with reflected candlelight. Bright red poinsettias graced several surfaces of the room, giving it a festive air. The tantalizing aroma of scented candles teased the senses. Cinnamon, vanilla, bayberry and other spices, infused the air, adding to the Christmas ambiance.

"Who gives this woman's hand in marriage?"

Cathryn and Kellie both stood, hands clasped, and spoke in unison. "Her daughters do."

Cathryn sat, watching as her mother bound herself legally and spiritually to Doc Barton. It turned out that having a Catholic wedding outside of a church was a simple enough procedure as long as you got prior approval and could find a priest with a few minutes to spare on Christmas Eve. Father Hebert had said the funeral masses for both their spouses, married all of their children and had witnessed them both in holy mass every Saturday or Sunday for years. He'd been more than willing to donate a few minutes to the cause, as long as they promised to be at the Christmas Eve mass later. All members of the newly consolidated family intended to attend as a group.

The entire ceremony took all of five minutes and that was with Father Hebert's personalized touches for two of his loyal parishioners. Within ten minutes, he was on his way back to his busy Christmas mass schedule.

Cathryn and Zach stood before her mother and new step-father, beaming with happiness for both of them. Cat pulled her mother close for a hug. "Mom, I'm so happy for you." She released her and stood before Doc Barton. "You know, Kellie and I put our heads together and finally decided what to call you. We've known you as a 'Doc' all our lives and can't quite separate ourselves from it. So, we've decided to call you 'Poppa Doc'."

Kellie stepped forward, her second baby belly beginning to take center stage. "That is, with your approval, of course."

Gavin Barton bellowed with approving laughter. "Poppa Doc it is. I love it, and I love you girls, too." He enveloped them both in his arms and leaned forward to kiss his new wife. "I think we're all going to be great as a family."

Much later that evening, after the wedding, and the mass, and the supper at Mom and Poppa Doc's place—Cathryn lit the last of the candles she'd accumulated in their den. Between the candlelight, the glow of the tree lights, and the soft crackling flames of the fireplace, the room was awash in the ambiance of golden amber. It sparkled and reflected brilliantly from every surface. She placed three candles on the coffee table and set a bottle of chilled champagne on one side and a bottle of sparkling grape juice on the other, with two glasses, and a corkscrew between them. She placed a delicately wrapped box in the center. Stepping back, she surveyed her handiwork and nodded in approval before sitting alongside her sleeping husband.

She leaned forward to whisper in Zach's ear. "Hey babe, wake up. It's almost Christmas." She sat back and watched him stir, stretch, and generally convince himself to wake. He blinked several times before he sat up and yawned.

"Dang, I was out."

She gave him a soft chuckle. "It's been a pretty long day, hasn't it?"

He nodded. "What's all this?"

"We spent all Christmas Eve with my side, and we're spending Christmas Day with your side. I thought we could have a little 'us' time between the two."

He nodded and yawned again. "What time is it?"

"Two minutes to midnight. I want us to be awake to ring in our first Christmas together."

His mouth spread in a slow smile. "I'm glad you did." He pointed at the gift box. "Does this mean I can give you your gift too?"

Her lighthearted laughter filled the room. "Let's save those for tomorrow morning. This is a gift for both of us."

He frowned. "But you know what it is, that's not very fair. I don't know how much I like the rules of this game."

She cocked her head and grinned. "I know what it is, but I haven't seen the results."

Zach shook his head. "Now I'm really confused."

"Okay, Zach. You remember how you made me promise not to get the results of a pregnancy test without you by my side?"

"Uh-huh."

"Well, We saw them together. We know we're

pregnant, but that box holds the official results of the ultrasound. I was adamant about Doctor Brown not telling me a thing. Both he and his nurse were quiet as a mouse. So sit up and open it so we can see the very first picture of our child, together."

Zach leaned forward and took the box in his hands, pulled on the delicate red and gold ribbon. He removed the gold foil covered lid, revealing a piece of folded paper. His stomach churned, filled with butterflies as he glanced at his wife, sensing how big this was. "You really haven't seen it yet?"

She crossed her arms tightly across her chest and shook her head. "I really haven't. Since you couldn't be there for the ultrasound I wanted to wait until we were together."

He paused, surprised at her reaction. For all of her claims to love surprises, he knew she didn't particularly enjoy having to wait for them. She'd completely turned the tables on him with this little stunt. He unfolded the sheet of paper.

Cathryn clasped her hands tightly together. "Read it aloud, please."

Zach cleared his throat and looked down at the paper.

"To Mr. & Mrs. Zachary Ferguson—

Congratulations on the exciting news of your pregnancy. Enclosed you'll find pictures from the first ultrasound of your—"

Zach stopped there and lifted his gaze to hers, his heart pounding in his chest, as adrenaline rushed though him.

Cathryn jumped up off the sofa, obviously too excited to contain herself. "Our what? Does it say the sex? I thought it was too soon for that."

"You really don't know?"

"No. What? Is it a boy or girl?"

Zach flipped the second slip of paper to stare at it, and

then stood beside her. He slowly turned it so she could see.

She squinted at the paper until her mouth gaped open. "Is that . . . oh, oh my God . . . Zach." She pulled the letter from his other hand and read the rest of it.

"*. . . pictures from the first ultrasound of your twins. Your due date is on or near July 4th.*"

She whooped just as she did during a hard-earned Saints win, then threw her arms around her husband's neck. He lifted her by the waist and spun her around.

"Oh God, I can't believe it." She waited until he put her down and they stood staring into each other's animated faces. "Dr. Brown said the home pregnancy test sometimes misses if you're not far along. From what this says I was already about a month pregnant when it showed that first negative."

"Talk about shock and awe!" he said, running both hands through his hair, unable to pull his gaze from his wife.

Cathryn raised her hands to her cheeks, pink with excitement. "Are you as ecstatic and terrified of this as I am?"

He nodded. "I think so. I mean, ecstatic? Hell yeah, I'm ecstatic. But terrified? Eh, not so much as you, I think."

"Why not? We don't know a thing about bringing twins into the world."

"We don't know a thing about bringing a single baby into the world. We don't have any expectations, nothing to compare it to. We'll figure it all out for the first time, and we'll do it just the way we heard the news. Together."

She passed her hand slowly, lovingly down the side of his face. "How did I ever think I could spend my life without you by my side?"

He gave her his best sexy crooked grin and kissed her lightly on the mouth. "I don't know. How did you?" Zach leaned in to touch his forehead to hers. "Merry Christmas,

Mrs. Ferguson."

"Merry Christmas, Mr. Ferguson."

"Are you feeling okay, Cat?"

She nodded, before giving him a long and leisurely kiss. "I'm so very good, Zachary. But I'm always better with you."

ABOUT THE AUTHOR

Photograph by Simple Memories Photography

Lori Leger lives in south Louisiana with her husband of eighteen plus years. Between the two of them, they have five wonderful children and a passel of grandchildren, ranging in age from six months to seventeen years of age. In March of 2012, she resigned an 18+year career in road design to write full-time. Lori is the owner and editor of Cajunflair Publishing Company. She has seven full-length novels, one novella, and four short stories published, with an article in a non-fiction book soon to be published. You can find Lori's works on *Amazon and CreateSpace.*

Lori Leger's Website: http://www.lorilegerauthor.com
Facebook: http://www.facebook.com/llegerauthor
FB Page: http://www.facebook.com/lorilegerauthor
Twitter: http://twitter.com/lleger641
Blog: http://cajunflair.wordpress.com
Pinterest: http://pinterest.com/lleger641
Goodreads:
http://www.goodreads.com/author/show/5171074.Lori_Leger

DEDICATION

This is dedicated to three particular groups of women:

First, to the mothers out there who juggle child rearing with all the pressures of daily life. As a mother of grown twins, with a previous single child, I remember how difficult it was to make time for my children, as well as catch a few minutes for myself.

Second, to the mothers who've never been able to hold their own children in their arms. There are so many couples out there, who strive every day to conceive. So many of those aren't able to, or if they do, aren't able to carry full term. My heart goes out to these women as well as their spouses.

Third, to women who've been victims of rape or attempted rape in any situation. I pray for true healing of your hearts and souls. It's a heinous and violent act, whether it's by someone you know or a complete stranger, in your own home, outside your home, or on a date. Please don't keep it inside to fester and cause permanent damage. Find someone to talk to, whether it's a professional or a trusted friend, as my character in the story did.

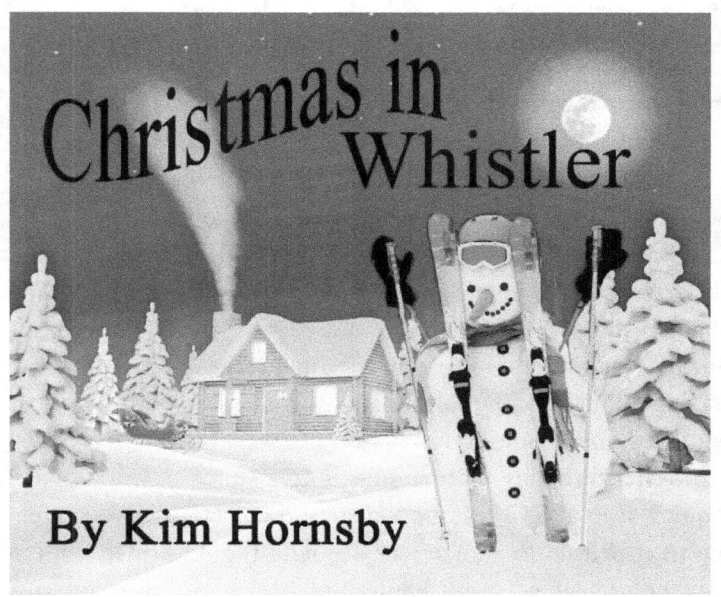

Chapter 1

Christmas in Whistler always meant snow. That's what Daria's friend Joanne said on the phone that morning. "Whether it's man-made by those big machines, or coming from the clouds, there will be snow for Christmas at Canada's best ski resort.

That was good enough for Daria. This year, she'd need a winter wonderland to distract her and, all things considered, Whistler sounded pretty close to perfect. "Okay, you sold me. I'm coming for the holidays."

The need to get out of town didn't completely present itself until the reality of Christmas wihout her children hit her smack in the heart, on the twenty-third. Her precious little girls were spending Christmas with their father and his girlfriend, Suzanne, who also happened to be the reason the family imploded. In the first place. Daria would be alone, four miles down the road from her daughters. Not allowed to see them.

On the not-fair-meter, she figured the needle would spike near the finish line. In the spirit of good mothering, she'd handed over her cherished girls at nine that morning to a man who'd cheated on her, and the woman he'd done it with. It wasn't easy to smile and wish everyone a very Merry Christmas but if she had anything to do with it, her innocent children would never know how their mother felt about Daddy and his girlfriend. And they'd never hear how Suzanne had taunted Daria in the final stages of the divorce, texting about her new family and how she looked forward to being an "instant mommy."

After throwing a few things in to a suitcase, Daria made a quick stop at REI for snow gear and then took off to catch the next Seattle to Vancouver, Canada flight. Armed with a new polar jacket, snow pants and boots, she guessed she could endure a snowstorm in Antarctica quite comfortably in her new getup. Jo had said to bring warm clothes.

Seeing her best friend would be golden. Jo's job as a structural engineer with a company in the Great White North had resulted in a temporary move to Whistler. From recent reports, Jo loved the small town life in the Canadian mountains. That morning, when Jo confessed she and her latest love had split, Daria half-joked that they'd be each other's shoulders to cry on during Christmas. Jo was gay and really wanted to get married and have children someday.

Long ago, when a teenage Jo had told her that she was gay, Daria was surprised, but it didn't change their friendship. Not one bit. After all, Jo had accepted Daria's secret without batting an eye. And seeing auras of energy around people's bodies was a strange claim. Daria had never let that tidbit slip out to anyone, except an Aunt who'd guessed the secret because she saw auras too, and Jo.

The plane touched down on Canadian soil and taxied to a stop. Daria had been fighting motion sickness for an hour and was still a little green around the gills as she cleared customs. Wheeling her single suitcase from baggage claim, she saw Jo's smiling face behind the glass partition and immediately felt better. Emotionally, anyhow. Daria returned the smile.

"Hey Girlfriend!" Jo hugged her like they hadn't seen each other in years, and pulled back to check for tear tracks on her cheeks. "No plane crying? That's good."

The two friends had been through high school and college love affairs together at the University of Washington and knew each other's telltale signs. Jo got puffy eyes, and Daria often had tear tracks long after the tears dried.

Talking their way through the traffic of Vancouver, they drove over Lion's Gate Bridge to the upper level highway. Conversation came whooshing out with topics ranging from Daria's daughters to Jo's work, to Seattle friends, and then fashion. Although the two women had so much in common, they had totally different styles. Daria was a petite blonde with a homecoming queen look, while Jo had a motorcycle queen look with dark hair and a Mediterranean olive complexion. Daria's ex-husband, Robert, used to say they looked like All American girl meets Rock Star. But when it came to their personalities, they were linked. In more ways than Robert knew.

The day they'd met in Redmond High School's cafeteria, Daria knew immediately she was destined to be a part of Jo's life. The aura around Jo was shining as brightly as if a spotlight shone on her back. According to Aunt Beatrice, that only meant one thing—a strong link. The only other person who'd had an aura like that was Aunt Bea. She'd taught Daria everything she knew about the strange ability before she died, and the rest Daria had learned through books and eventually online. Reading auras was an unusual ability and Daria had kept the secret all her life, like she was an axe murderer or worse. Robert didn't know, and for good reason—five of his aura's seven layers spelled bad news. Always had. Daria had chosen to ignore that fact when they fell in love.

As they turned at Horseshoe Bay to head north, Jo's aura was still spotlight white and pulsing with layers of blue and shades of yellow, signifying happiness and opportunity. She could easily ignore a person's aura after years of this sight. The winter sun pierced the inside of Jo's SUV as the car sped along the road. Six days stretched out before the two friends like a prospective trip inside a time machine. Daria was headed to a time when she didn't have children, a time when she wasn't married, when she and Jo were young and carefree. She was in a different country with no responsibilities for a week, beyond being a good friend. Her heart felt light for the first time in a long while. "I feel like my old self," she exclaimed to Jo, who responded with "Atta Girl!"

The drive was stunningly beautiful, like a movie scene where a train winds through the anow-capped Rockies on a sunny day. On the left, an ocean sound loomed far below, and on the right, the sheer wall of rock, probably blasted out decades ago to form the road. At a town called Squamish, Daria confessed she'd have to call it Squeamish due to the twisting road and her returned motion sickness. Jo laughed. "Not long now," she said. Then the road opened up and straightened.

"There's the white stuff!" Jo said, pointing to closer mountains with fluffy clouds circling their peaks.

"It's so beautiful. I think I'm going to cry." Daria's excitement about being in a snowy ski village for Christmas increased with every mile.

When they pulled into the Whistler city limits at 4 p.m., the sun was just dropping behind the mountains, casting a dark shadow on everything inside the basin. Six-foot snow banks bordered the sides of the road. Once past the Function Junction Industrial Area, Jo slowed the car and they wound their way past signs for housing development turnoffs. Traffic was thick on the other side of the road.

"All this is day-skiers driving back to Vancouver," Jo said, motioning towards the snaky line of cars.

With log homes, snow banks, cars loaded with skies, hotels, and restaurants, the initial view of the Whistler area, called Creekside, was everything Daria expected in a ski resort, and so much more.

"It's storybook beautiful."

"Wait until you see the town. This is just a tease," Jo said.

So far, Whistler was unlike any other place she'd ever seen. Not that she'd ever been in a world-renowned ski resort before. Over the last five years, Daria had successfully avoided skiing with Robert, saying she got too cold and didn't like to make her toes suffer that way. He'd been the parent to start the girls on skis and she'd been the parent who did everything else with their daughters. Aside from eight Sundays with his girls in ski season, Robert avoided fatherhood if he possibly could. Instead, he pursued his career at a software company like his life depended on it. The upside to her daughters' Dad never being home was being able to afford skiing, and the lavish lifestyle he provided. Not that any of that mattered to Daria, or the girls. They'd have preferred his time. The house was too big to clean herself and she now depended on a weekly cleaning lady to help out. Daria planned to move eventually, create some distance between herself and Robert and find a smaller place for the three of them.

"I have a confession to make," Jo said. "It's a little negative and a big positive." Jo looked over at Daria who braced herself for terrible news. "I told a little white lie to get you to come to Whistler for Christmas."

"What?" Daria's heart jumped and she stared at Jo reproachfully, hoping it had nothing to do with Robert.

"Sheila and I didn't break up. We just had a fight. Everything is okay now." Jo looked so apologetic that Daria had to laugh.

"I didn't know if you'd still come if you thought you were going to be hanging around with a couple, but Sheila is so busy this week that I'll hardly see her."

Daria reached over to touch Jo's shoulder. "I'm glad things are still good with Sheila." She was. "Don't worry, I'm here now. It just feels good to get out of town." She fidgeted with a tissue in her coat pocket. "You're saving me from driving over to spy on the girls as they go in and out of Robert's place." This dynamics of the week would be different with Jo still part of a couple, but that could be a good thing.

"We're staying at Sheila's house, not my condo." Jo grinned at Daria. "That's the good part. Her house is amazing! Wait until you see. Sheila's the owner and chef at one of Whistler's most popular restaurants, Sushi Yo, and has money."

Jo steered the SUV into a housing development called Blueberry Hill and two turns later parked in the short driveway of a mountain chalet. Daria whistled, the house must've cost a lot of Canadian bucks. "This is Sheila's house?"

She got out of the car and stood, taking in the sight. The neighborhood resembled a group of small lodges, all unique in design, but well suited to the mountain theme. Sheila's home was constructed with huge wooden beams and a granite rock front. It had to be five thousand square feet, for what she could see.

"Nice digs, eh?" Jo joked. "Come on."

She followed Jo up the snowy driveway, silently praising her boots' heavy treads. Catching a peek between houses, Daria saw nothing but the massive monstrosity of Whistler Mountain in the distance and assumed from their drive up the last hill that the house was built on the edge of a cliff.

"Sheila's at the restaurant. She won't be home until late tonight." Jo said with an infectious smile.

After stepping out of her boots, Daria followed Jo into the main room and gazed at the view through twenty foot windows. The mountain loomed in front of them, almost too close to get a good view. The peak wasn't visible. Below the cliff lay a snowy field.

"Mountain ahead, golf course below. The town to the left." Jo pointed to where twinkling lights punctured the dusky light. "We'll go to Whistler Village for dinner, but not Sheila's restaurant. We can't get in there for weeks, unless we want to sit at the bar." She motioned for Daria to follow her.

Although she kept thinking how much Robert would love this place, Daria pushed those thoughts to the back of her mind and followed her suitcase down the hall.

"You'll sleep in here this week." Jo motioned to the doorway ahead of them. "Sheila's son Javier is at the end of the hall and we're on the other side of the living room in the master bedroom. I've pretty much moved in, and not because of the house." She grinned. "Wait until you meet Sheila."

Darla took in the cozy snugness of the guest room. It was just large enough to accommodate a twin bed covered with a bear-themed comforter, a rust-colored chair by the window and a dresser with a deer antler lamp. "This is perfect. Oh Jo, it's so cozy and lovely." She pulled Jo into a hug and felt the warmth of her aura. "This is absolutely perfect. You're sure Sheila is okay with me being here. After the fight and all?"

Jo pulled back, her face tinged with disbelief. "Are you kidding me? Of course she's okay. I wouldn't be with anyone who didn't like my friends. Besides, *she* has a friend coming to visit tomorrow. And, if you're worried about us fighting it was only that she worries I'll be gone in nine months when this contract ends." Joanne's eyes sparkled. "I'm so in love with this woman, Dar, I may end up living in Whistler."

"Oh, my Gosh!" Daria was happy, but she'd reserve her excitement until she actually met the chef and saw her aura.

Jo knew what she was thinking. "Don't tell me if the aura is bad, okay?"

"I may not see anything right away, you know that. Or, it may only have to do with me and my relationship to her."

Jo knew that part of reading an aura had to do with interpretation, and nodded.

"Where's the boy?"

"With his Dad or on an overnight, or something."

"I'll need to Christmas shop a little before the 25th." Daria loved Christmas, loved presents, Christmas food, loved to decorate trees, and everything that came with the holiday. "I want to get a few things." Just because her kids were with Robert, didn't mean she couldn't now get into the spirit of the holiday. Walking back into the family room, Daria looked around. "Where's the Christmas tree?"

"Sheila and I have a fake one in the bedroom, haven't had time to do a real one."

Daria's eyes widened. "Let's get one now!"

Daria rubbed her arms to warm up. It was cold in town and the ski jacket she'd worn didn't help warm up her legs in jeans. The village core was pedestrian only with roads circling the outside hub. Bundled in their winter gear, she and Jo wandered the snowy promenade, ducking in shops and talking about what to have for dinner.

The snow made Whistler Village a Winter Wonderland and the word 'enchanting' came to mind as they walked under a twinkly lit arbor into an Italian restaurant. Seated at a window table, they ordered shrimp fettuccini, garlic bread and salads. Daria hadn't eaten a meal all day. Waiting for their food, they laughed about the old days when they couldn't afford a hamburger let alone this meal, or the expensive bottle of wine that sat between them. Daria had recently lost a few pounds, no doubt due to her worry about a Christmas away from the girls, and felt no guilt in overeating when the calorie-laden fettuccine was placed between them.

After dinner, when they exited the restaurant they heard singing. A group of carolers stood just around the corner, singing "Oh Come All Ye Faithful," dressed in period costumes. The movie It's a Wonderful Life came to mind and they stood listening for a few songs. The perfect ending to their dinner.

Once a ten-foot Scotch pine tree was loaded on the top of Jo's car, they drove to the drug store for decorations and a tree stand. Soon, the two friends were back at the house chuckling about how Jo had always been useless with anything artistic. She could hammer her way through a kitchen remodel but drawing a picture, decorating a house or artistically designing a Christmas tree was not her forte.

"That's what I'm for, remember?" Daria laughed, as they lugged the tree to the front door of Sheila's house and brushed off all the snow. "You're the engineer and I'm the artist." Daria had studied costume design at school, not that she'd had much of a chance to use her talent so far. Her dream ended when Robert came along with *his* dream of having a stay-at-home wife and eventual mother to his children. She'd given up the idea of doing all three too easily, but never regretted a moment of being a stay-at-home mom to her daughters.

Once they secured the tree in the stand by the family room window, Daria insisted Jo sit down, with a glass of pinot grigio, and watch her decorate. First the lights, then the red bows, then she asked Jo if she wanted to fasten the Twelve Days of Christmas ornaments.

"No thanks. I wanna watch," she said, pulling a fuzzy brown throw blanket over her legs.

"That's what he said," Daria laughed. They'd had this joke for years, silly as it was. She stood back to get an idea of where to put the ornaments, sipping her long-stemmed glass of pinot. The wine's effect was heady, and as she worked on the tree she worried she'd wake up tomorrow to a tree with upside down decorations all on one side. "Looking good so far?" she asked Jo. Her buzz was enough to keep her happy but not so much that she was slurring her words. Not having had anything to drinks in months, Daria realized what a lightweight she was at drinking wine.

The plan was to keep the tree lit for Sheila's arrival after midnight. Daria wanted to meet this Sheila but somewhere around 8:30, knew she would never be able to stay awake.

"You'll see each other at the coffee pot in the morning," Jo said.

While someone on the stereo sang about a little drummer boy, Daria added the final ornaments and strung garlands of gold balls in loops around the tree. Jo ran back from the kitchen with a set of chopsticks, a red cheese grater, a potato peeler, and other kitchen gadgets.

"Is this okay or will it spoil your design?" she asked, after placing them all over the tree.

"Oh My Gosh, it's perfect!" Daria was pleased that Jo had added her own touch in honor of Sheila being a chef. They had garland left over, and together they strung them around the room with the extra light strings.

Turning off the house lights to see the Christmas twinkles, Jo and Daria made "oooo" sounds in appreciation of what they'd done. Standing arm in arm by the bountiful tree, Daria gazed out at the tiny lights of Whistler stretched to their left. Although the mountain itself, was mostly dark, little lights dotted the base, and a string of snow cats' spotlights headed up the mountain to groom the ski runs.

"Oh, Jo, this is absolutely the best thing I could've done today." Tears threatened but Daria would not let them fall. No tears on this adventure.

Daria woke to the sound of coffee beans grinding on the far side of the house. She had mother's hearing and unfortunately, not even the ear plugs she'd packed cancelled out the faint sound. The bedside clock read 7:23 and she burrowed back into the fluffy quilt for another few minutes. She had time.

Jo didn't work this week and today they planned to go Christmas shopping. Last night Jo had agreed there'd be no skiing for their first full day. Daria was thankful her day of falling on her butt had been postponed and took her earplugs out to listen for Jo's voice.

Once she heard voices and footsteps padding along the hallway floor, Daria swung her legs over the side of the bed and grabbed her robe. The house had cooled off over night and she quickly wrapped her fluffy robe around her body. Apparently Sheila liked the house cold for sleeping but Jo had said to hurry out to the kitchen in the morning where they'd stand on a heated floor, waiting for coffee as the house warmed.

Daria brushed her shoulder-length straight blonde hair, took off the last remnants of yesterday's makeup, and headed out to the kitchen to meet Sheila. Laughter trickled from the kitchen, as she traversed the family room. Stopping to gaze out the window, Daria saw that the valley and mountain were still shadowed. It looked like a gorgeous day, with the sky above the mountain as blue as a robin's egg.

"Tell me what you want or I'll tickle it out of you." Jo's voice teased from the other room.

Daria rounded the corner to find Jo embracing a dark-haired beauty in front of the stove. "Good morning ladies!" she said.

Jo gave Sheila a kiss on the cheek and they broke apart. "Daria! Sheila, this amazing apparition in the doorway is Daria."

Daria approached the women and smiled warmly, extending her hand. "Sheila, I'm so happy to meet you. I've never seen Jo this . . . this . . . " She looked at her beaming friend, ". . . this giggly in love."

A faint aura of light emanated from Sheila, shades of blue and a pulsing red. That was good. Daria nodded at Jo.

"Well, it's mutual," Sheila said with a noticeable accent. Jo said she was from Brazil originally. "I'm excited to finally meet you too." Sheila had a smile as lovely as her face. Her thick black hair hung in curls across shoulders which were covered by a pink sweater. The three women stood smiling at one another until Daria broke the spell.

"Thank you so much for inviting me to your home for Christmas. You have no idea how much this means."

Sheila nodded, looked at Jo, and spoke. "I do. I'm a mother. We're going to try to distract you from not having your daughters this week." She touched Daria's arm. "Now I need real coffee, not this weak dribble Jo likes." She crossed to the espresso machine, while Jo looked expectantly at Daria.

"Beautiful aura," Daria whispered to her friend. An aura wasn't always obvious and reading one took some skill. For one thing, you had to concentrate sometimes to really see the energy emanating. And Daria's gift wasn't textbook exact. Sometimes she read an additional eighth layer of energy that related to how the person reacted to her, something she'd never heard about through her research. Usually, she dialed down her ability when meeting someone new. Jo got her friend a cup of coffee and Daria took off her slippers to truly enjoy the heated kitchen floor.

Sheila's son, Javier, was a typical eleven-year-old boy, aside from the fact that he was a beautiful kid with gorgeous dark skin, black eyes, and enviably long eyelashes. He hadn't wanted to go shopping with his mother. Yet when he returned from his sleepover, he agreed, as long as he could go skiing with his father later. Sheila promised she'd have him at the base of Blackcomb, one of the two skiing mountains, by one p.m. to meet his Dad.

With a long list of to-do's, the four set off for Whistler Village and its charming shops. Daria had a stroke of luck discovering a Kendama game in the yo yo section at the village toy store. She'd heard that preteen boys liked these things and Jo whispered that Javier did not have one. She also picked up toys for her girls—a bear and a moose with "Whistler, Canada" embroidered on the chest along with *I'd rather be skiing* T-shirts. She added ponytail holders and hair bows to her basket because the girls loved them and threw in little purses with sparkles and zebra print trim. She'd scheduled a Skype call with them later in the day and hoped that Suzanne, the instant mommy, wouldn't participate.

The sky had clouded over by the time the foursome left the lunch restaurant. The weather report called for snow on Christmas Eve, and the prospect of flurries excited Daria. She mentioned that if there was enough snowfall, she'd satisfy her Christmas wish to build a snowman. Javier said he'd help later and took off to meet his father. Sheila promised Jo she'd be home by four o'clock, when her friend would arrive from San Francisco.

"Old friend from college days, I think," Jo said to Daria as they walked to the car. "Oh and tonight is a Christmas Eve party is scheduled for 7 p.m. It's casual, jeans and sweaters. Some of this group will come straight from skiing."

Daria hadn't brought many clothes except yoga pants, casual shirts, the clothes she wore on the plane, and her ski stuff. Luckily, at the last minute, she'd packed her high-priced designer jeans and a few fun tops, one of which would do for the Christmas party.

Arriving back at the house with their packages, Daria joked that it was almost like when they'd shared an apartment in college except now they shopped with their choice of credit cards.

"You still doing okay for money with Robert and everything?" Jo set her packages on the dining room table.

"Yes. Luckily Robert's guilt was strong enough to give me the house and a generous settlement." Daria pulled the wrapping paper out of the bags and organized a wrapping station on the table. "I've taken on a few costuming projects for a local theatre group and hope to break into that market. Make my own money eventually."

While they wrapped presents, they talked about Daria's designs for a post-apocalyptic play that was in pre-production in Seattle. "The clothes are grim and grey then set their gifts under the pine tree. The Christmas tree smelled heavenly, its strong pine scent filling the room.

Daria wondered what her daughters were doing. Most likely, they were very excited about Christmas Eve being only five and eight years old. She'd told them they would have their own Christmas with Mommy on New Year's Eve at their house, but at the last minute she'd given Robert half the Santa toys in case he didn't get them things they wanted. Tonight, she'd show them their stuffed animals on Skype. They were so young to be separated from their mother at Christmas. She could count on one hand the years since preschool. For Daria's tender heart, it was a chore to trust that Robert knew what he was doing with them, considering he hadn't been around enough to really know them.

The divorce with Robert had been hurtful but, as luck would have it, over quickly. The most pain came from knowing a strange woman put her young daughters to bed when they stayed with Robert. A woman who played a large part in the family's break-up, and a woman who had an aura that read like the wicked witch of the west. But, for her daughters' sake, she had to pretend to like Suzanne.

"I'm glad Daddy has someone wonderful to love him," she'd said, gritting her teeth and smiling at her beautiful daughters after they'd gushed over Daddy's pretty girlfriend. Lying didn't come easily but she'd read that the best thing to do for her kids was to pretend to like the girlfriend and trust that Robert wouldn't do anything to put their children's safety in jeopardy. He was their biological father and he had legal rights. Giving him a week with them at Christmas was something she had to accept.

Even though she was now regretting her decision, Robert got Christmas this year because Daria wanted the February break so she could take the girls to Maui with her parents and the rest of the family. A reunion of Daria's big extended family had been in the works for a year and she was determined her girls wouldn't miss the fun of playing on the beach with their cousins.

While putting the finishing touches to her makeup and hair for the party, Daria heard a man's voice in the front hall. Judging from all the laughing, he sounded like a funny guy. Jo said something about needing more of this in Sheila's life and Daria wondered what she was talking about. Daria strained to listen while she added a pair of red bead drop earrings and then stood back to check her reflection in the mirror. She hadn't gotten dressed up since Robert's birthday, last March. A night she now referred to as the "beginning of the end" seeing the event concluded with him saying that he wanted a divorce.

Tonight she looked much better than that fateful night. She wore slim fit jeans with a tight, red-patterned top and a pair of extremely expensive boots she'd bought out of spite the day after Robert's revelation. Her hair hung in soft curls along her shoulders and her eyes glowed with a brightness that hadn't been there two days ago. Canada's mountain air obviously agreed with her. Swiping some lip gloss across her mouth, she turned from the mirror, satisfied with the results.

Stepping into the sunken living room, Daria's gaze fixated on a man wearing jeans and a sky blue dress shirt. He stood in front of the window with a beer in hand, talking to Sheila about something that had her laughing. It looked like the first guest had arrived. Daria wondered if she should disturb the twosome by the window. They seemed so happy. Outside, the approaching darkness cast a grey light on the landscape, and lights burned brightly on all over the village. The lit Christmas tree cast a colorful glow across the room and Daria was happy they'd made the effort to get this tree.

When Sheila saw Daria, she cut her laughter short, motioning her over. "There you are. I want you to meet my good friend, Pierre Charbenaud."

The man transferred his beer in order extend his right hand. "Hello."

Daria hesitated before taking his hand. She almost froze but eventually took his hand. "Nice to meet you, Pierre," she said. In all her thirty-two years, Daria had never seen an aura like this before but she'd been warned of its existence. At first sight, the aura looked like a warm glow, like candlelight that drowned the other layers. Once she took his hand, the glow ignited and became a low orange flame. She nearly jumped back at the appearance of the flame but managed to hold it together. If she hadn't been so distracted by his aura, she might have noticed his handsome face, especially when he smiled. But her immediate attention remain locked on the unusual glow surrounding the man.

"Sheila tells me you are from Seattle. Is this your first visit to Whistler?" he said with a slight accent that she suspected was French. His name certainly sounded French.

"Yes. It's lovely," she said in a weak voice.

"Are you feeling okay, Daria?" Sheila asked, resting her hand lightly on Daria's arm.

Just then, Jo burst into the room. "Here comes the food!" Sheila excused herself to accompany the caterers to the kitchen.

Daria recovered quickly. "You looked familiar at first. That's all," she shrugged.

"I have one of those faces."

Daria nearly laughed aloud at his comment. Pierre Charbenaud did not have an ordinary looking face at all. He had a drop-dead, gorgeous face, completely unique in a handsome, movie star way.

"Do you think we should try to help Sheila, or stay out of their way?" Pierre nodded towards the kitchen.

"I think they'll call us if we're needed, but I would like a glass of wine." She nodded to his beer. "While I'm going that way, do you need another one?'"

"Yes, why not?"

In the kitchen, Daria pulled Jo aside. "Pierre has a very unusual aura."

"Good or bad?"

"Good, maybe." She poured two glasses of wine. "At the very least it's intriguing. What does he do for work?" She gave one glass to Jo.

"Wine snob, or something."

"That's a job?" They laughed and Daria grabbed a beer from the fridge. "Let me know if you need help with the food or anything. I'll be waiting for instructions." She made a face and scooted out of the way as Sheila ordered everyone around like the chef she was.

A small terrier dog greeted her in the great room as she entered, its ears flopping as it jumped up to her knees. "Hey! Where did you come from?" She looked to Pierre who whistled for the dog.

"He's mine. Name is Scruffy," Pierre said.

"Was he here before?" She scanned the area, as though she might have missed something.

Pierre laughed. "No he was outside taking a tinkle in the snow. Not his favorite thing to do." He picked up the little dog and ruffled his fur. "I'm not sure if he's ever seen snow before. I may have to find him doggie boots for this week."

Daria handed Pierre his beer and they sat down on the couch. Scruffy settled at Pierre's feet.

Pierre's aura was back to being a faint flow of yellow light and she still wasn't sure why she wasn't seeing the usual seven layers, including unwanted energy that came from everyone. As they sipped their drinks, they talked about Whistler and Daria soon realized that Pierre was the other houseguest, not a party guest. And, he was indeed French. The chardonnay made a warm path down her throat to her tummy.

"Sheila said that you and Jo go way back. Went to college together in Seattle?" he asked.

The conversation eventually led to Seattle, which led to the subject of her children. "I have a Skype call with my kids in about twenty minutes." She checked her watch. "I'm a little worried that my ex-husband's girlfriend might try to high-jack the call. I'm going to drink this wine fast." She took a big gulp, swallowed, and smiled at Pierre apologetically.

"Where are your children?"

"With their Dad in Seattle; Woodinville to be exact."

"Ah, home of Chateau Ste. Michelle."

He *was* a wine snob. "Yes, are you interested in wines?"

"I am. As a matter of fact I'm a vintner." He must've noticed her puzzled expression and explained. "I grow grapes and produce wine. I live outside San Francisco and have crops in Napa, along with a winery."

Much more than just a wine snob. "Oh, how fun. I live very close to the Woodinville wine tasting center." They talked about wine until it was time for Daria to set up her laptop for the call. "Excuse me while I try to hold my composure for the sake of my daughters." She disappeared to her bedroom, her heart beating fearfully against her chest in anticipation of what could happen during the call.

The girls were giggly and excited, and Daria's heart ached to be with them. When Suzanne barged in to tell the girls it was time to go caroling, Daria fought back her urge to argue that this was more important than singing bloody Christmas songs. They were talking to their mother, for goodness sake.

"Oh, hello Daria. Aren't you just down the road? Why are you calling?" Suzanne had stuck her head in the picture and the girls moved over and almost out of view to accommodate.

"I'm in Whistler, skiing. I promised my girls I'd call them on Christmas Eve." She held up the stuffed animals. "Look Sunny, I bought you a cute little moose. And this bear is for you, Rosey. Aren't they fun?"

The two little girls reached for the screen and pretended to stroke the animals, giggling.

"Don't touch the screen girls. You'll leave finger prints." Suzanne sounded annoyed.

Daria didn't know why she did it, but her split-second decision cleared mission control in her brain and she found herself asking her darlings if they'd like to meet a friend of Mommy's.

"Yea!" They nodded as Sunny bounced around in the chair.

"Just a sec." Daria stood and peeked around the corner where Pierre was by the tree, changing the music. "Pierre, wanna meet my girls?" When he looked over, she gave him a desperate look and ran back in the bedroom in case Suzanne signed off. The girls were waiting in childish innocence. Daria smiled at them. "His name is Pierre and he has a cute little rescue dog." Suzanne had a very expensive

French bulldog that she paid thousands of dollars for and babied like a newborn.

The girls said, "aww, what's the dog's name?" Pierre peeked around the corner with Scruffy in his arms and advanced to Daria's chair. Suzanne inserted herself between the two girls and moved the laptop back to accommodate all three. Daria knew Suzanne well enough to know that she wasn't going to miss seeing a man in Daria's life. Game on.

"Of course I'd like to meet your girls." Pierre sat on the edge of the chair with Daria, putting his arm along the backrest. *Oh yea. This was good.*

"Pierre, this is my sweet little angel, Sunny."

The littlest one held up her hand and waved.

"And this is my biggest angel, Rose." Daria couldn't believe she was doing this.

"Nice to meet you." He pretended to shake their hands and they did the same on their end. "And this is my furry angel, Scruffy." He held up the dog's paw to wave and everyone laughed but Suzanne.

"Can he do any tricks? He's so cute!" Rose said.

"He can dance but I need a treat. Maybe tomorrow when you talk to Mom, I'll be more prepared." Pierre smiled at the girls warmly, like he was used to children and Daria wondered if he had any.

"Are you skiing too?" they asked Pierre. "Mommy can't ski."

"I am going to teach mommy to ski, as a matter of fact. I'm a ski instructor."

The girls looked impressed while Daria tried to appear like she knew the man sharing her chair was a ski instructor. "There is so much snow here, my darlings. It's snowing now. I'm going to have to bring you girls here to ski."

"Will Pierre teach us to ski moguls?" Rose asked excitedly.

"I sure will." He spoke before Daria could think of an answer. "Moguls are just bumpy friends who like their back scratched."

The girls giggled.

Pierre's adorable French accent was just enough to see him through Suzanne's eyes as a gorgeous ski instructor. How could Suzanne not wonder what Daria was doing with this man?

The girls told Pierre that they already knew how to ski because they skied with Daddy. Then Suzanne got a strange look on her face and called to Robert. "Robert, come meet Daria's new friend, Pierre."

"Oh, I'm not so new, am I, Ma Cherie?" Pierre put his arm around Daria's shoulders and she snuggled in to his warm side. *Thank you Pierre Charbenaud, whoever you are.*

"No, not new at all," Daria said. *Oh this was good.* "I've known Pierre since first year in college." She'd met Robert during her second year. That tidbit would have Suzanne questioning Robert all night.

"Move over girls." Robert slid in beside Suzanne who immediately put her hand in his lap, inches from his crotch. Daria almost laughed out loud. "Daria." Robert's expression was stony and she couldn't read auras on the computer.

Pierre held firm, smiling at the foursome on the screen. "Nice to finally meet you, Robert." He glanced back at Daria, fondly. *Keep it congenial, the girls are watching.* "Seems like the girls are really looking forward to Santa coming tonight." Daria tried to ignore that Pierre's leg pressed alongside hers in the chair.

"We're looking forward to it too." Robert continued to stare, stone-faced.

Suzanne turned to the girls and said clearly, "We don't still believe in Santa, do we?" She laughed, scrunching her nose like she'd smelled something bad. "You're big girls now, aren't you?"

Daria wanted to slap her. "Suzanne! Of course we know all about Santa and how some kids don't believe, but how do all the presents just get in the living room on Christmas morning?" Daria's laugh was forced. "We've had this talk, the girls and I and we are big believers!"

"And who eats the cookies I always put out?" Pierre looked unfazed by Suzanne's ugly comment. "Where do those go? And the milk?"

"Absolutely true, Pierre." Daria would've marched Suzanne from the room clutching her scrawny arm, if this hadn't been a Skype call. "Robert, no offense but I've seen enough of the grown-ups. Time for just me and the girls now." Daria faked a laugh as two small faces came back into view, happy, excited, and obviously unaffected by Suzanne's direct hit to their mother. "Now sweeties, get to bed in good time tonight so Daddy doesn't have to listen to you giggle and talk. Then you'll be in good shape for Santa's presents tomorrow." She thought of the toys she'd left with her ex-husband.

Robert spoke off camera. "Let's do both Suzanne. She brought them over."

"Daddy, I can hear you talking," Daria said in a sing-songy voice. "If it's a secret present you're talking about, remember the girls can hear you too."

Suzanne poked her head through the two squirming girls. "We're doing our own Santa thing. We'll just give you back yours."

What? Suzanne wasn't giving the kids her Santa gifts? What the hell? Daria's blood pressure jumped and her anger threatened to explode.

Robert interrupted. "Say good-bye, girls. Daddy wants to say a special Christmas Eve wish to Mommy." The girls said their good-bye's, blew kisses, and ran off to the hall to get their coats for caroling.

With just Suzanne and Robert left, Daria tried to be civil. "You have your own gifts for the girls? They specifically asked for the things I brought over. Just remember that. They might be disappointed if they don't get some things on their list."

Pierre took her hand in his and pulled it over to his lap. Squeezing ever so lightly.

"Daria, Suzanne got some terrific toys and we'd like to do our own Christmas, not yours."

Suzanne interrupted. "I know you like to control everything, Daria, but you have to let us parent the girls too."

Pierre almost cut her off. "Suzanne, this is between Daria and Robert. Not us. Let's let them speak."

Suzanne's look of shock was priceless. "Who the hell are you, Pierre? Who do you think you are talking to me like that? I've been around for a year and have dried those girls' tears when they were sad, read them bedtime stories, and fed them mac and cheese that I made by scratch. Something their real mother doesn't even bother to do!"

Robert looked shocked. "Honey, don't. It's not the…"

Daria broke in, talking overtop of her ex-husband. "How could you have been around for a year Suzanne, when Robert and I have only been separated for eight months?" Daria knew the answer.

"I'm out of here. The girls and I are going caroling." Before she was out of the chair, Pierre spoke.

"Suzanne and Robert, you're making it very hard to share our happy news with you." Pierre smiled lovingly at Daria.

The curiosity on Suzanne's face made Daria want to say something that would stick in her craw, something that would make the woman see her as something more than a victim to be bullied. Daria turned to Pierre and whispered loud enough for Suzanne to hear, "That's okay, darling. We'll tell the girls ourselves, when we get there." She then turned to the computer screen. "Goodbye, Robert," and hit the 'end call' button.

They sat for a few beats before Daria let out the long breath she'd been holding. She turned to Pierre and laughed. "What have we done?"

He raked a hand through his hair. "I'm sorry I said that, but I couldn't resist." He searched her face. "Suzanne's a piece of work."

"Yes, she is. It's all right if she tells the girls we have news." Daria was working through all the what-ifs in her head as she stood up and looked out the window. "Thanks for playing along. I really appreciate it." The worst case scenario would be that Suzanne told the girls that Mommy was getting married. Knowing her children as well as she did, they would be excited to think their mother had a boyfriend.

"She hates you, doesn't she?" Pierre stood and set Scruffy on the floor.

Jo poked her head in the door. "What's going on? You guys looking at YouTube videos?"

"Pierre and I told Suzanne and Robert that we have news." Saying the words aloud made Daria wonder what else it could mean besides an engagement. What was Robert doing at that very minute—probably holding back Suzanne from spilling the beans? "You know you have to come to Washington with me now and pretend we're a couple."

"Didn't you two just meet?" Jo looked confused.

"I'm kidding Jo."

Pierre shrugged. "It just so happens I'm driving to Washington on the twenty-ninth to do some business." Pierre sounded ready to continue the façade.

Daria looked at Jo, fury rising to the surface again. "Suzanne all but told the girls there's no Santa."

"And she told Daria that she'd been involved with her husband four months before their separation," Pierre added.

Jo looked like *she'd* been told there was no Santa. "You've got to be kidding me!"

"And she insulted Daria's mac and cheese," Pierre said.

"I forgot that." Daria looked hurt. "She really *is* nasty. I make terrific mac and cheese with four different cheeses and whipping cream! She is one nasty skank. I'm not making this up, am I?" Daria picked up her phone and began punching in numbers. "I'm texting Robert to tell Suzanne not to ruin his daughter's Christmas by telling them about Santa."

"I think we should go to Seattle after this to play a good old fashioned New Year's joke on Suzanne.

Daria smiled. "Thanks for being in my corner, Pierre." She read the text from her ex-husband *"Don't worry about the girls. R U getting married? Do the girls know?"* She typed back. *"No,"* and left it at that. Robert could interpret it any way he wanted but after two minutes of talking to Pierre about Suzanne's penchant for making Daria's life miserable, Robert wrote more. *"I won't tell them anything."*

Daria grabbed her glass of wine from the dresser, downed the last of it and made an announcement. "I can't do anything from Whistler. If everyone will excuse me, I'm not going in to the bathroom to cry or wring my hands and worry. I'm going to have another glass of wine and see if Sheila needs me in the kitchen."

Walking across the Great Room, she allowed herself to glance at the twinkling lights of the village out the window. It was Christmas Eve, she was at a ski resort far away from her girls, and Robert assured her they would have a wonderful Christmas. She had to let it go for now. Taking a deep breath, Daria turned toward the kitchen, and went looking for the wine bottle.

Jo had changed into a pair of black jeans and a sparkly top, a bedazzled look that left Daria staring. Tonight, sparkles won over the tough chick look. She even wore dangly earrings. "Nicely done, Joanne," Daria said looking her up and down. She was pleased to see her friend make such an effort. Sheila was dressed similarly and Daria smiled to herself.

The party was in full force a half hour later. Guests arrived in large groups, stomping the snow off their boots as they entered the foyer and Christmas music played loudly in the background. Lights twinkled in the living room over a bar that had been set up next to the Christmas tree. When Javier walked through the door at 7:40, Daria happened to be near the hall and heard his mother speak to him in in rapid Spanish.

"Spanish is a beautiful language." Daria watched the two move from the front door, to Javier's room.

Pierre chuckled. "Even when she's chewing him out for being late?"

Daria looked at him, questioningly. "Really? It sounded so melodic."

"It's Portuguese, by the way."

"Is it similar to French?"

He seemed to understand what was being said. "No. But I had a girlfriend from Brazil and I'm familiar with the conversation that starts with 'Where were you? You're late.'" His eyes twinkled.

A party guest named Bernadette laughed at Pierre's comment. She was clearly putting the moves on the dashing Frenchman, agreeing, laughing, and thrusting her bosom his way. Daria needed a glass of water to clear her head a bit. She was beginning to slur her words—time to slow way down and see if Pierre looked as amazing when she was totally sober.

Close to sixty people came and went during the four hour party. The sushi was out of this world delicious and Daria ate too much. Since the divorce she hadn't gone out for sushi and remembered how much she loved sashimi rolls. Sheila's team had prepared other finger foods like crab cakes with a mustard aioli, feta and parmesan stuffed mushrooms, teriyaki beef kabobs and chicken tacos. The food was hard to resist and the alcohol supply seemed bottomless. All car keys had been thrown into a glass urn at the front door table and Daria imagined there'd be a lot of taxis called to Sheila's address tonight. A teetotaler named Owen was in charge of handing back car keys or calling taxis and he walked the premises calling out, "Friends don't let friends drive drunk."

During the festivities, Jo introduced Daria to six bachelors who all lived in or near Whistler. Daria smiled and talked with each one like she had no idea what Jo was up to. Finally she took Jo aside to ask her to put a halt to the one-woman crusade to get her a Christmas hookup. "I'm having a wonderful time! Call off the bachelors, please." Jo continued putting out fresh plates of sausage rolls and cheese puffs.

But at 11:30, Daria was a little bit tipsy, and decided a walk in the snow was just what she needed to clear her head. On her way to retrieve her coat from her room, she saw Javier still awake at his computer and mentioned that she was heading outside to make a snowman. His eyes lit up and his mouth dropped open. "Tell your Mom you're going outside with me, and I'll meet you at the front."

One more thing before she walked out the door. She grabbed a carrot from the fridge and rounded the corner to the front door, almost running into Pierre. In the dim light of the hall, he looked especially handsome, but then, she was still feeling the wine's effects.

"Leaving?" he asked.

"Javier and I are making a snowman."

"How fun. Javier must be excited." The look in his eyes made her blush and Daria was glad she was bundled up and on her way out. "I better get outside before I have heatstroke." Waving her carrot, she slipped out the door.

Javier joined her soon after on the snowy front lawn where she'd started to roll a big ball for the snowman's base.

"Let me help!" he called, running up to her.

Pierre walked outside next. "I brought a hat and mittens."

Three snowballs later, they had their basic snowman and added the twigs for arms, stones for eyes and buttons, and the clothes that Pierre brought. They stood back and surveyed their work.

"Magnifique," Pierre said.

"He's one handsome snowman," Daria added.

"He's kind of small but he's got a lot of charm," Javier said with a smile.

"Is he small? I've never made a snowman before." Daria's confession brought looks of surprise from the boys.

"Well then, we need a photograph." Pierre pointed to the front door where several people were leaving the party. "Go get your phone. We'll take a picture so you can send it to the girls tomorrow." His smile stretched from ear to ear.

Daria ran inside thinking what a good idea that was, but a text from Suzanne had her heart leaping into her throat. *The girls told me that they love me, tonight. Ahhhh.* It would've been a lovely announcement if anyone else had sent the text, but from Suzanne, the words were meant to hurt. And, on Christmas Eve. Fighting back tears, Daria continued outside and forced herself to remember that she wanted the girls to love Suzanne, take her into their hearts. It was for their own good.

"Come on Javier, get in this shot with me." Daria stood by the snowman that Pierre was now calling Monsieur Neige, and they posed for a photo. Javier switched places with Pierre, and just before the photo was taken, Pierre put his arm around Daria and planted a kiss on the top of her head.

"That one is for Suzanne," he said, his eyes twinkling. "I just hope I'm handsome enough to look like your boyfriend."

"Oh, you're handsome enough," Daria whispered. He was for sure too handsome.

Javier put a sign on Monsieur Neige that said "Merry Christmas, DO NOT TOUCH ME—I have a cold." The last part was Pierre's idea and they laughed about other things they could say with plays on words like "frozen," "ice," and "manly bits." Just as Javier disappeared inside, a few flakes of snow fell in the yard. Looking up, Daria saw that the sky was filled with flakes on their way to the ground.

"It's snowing!"

"Oui," he said. "Joyeux Noel, Ma Belle." Pulling her into a hug, they stayed in the yard watching the snow lazily float past the street light in front of the house.

Finally she broke the silence. "I want to go for a walk in the snow. Will you come with me?"

"With pleasure." He kissed her head and they set off down the cul de sac, the magic of snow adding entrancement to the night.

Pierre pointed the way down the hill and within minutes they ended up at the golf course, below the cliff. Seeing the wide expanse of pristine, white snow, Daria had an idea. "Let's make snow angels! Do you know how?"

Pierre assured her that he was the "French champion, king of snow angels," and grabbed her hand to lead her to the clean snow away from the trampled path. "We have to make it look like we dropped out of the sky," he said.

Daria wasn't sure what he meant but followed him to an area that was well-lit by streetlights, revealing the smooth surface of an untouched landscape. Once they selected their spots, they turned and fell backwards. Next they flapped their arms creating the angel wings. When satisfied, they stood in their last footprints, and Pierre told her to hop to the next footprint and cover up the last one. They erased their tracks and stood staring at their side by side angels.

"They are so beautiful. My wings turned out perfectly." Her voice was hushed.

"Perhaps because you are so close to an angel yourself."

Pierre's words touched something in her heart and she turned to him to make sure he wasn't kidding. Robert would have said it sarcastically and then expected a laugh. "That's a sweet thing to say." If she'd been able to read an aura outside in a snowfall, Daria was pretty sure Pierre's would still be glowing yellow, like candlelight, but there wasn't an aura around Pierre, just a sense of sweetness. According to Aunt Beatrice, the only people who exuded that aura, without layers, were people who were meant to be a soul mate. She wasn't sure if her aunt said that because it was the state of Uncle Art's aura, or not.

Looking into her eyes, Pierre's smile looked very boyish, almost mischievous and Daria knew they would kiss. The inevitability of sharing something physical was as clear as the angels in the snow in front of them. He leaned forward, his eyes on her mouth. His lips were cold and she imagined hers were, too. As Pierre deepened the kiss, his warmth seeped into her. Gloved hands cupped her face and she allowed herself to let go, to enjoy, to participate. His mouth was soft, sensuous. As suddenly as it began, it ended. He pulled back. Not far, but far enough for her to see worry in his eyes.

"I'm not taking advantage of a woman under the influence, am I?"

"A little," she said, then realized how it sounded. "I mean you're not taking advantage, but I am a little under the influence of many things tonight. Wine, Christmas, the snow . . ."

His gorgeous eyes studied her face and then he smiled. "Me too. But I'm also under the influence of you." He kissed her forehead. "I'm French, and we love to kiss." He kissed her lips tenderly. "And you do this well," he said, moving his kisses to her neck.

"Hmm, I haven't been kissed like this in so long." Daria thought she might just rip off her outer gear and let him have his way with her right there. His kisses were taunting, sexy. His mouth moved back up to her mouth then laid one on her lips. He deepened the kiss and opened his mouth to explore with his tongue. Daria was right there with him. She hadn't felt this passionate in years, maybe not ever. Pierre was French and they invented this move, she told herself. As the passion escalated to a feverish pitch, Daria knew they'd have to slow down. They were in the middle of a golf course in the snow, under a streetlight, making out.

Finally, she pulled back and Pierre grinned at her. "Mon Dieu, you do that well."

"I was thinking the same thing."

He pulled her in for an embrace and they watched the snow fall. "Our angels will be covered soon," she said.

"They'll still be there, and we'll know." He kissed her forehead once more and took her hand. "I'm afraid we weren't very angelic."

They walked across the snowy field and looking up she found Sheila's brightly lit house by the tree in the window. Two people who she assumed were Jo and Sheila stood at the front window of the Great Room. Although it was far away, Daria was pretty sure they'd been seen and Jo would be smiling.

Arriving back at the house, they found the partiers gone, silence. The caterers had earlier filed out during the construction of Monsieur Neige and the house was now dark except for the Christmas tree casting a magical glow on the gifts beneath it and across the room.

Pierre and Daria hung their wet clothes in the laundry room, whispering about how they'd need everything dry to ski tomorrow. "What is the plan? First thing, or noon, or what?" Daria laid her mitts on the floor near the heating vent.

"I can't imagine we'll ski first thing," Pierre said. "And even if those three want to ski early, I'll stay with you and use you as my excuse to not hit the slopes until noon if you like." He snuck a quick kiss. "It's past midnight. Christmas day now. Merry Christmas." His grin widened to a glorious smile. A smile genuine enough to reach his eyes. Warm enough to melt all the snow outside.

"Joyeux Noel," she said, then giggled. "Was that right?"

"Oui." He nodded. "Let's get another drink. I'm not ready to sleep."

They headed to the kitchen. Now that she'd totally sobered up, Daria wondered if it was a good idea to drink before bed. She voiced her concern. "I think I just need water."

"How about hot chocolate?" Pierre pulled a box of cocoa packets out of the cupboard and held them up like he'd found gold.

"Good idea." Daria found mugs and heated milk in the microwave while Pierre watched her from a bar stool at the kitchen island. Pierre was cute. Fun, too. Kissing had been something special for her. She wondered if that was the meaning of the aura—a compatible physical partner.

They sipped cocoa in front of the tree. Daria told him all about costume design. They talked until Daria couldn't hold in her yawns any longer. It was time for bed. She had to call the girls in the morning and it was approaching one a.m. Pierre kissed her deeply enough at her bedroom door to make her belly flutter, and then they went to their respective rooms.

Somewhere between brushing her teeth and getting into her nightgown, Daria had the wild idea to just fling herself at Pierre. The temptation to walk down the hall, knock softly on his door, and ask if he'd like company, was too much for her to resist. Especially after all she'd been through in the last nine months with Robert and Suzanne. She needed something and Pierre was the type of man she could trust. He knew more about her current life than Robert did at this point. Not that she'd ever sleep with Robert again. This vacation was about having fun, trying new things, stepping from her comfort zone. Her heart beat wildly against her ribs at the thought of asking Pierre to sleep with her.

Tip toeing down the hall, Daria considered backing out of this crazy idea. But no, no chickening out. She stood at Pierre's door wondering if he was asleep. Would he even answer? And if he did, what would she say that didn't sound cheap or cliché? Oh Geez, she didn't even know what to say! *Can I come in* didn't quite cut it. *Can I spend the night* sounded needy.

But then, she heard Pierre's voice from the other side of the door. "Merry Christmas Sweetheart. I love you. Call me in the morning when you wake up." Was he leaving a message on voicemail? Oh, no! Had she even asked him if he had a girlfriend? She'd assumed if he had, then he'd be with her for Christmas.

"I miss you. And, uh, I wanted you to know how much I love you." There was a pause and then Pierre said the words that changed her plan to sneak back to her room. "No father could be more proud of his daughter."

Daria's eyes widened, her heart beat fast. Pierre was a father. No girlfriend. Relief. But those few sentences had changed things. Allowed her to reassess her motive. Thinking time. There was too much she didn't know to just fling herself at Pierre.

Just as she started to turn to head back to her room, the door opened and Pierre stopped in the doorway, no doubt shocked to see her standing in the hall.

"Daria? Are you okay?"

Damn. She couldn't think of anything that would explain why she was in front of this door looking like she was about to knock. "I was going to . . ."

"Knock?" He looked confused.

"Yes." She let out a deep breath she'd been holding. "I wanted to ask you if . . ." but she couldn't think of a good lie fast enough.

"I was just going to the kitchen to get a glass of water." He smiled compassionately. "Shall I just forget I saw you here? Were you leaving?" He looked at her feet and smirked.

"I was. Good sense has taken over." She looked down the hall, blushing.

Pierre moved toward her and encircled her in his arms. "Ah, Cherie." He kissed her hair. "Do you want to come in to talk?" He drew back and she shook her head. "Do you want to come in for another reason?"

If she thought she could resist him before, she knew she now wasn't physically capable of turning around. She wanted this man, even if it was only for one night. She wanted to feel loved. And Pierre felt safe.

"Come in, Cherie." He held the door open and Daria walked into his bedroom.

Christmas morning dawned, and it was still snowing. Daria met Jo at the coffee pot just after eight and learned they might not ski until the following day.

"Sheila has a headache and I feel lazy today."

"Let's play it by ear then," Daria said, feeling grateful for another day of not making a fool of herself on the slopes.

"We saw you and Pierre on the golf course last night." Jo's face was bright with animation.

"He showed me how to make my first snow angel." She didn't want to reveal too much, just in case. "Did you see our snow man out front?"

Jo nodded and waited for more.

"My first snowman."

"Was last night a first for other things?" Jo poured the perfect amount of milk in Daria's coffee cup.

"First time away from my kids at Christmas." Daria took a sip.

"First time you made love with a Frenchman?" Jo looked over.

"No." Jo could take it any way she wanted but whatever way you looked at it, Daria's answer was no. She hadn't made love with a French man. She and Pierre had only talked. They actually lay down on the bed, holding hands, facing each other with Scruffy snoring between them. After fifteen minutes of talking, he told her very politely that he wanted to make love with her but sensed it was a last minute decision on her part. She hadn't argued the point.

Daria knew rejection when it was in the air in front of her. "Okay then. I'll be getting back to my room." She rose from the bed.

"Ma Cherie, if you still want this tomorrow night, then there will be nothing standing in the way, but tonight, we are under the influence of Christmas. And spontaneity," he added.

Although his intentions were honorable and he'd exhibited self-control where she hadn't, she entered her room wondering why Pierre could resist her. Obviously she wasn't tempting enough.

"What do you mean, 'no'?" Jo pinched her friend on the arm. "You will tell me what that means, right now!"

"It means I like him, and think the feeling is mutual." They took their coffee into the great room and sat by the tree. "We'll see if that's still the case today."

By the time Sheila rolled out of bed to say hello and disappeared into the kitchen for espresso, Pierre was just coming back from a run.

"You jog in the snow?" Daria thought he'd been in his room asleep.

"Merry Christmas, everyone," Pierre was the epitome of athletic health. Scruffy jumped around, happy to be back in the warmth of the house.

"Pierre runs, just like you, Daria," Jo whispered.

"Zip it please, Jo." She shot her friend a look.

"He's a jogger, Daria," Jo teased.

Daria laughed and left the room to see what she could scare up for breakfast. She'd received a text from Robert saying the Skype call would be postponed until tonight. *The girls are busy with their toys right now,* Robert wrote. She could only hope that her daughters had the gifts they'd asked Santa for at the mall last week. And that Suzanne hadn't revealed that Santa was just a myth.

"Is it okay if I make eggs and toast?" she asked Sheila, who smiled and poured espresso into a tiny cup.

"Absolutely." Sheila said. "Did Jo tell you I don't want to ski? You can still go. All of you."

Pierre walked in and shrugged. He brushed against Daria as he leaned over to grab a mug from the cupboard and winked, smiling out one side of his mouth, mischievously.

Javier ran into the kitchen, asking why everyone let him sleep in, and led the group to the Christmas tree. Santa presents had been left for Javier with a stocking bursting with toys and candy. The group settled around the tree and opened presents, littering the carpet with torn wrapping paper. An hour later Daria served a breakfast of scrambled eggs, bacon, and toast with fruit salad. Sitting at the table they made a plan for the day.

Sheila and Jo would stay with Javier to have a quiet day and get the turkey in the oven for the evening's meal. "Just us five, no big party tonight," Jo assured Daria.

Pierre wanted to ski and offered to show Daria the basics. "It'll be fun. I won't leave you on your own." She must've looked frightened. "I used to teach during my college years," he added reassuringly.

His aura was still a faint flickering of candlelight-- a contrast to Jo's layers of pink for gay energies, blues for her structure and organizational mind, a small brown layer for being grounded to earth.

After borrowing Jo's gear, Pierre and Daria left the house with the intention of going skiing. Once the front seat was cleared of papers and brochures that Pierre called "business mess", she hopped into the passenger seat and they sped off down the newly plowed street.

"I bet Sheila pays more taxes than the folks who have to wait to get their streets plowed today," he joked.

Pierre looked good enough to eat in his ski gear and Daria was happy that her feelings for him hadn't changed since the night before. At the first stop light, he leaned over and kissed her. "Did you sleep well after I kicked you out?" He grinned.

"Ouch." Daria made a motion to put a knife through her heart. "I did. But my ego is suffering today."

He looked at her as though she'd told him he'd never smile again. "Oh, my darling, no." He pulled the car onto the shoulder of the road, put it in park and turned to face her. "Do you have any idea how difficult that was? How much I wanted to pull you into that bed and make love to you?" His aura flashed orange and she hoped that meant what it usually did--sensuality. "After the call with your children, I knew you needed to feel loved. But I also think that you are a mother who doesn't act impulsively and I wanted you to be sure. Not regretful and avoiding me today because of embarrassment."

She nodded. "You're right."

Satisfied that she meant it, he pulled the car back onto the deserted road.

"Thanks for ending what could have been a mistake last night." She rolled her eyes. "I would be so embarrassed and regretful if you hadn't seen it for what it was." She looked over to see Pierre staring straight ahead, his jaw clenched.

"What was it?" His voice was suddenly cold as they turned left and headed down the hill they'd walked the night before.

"It was me, almost throwing nine wonderfully fabulous months of celibacy down the drain."

He smiled and glanced at her. "That long?"

"Like you said, I'm a mother."

"Ma Cherie." He was grinning now. "How do you think women become mothers? Not through celibacy. Besides, even mothers need romance." His look made her want to snuggle in to his side. Pulling on to the main road, there were no other cars in sight. It was Christmas morning and Daria wondered how many people would actually make it up the ski mountain on this day.

"So Cherie, you are thankful you left my room last night?" Pierre could do that thing where one eyebrow goes up but not the other and she almost laughed at him.

"I am."

"And tonight, you will be knocking at my door again, but I won't turn you away."

"Maybe or possibly you'll come to *my* room tonight." She flashed him a sexy smile she didn't even know she knew how to make, and he pretended to clutch his heart.

"I have the queen-sized bed and larger room," he added.

"Oh, if we end up in the same bed tonight, you can bet there won't be more than one imprint in that mattress." Where was she getting this stuff?

He laughed as he continued to maneuver his SUV through the village. Once parked they grabbed their equipment and walked the length of the village to buy lift tickets. "I ski here in the winter. I know exactly where to take you to start your career in downhill racing, I mean skiing," he joked.

"Be gentle, it's my first time," she said, purposely using the double entendre.

He chuckled. When they reached the ticket window, Pierre bought two tickets. It was quiet on the mountain and they didn't need to wait in line to get on the Whistler Gondola. The view of the village below from the high speed, glassed-in lift was absolutely awesome like looking at a snow globe with a picturesque village inside. "We'll get off at the half-way point," Pierre said, kissing her on the nose.

Daria was anxious about her first time on a ski run. She didn't want to look stupid in front of him, but wanted to be able to tell the girls on the Skype call later that Mommy had skied. She fastened her helmet, thinking it would flatten her hair to all heck, and stepped into her skis. This was it.

Turned out, Pierre proved to be an excellent instructor and Daria had a talent for the sport. After an hour of practicing the pizza move, Pierre said she was ready for a green run. "We'll do a slow meandering route that leads back here." He made a multi-curved "S" in the air and nodded at his student. "I might have you ski between my legs at first to get the feel for it."

Daria rolled her eyes and smiled. "Oh please. Is that really a teaching method?"

"Why do you think I became an instructor?" He smiled and carried her skis to the Gondola where they boarded and continued to the top of Whistler Mountain.

The clouds were high above the mountain's peak, and as they reached the top, Daria was overcome with the beauty of the mountains. Why she'd never tried this sport before, was a mystery. Her toes were nice and warm thanks to Jo's expensive boots. Actually, she was a little on the warm side with Pierre pressing against her back, encircling her chest with his arms. Luckily, they had a gondola car to themselves, and their make-out session on the way up had been totally private. "You Frenchmen are very physical," Daria cooed, as Pierre pulled at her turtleneck and kissed the side of her neck.

"I told you we like to kiss." He moved to her lips, then kissed her passionately, his tongue searching her mouth.

The primal need she had for Pierre was thrilling but when she opened her eyes, she saw the gondola station in sight and broke the kiss. "Almost there."

Pierre zipped up his coat, buckled his boots and they were at the station. "And so it begins."

After a quick shower back at the house to warm her tired, cold muscles, Daria put on jeans and an angora pullover and headed to the bathroom to do her makeup and hair. Tonight, she wanted to look especially good. Daria was proud of how well she'd done today. By the end of the afternoon, she was skiing on her own, making turns, skiing. She and Pierre had skied the whole mountain, from the peak to the valley on the last run and even though it took them an hour with five stops to look at the scenery and flirt, she was extremely relieved and proud.

Jo peeked in the bathroom while Daria styled her hair and held up both thumbs. Daria nodded, knowing exactly what she meant. "How was your day, Jo? Relaxing?"

"Yes. Sheila's always so stressed out with the restaurant, she just wanted today completely free to hang with Javier. Dinner is at six by the way." Jo's jeans slung low on her light framed hips, her hooded sweatshirt tight enough to show her flat tummy.

"I want to make the gravy, or set the table, or carve, or mash, or contribute in some small way." She and Pierre had stopped for pies and ice cream on the way home from skiing. "Let's do something while Sheila is still busy." As far as she knew Sheila and Pierre were still in the deck's hot tub with Javier so the chances of being able to help get things underway was good.

"You know Brazilians don't eat until like nine, right?" Jo smiled apologetically.

"I thought you said six?"

"Sheila says six but look, it's five now and she's still in the hot tub."

"Won't the neighbors be here at six?" Daria liked that Sheila had invited her next door neighbors, Merv and Shoshanna, for dinner even though they'd already celebrated Hanukah.

Jo nodded. "Yes, but we have appetizers until the turkey is ready. I think we'll eat around seven."

"Let Sheila soak in the hot tub. We'll set the table in a few minutes." Daria put the finishing touches to her hair, sprayed to hold it in place and turned to Jo. "Let's get a glass of wine because I'm Skype calling the girls in ten minutes and that means Suzanne."

"I'll stand off camera making funny faces, if that helps." Jo was serious.

Back in her guest room, Daria initiated the call to her ex-husband and their daughters. Suzanne answered with Sunny and Rose sitting on the couch in front of the camera. "Robert is busy assembling toys and won't join the call," Suzanne said in her prissy, I'm-better-than-you voice. Daria knew it would be a strain to get enough time, or quality time with her girls. Robert usually monitored Suzanne's bitchiness. Poor Sunny was having a meltdown about something she got for Christmas not being the right thing and Rose was trying to tell her sister that Daddy said Santa would come twice.

"That's right, Sunny." Daria's heart melted at her daughter's tears. "You are twice as lucky as most children this year because Santa is giving you a second Christmas next week. Look at me, darling. Look at Mommy and listen to what I'm saying. Sunny looked at her mother's image on the monitor. "Santa is coming again and who knows what he'll bring you at our house!" Daria could almost feel Suzanne's bad energy just off to the side, even though that was impossible. "My sweet little angel. Guess what Mommy did today for the very first time, that you girls already know how to do so well."

"Ski!" They both said. Sunny sniffed and forced a little smile.

"Oh, how did you know? I have pictures of me falling down the mountain, not as graceful as you, I'm sure, but I was very proud of myself."

"Did your new husband go too?" Sunny asked.

"Who, Pierre? He's not my husband. He's my boyfriend. My very handsome and wonderful boyfriend."

Their faces lit up. "We like his dog!" Rose said on behalf of the two.

"Oh, me too. Scruffy is cute, and yes, Pierre went skiing too. He helped pick me up when I fell because he skis very well. Much much better than Daddy!" She couldn't help herself.

Just then, Suzanne poked her big head on the screen and said, "Time for dinner, my little girls." The fact that she cut short the conversation was bad enough but calling them her little girls was nasty.

"Is that Suzanne ending your Christmas call?" Pierre said from the doorway.

Daria looked over to see a scantily clad Pierre in swimming trunks, in all his six-pack, muscular glory. She tried to suppress an audible gulp. "Yes, the girls are finished talking and they have to eat dinner." Daria smiled at the camera to let her daughters know they could go and she wouldn't be disappointed. On screen, she saw Pierre move in behind her, bare-chested and flaunting the fact that he obviously worked out. He wasn't a hugely muscled man but definitely toned and worth looking at. His chest had just enough hair to lead down, down, into the trunks. Suzanne's hand was at her throat.

The girls giggled and said he looked naked. "Oops, Pierre, did you lose your shirt for Christmas?" Daria covered her mouth in mock fun and Pierre leaned into camera view to say hello to the girls.

"Sorry Ladies," he said in his sexy French accent. "I was in the hot tub outside and the rule is no shirt, just like swimming. Have you girls ever been to a swimming pool?" They giggled a yes, and Daria watched Suzanne watch Pierre, off to the side. She'd hopefully be envious. Robert had become a little doughy since he'd taken the IT job, and more so since he wasn't with the family on a full time basis.

"They love to swim." Daria touched Pierre's arm. "Merry Christmas, my darlings," Daria said blowing kisses.

"Love you, Mommy!" They called as Suzanne reached forward and the screen went black. She'd cut them off.

Daria's head fell to her chest and her tears fell.

Pierre stroked her hair. "She's not worth it, Daria." He touched her shoulder, squeezed a little. "The girls are happy. They're fine." He moved in front of her and squatted to look in her face.

Daria sniffed, forced herself to stop crying. "I know. They are just so precious and she's using them to get to me. I don't know why, but it's not right and every time I try to tell Robert that he's the parent, not Suzanne, he gets defensive. She has some sort of spell over him. My poor babies."

"They aren't poor babies, Daria. They don't look like they're being mistreated. Those two girls are better off than most of the children in the world and you have to remember that. Kids are resilient." He took her hands in his and continued. "She's trying to make you feel this way but the kids have no idea. Do you understand? Your children are happy, normal kids. Don't let her take away your happiness." He kissed her cheek. "She's a mean person but guess what? It's only a matter of time before Robert gets the message too. Come on, Ma Cherie, chin up."

Daria lifted her chin and smiled weakly. "I don't care if he ever gets the message except that I worry about the children. It's just hard. I'm sorry you are a part of this." She took a deep breath, and chuckled. "I just met you yesterday. Poor you." She gazed into his compassionate face. "Thank you, Pierre."

He nodded once. "I hear Christmas dinner is almost ready and then after that, Javier wants to give Monsieur Neige a makeover. Apparently our snowman gained some unwanted weight today during the snowfall." He kissed her lips, smelling like chlorine. "Are you in or out?"

She wiped the tears from her cheeks. "I'm in for both dinner and snow."

"Good girl." Pierre nodded at her and left the room.

It was difficult to watch him leave her bedroom. She'd had no idea that through all those layers of ski clothes or even jeans and a shirt, that Pierre was in such good shape. A shiver shot through her body, thinking about how she'd kissed him so passionately in the snow last night, and on the gondola today. It was her call tonight. Isn't that basically what they'd been teasing about all day? If she wanted.

Christmas dinner was laid out on the dining room table overlooking the lights of Whistler Mountain. Earlier, Daria had made place cards from ribbon and leftover present cards, as well as a centerpiece from pine boughs and ribbons and candles. The table looked lovely. Merv and Shoshanna were a delightful couple, holding hands between courses, looking fondly at each other. Javier told jokes, Jo told stories of the crazy guys on the construction crew and even Pierre talked about his winery. He'd brought bottles of crisp chardonnay for them to enjoy with the turkey.

"A light peachy taste with just enough sweetness," he said.

Daria was impressed. It was good wine. And she noticed that the label was nicely done. Of course, the designer in her noticed the label as much as the taste of the wine, but when she mentioned the colors and graphics of Black Lab Winery, Jo teased her.

"Ah, but the label is very important," Pierre said. "Like the cover of a book." He smiled at Daria. "We chose the name and logo very carefully with months of testing. My partner Sam has always had a Black Labrador Retriever and market testing showed that customers react strongly to the image of a dog on anything and especially the loyalty and sweetness of the Black Lab."

Daria looked over at Scruffy, who'd been told to go lie down. "Won't Scruffy take offense?" she said.

Pierre took a sip of wine. "What makes you think Scruffy isn't a Black Lab?" Javier laughed loudly, but Pierre kept a straight face. "After all, I found him on the streets. Who knows what he is."

"Tell Daria how you found him," Sheila said.

"Actually, it was only three weeks ago. I was walking along, in downtown San Francisco, on my way to meet with a client and I stopped to put money in the hat of a homeless man sitting on the sidewalk."

Everyone stopped eating to listen.

"We got to talking, I sat down with him and learned that he was actually a very interesting man, living on the streets with his little dog. With no hint of self-pity he told me that life was tough and he felt badly for the dog. As I sat with him, very few people actually stopped to give money, even though his sign said 'short on luck, please help'."

Daria felt tears threaten.

"The man's name was Gabriel, like the angel, and he told me he once owned a corner grocery store but had lost his business, his wife, and his home. He'd been on the streets for almost nine years. He couldn't have been more than sixty." Pierre cleared his throat, took a breath and continued. "He said his dog had mange, needed to see a vet, and I offered to take the little guy. After my meeting I went back to get the dog and drove him over to a vet, got him some salve and pills. When I brought Scruffy back to Gabriel later that day, he was gone. I looked for several days and when I finally found someone who recognized Scruffy, he told me that Gabriel had passed away. He'd had terminal cancer." Pierre stopped and cleared his throat again. "I like to think he wanted me to take Scruffy, knowing he didn't have much time left."

Daria looked over at the dog sleeping peacefully by the fireplace. *Lucky little guy.*

Sheila spoke. "And Pierre made arrangements for Gabriel's funeral so the man wouldn't be buried in some public plot. He not only rescued Scruffy," she said directly to Javier, "but he rescued Gabriel as well."

Tears had filled Jo's eyes. Daria was next.

"And that's why Scruffy sleeps with me on the bed, and I let him lick my face in the morning." Pierre made a face and Javier laughed again.

Daria was touched by the story, overwhelmed by Pierre's compassion. "And that's why Scruffy might very well be purebred Black Lab?" she added.

"Exactly." Pierre finished his wine and poured everyone a round.

"And that's how I know Sheila." He glanced at the head of the table to the hostess. "She rescued me."

He didn't elaborate and Daria wondered what he meant, but just then Javier coughed on a piece of something and Sheila jumped up to pat his back. She would ask Pierre later how Sheila saved him. If there was a later. And, if there wasn't going to be a later, Daria knew at this point, she'd be very disappointed. She liked this Frenchman, a lot. Much more now than when she'd snuck into his room the night before. In some ways, Scruffy's story changed everything. Tonight could no longer be a simple one night fling with a stranger, or even a fleeting romance. Daria knew the sweetness of this man. He'd displayed that with her girls twice and he'd been compassionate enough to rescue Scruffy. She'd even seen tenderness over how much he owed to Sheila.

Christmas songs played in the background, and a choir sang about a King who helped a poor boy trudge through deep snow on Christmas day. The traditional dinner had been scrumptious with turkey, gravy, creamy mashed potatoes, stuffing, and a "medley of fall vegetables," Jo had announced proudly. Daria had never seen her friend cook anything beyond Top Ramen and Kraft Dinners and was impressed by Sheila's influence. When praised about such a wonderful meal, Sheila insisted that turkey was the easiest thing to cook, and next year Jo would prepare the main course.

"It's a date," Pierre said and laughed.

Daria had purposely eaten lightly, thinking that if she ended up naked with Pierre later, she didn't want to have to hold in her rounded tummy.

Over dessert, Pierre stood to toast the host before they dug into their apple pie a la mode. "I'm grateful and honored to be here with Sheila and Javier on this very special

Christmas day. And Jo," he smiled at all three. "In the bosom of this loving home of mother and son. I'm sure I speak for Daria when I say how thankful I am to be a part of this Whistler Christmas. And for Merv and Shoshanna to say thank you for including us!" He raised his glass of wine and everyone followed, even Javier who had a small glass of wine at his place setting.

Daria gazed at Pierre over the rim of her glass, catching his attention. He winked knowingly, as if to say "we'll talk later." There was so much she wanted to know about him. Was it wise to take on more than she could handle? What if she became totally smitten with him after tonight? Would it be worth it to be heartbroken over this man after a few days of romance? She wasn't sure, but she also wasn't stupid. She saw their relationship for what it was. This was a moment of time where their lives crossed, not the beginning of a long relationship.

When the group moved to the living room fireplace where a roaring fire had been stoked. The cedar logs crackled and popped in sunset flames as Pierre stayed close to Daria, settling beside her on the couch with Scruffy.

"We should get a dog," Jo looked at Sheila, excitedly.

Sheila shot her an 'are–you-crazy?' look but Javier yelled "Yes! Let's get a dog, Mom!"

"Jo, did you have to say that in front of him?" Sheila looked only slightly miffed. "We'll see," she said, looking at her son reproachfully.

Pierre had left a few inches between he and Daria and Scruffy eventually settled in that space. Daria wanted to hold Pierre's hand but she also did not want everyone to see. Instead, they both petted Scruffy, their fingers touching.

Merv and Shoshanna held hands while gazing into the fire. Seeing them together made Daria remember how she'd longed for that type of marriage with Robert, one that would have lasted throughout old age. Had Merv and Shoshanna experienced rough patches over their forty years of matrimony? In her own marriage, the affair with Suzanne had been more than a rough patch, and even if Robert hadn't asked for the divorce, she would have, knowing he was sneaking around with another woman. Just recently she'd finally owned up to her half of the problems in their marriage.

Daria didn't know how any marriage could sustain the libido suck that came with parenting. Not that Robert had participated much on the parenting side. He'd been disappointed to have girls. She'd always known that and it was the one reason she'd kept the upper hand with the girls, always controlling his time with them. Consequently, during the marriage she'd turned into a sexless, cold fish when she realized that Robert didn't love their children with the fierceness she did. She'd drifted away emotionally, doubtful they would ever recapture the passion they'd once shared. Of course, he'd turned to another woman. Hopefully, Merv and Shoshanna had never experienced the complete distrust and dislike that she and Robert had for each other.

When Merv stood and held out his hand for his wife, they announced their departure. Pierre walked them home shortly after ten o'clock and Daria followed him outside with Javier to check on Monsieur Neige. The sign had fallen, but the snowman looked remarkably well-preserved, considering he'd been exposed to fresh snow all day. Javier shook off the mittens and hat, while Daria dusted the snow from his face, laughing that he'd had a big Christmas dinner and had gained an inch all around.

Once satisfied, Javier went inside while Daria waited for Pierre to return. When he walked up to her, she offered her face for a kiss and he obliged.

"I haven't kissed you in hours," he whispered against her lips.

"I noticed." His smile was contagious. "I like you."

"I noticed."

When they opened the front door and took off their coats and boots, Javier had retired to his room and Jo and Sheila were on their way to bed. "Tomorrow, we ski!" Jo announced.

"Looking forward to hitting the slopes. How about you two?" Sheila said.

"If Pierre hasn't had enough," Daria said with a grimace.

"Not at all!" he looked at Daria as though his feelings were hurt. "You are my star student." He playfully poked her side.

Jo and Sheila left their guests alone on the couch in front of a dying fire and went to bed. A low flame and orange embers remained in the fireplace. Pierre moved closer to Daria and took her hand in his two. Suddenly she wasn't sure she could go through with this. Earlier, Jo had questioned her about the long term emotional investment but Daria said she just wanted to feel like a woman again, not marry the man.

Pierre kissed her hand and asked her if she'd had a good day.

She stared into the fire. "I did, thanks to you. And, of course to Jo and Sheila." An ember fell and the last of the log broke into pieces. There was one last puzzle piece to add tonight in order to make a decision about Pierre. "I've been wondering all day how you know Sheila. I'm not sure I heard that story."

He took a deep breath, as though contemplating his choice of words. "It's a long story."

"I have time." She turned towards him and saw a sadness in his eyes.

"Sheila was best friends with a girl named Anna, growing up in Brazil. When I met Anna in Colorado, sixteen years ago, the two were cocktail waitresses and I taught skiing. Anna and I dated for a few months, then the season ended, we broke up and I moved on to live in Napa. Eleven years ago, I got a call from Sheila to say she was in San Francisco on a chef training course and would like to see me. Long story short, she told me that I have a daughter, living in Portland Oregon.

Daria held her breath, waiting.

"Anna did not want me to know but Sheila couldn't keep the secret anymore. Needless to say they aren't friends anymore."

"Did you go to Portland and meet your daughter?"

"Yes and no. It took a while to get Anna to let me see the child. She didn't want some bum ski instructor showing up to mess up her daughter's life, and seeing it from that angle, I didn't blame her. But by that time I'd partnered with Sam and we were making our own label. Not Black Lab wine but another one," he clarified. "At least now I looked good on paper. I met my daughter, Jessica, when she was almost five. I had only seen her from a distance before that. I used to fly to Portland, rent a car, and just watch her from across the street at her preschool playground. " Pierre's face lit up, his eyes sparkled. "Now she's fifteen and we have a pretty good relationship."

Daria couldn't help but smile. "That's wonderful." How had he gotten through the years of not being able to see his daughter?

Pierre got off the couch to add a log to the fire. "It was frustrating, but Anna needed me to prove I was worthy of our wonderful child. I had been irresponsible and selfish when I dated her. Besides, she'd married and Jess had a stable home life. Telling her that she had two Daddy's was not something Anna was willing to do." He sat back down.

"How did it play out?"

"I was introduced as her Godfather and we told Jessica that if anything happened to her Papa, I would take over. I made lots of trips to Portland to take her to the zoo, to the beach, even skiing. And ever since then, I've kind of beaten a path from San Francisco to Portland." He clapped his hands and rubbed them together.

"Does she know you are her biological father now?"

"Yes. We told her when she was ten. Me, Anna, and Bill, her father."

Daria thought about Pierre's complicated situation. "You're in a parenting triangle like me," she whispered.

"Yes. But. There's more to the story. I was married when Sheila told me about my daughter. My ex-wife, Rachel, never did wrap her head around the fact that I had a child. We'd barely been married a year when I heard about Jessica. We didn't make it through the second year." He thought for a moment. "In my triangle everyone loves Jess. Bill is a wonderful person and parent, kind of different from Suzanne. Our situation is different. Anna and I were never married, never co-parented, and I didn't even know my daughter through her early years."

"Do you hold resentment for that?"

"I did, but I had to learn to let it go. It took a while, but now I don't worry about not knowing Jess when she was a baby. I see Anna and Bill a lot. They hold the key to Jessica and I won't ever do anything to get on their bad side."

Daria thought back to Pierre telling Suzanne on Skype to back off. He had about ten years of this on her. True, Suzanne was not nice to her but she believed that Suzanne liked her children. Maybe even had learned to love them.

"Jessica and I were going to come to Whistler and ski this week. It's kind of our thing together. She's a good skier. But teenage girls have social commitments and at the last minute, Anna phoned to say that Jessica had a Christmas party to go to and didn't want to miss it." He ran his hands through his hair. "When I leave here, I'll go to Portland for a few days to see her. We might go to Mount Bachelor for a day of skiing. And, she knows I'm always here for her."

Daria was dumbfounded. Pierre's love for his daughter was so unselfish. How had he managed that when she felt so frustrated with her easy situation with Robert and Suzanne? Daria passed her hand along the side of his face, leaned in to kiss him lightly on the mouth. "You are a good father, I can tell." She rested her head on his shoulder and he reached up to stroke her hair.

"It's not easy, parenting, right?"

"No. it isn't. Like skiing, it takes practice." She smiled. "And now you are stuck with me, a beginner, instead of your daughter."

"I wouldn't call it stuck when I spend the whole day devising ways to get you alone like this to kiss you." His hand tenderly cupped her jaw, and moved to her hair as they shared a brief but sweet kiss. When they broke apart, Daria had to ask the question that had been on the tip of her tongue all day. "Are you in a relationship, now?"

He pulled her to his warm chest and she buried her face in his shoulder. "No, I'm not. And I'm assuming you aren't either if you've been celibate for nine months."

She grinned. "Longer actually. Probably more like a year." Robert hadn't made love to her in the last few months of their marriage and once she found out about Suzanne, she was thankful he was always too tired, too drunk, or too distracted.

"Would you like to do something about that, Ma Cherie?"

She pulled back and trailed a finger from his neck to his belly button. "I would."

The next morning she woke up beside the most beautiful, sexy man she'd ever had the pleasure of knowing, her leg draped over his and the full length of him pressed into her side. She opened her eyes, immediately breaking into a smile.

"I see you smirking," he whispered. His hand came up under the covers, to lie flat on her tummy. "Happy Boxing Day."

Daria turned slightly to see him better. "It is a very happy one . . . so far." She grabbed his hand and brought it to her lips. "That was a very nice Christmas present, Pierre."

He moved in, removing all space between them. "I have a Boxing Day present for you, too."

When they heard Javier's voice out in the hall, they knew it was time to get ready to ski. "Shall we pretend to come out of our own rooms, or do we care?"

"I only care for Javier's sake," Daria whispered.

It turned out that everyone was in the kitchen when they opened the bedroom door. Pierre took Scruffy outside and Daria went back to her room. After pulling on her yoga pants and a T-shirt, she headed for the heated kitchen floor.

Jo and Sheila were dressed in their base layer leggings and tops, talking about whether to ski Blackcomb or Whistler. Daria entered the room, noting the mischievous smile on Jo's face.

"Blackcomb," Javier said. "It's going to be sunny and I want to do Seventh Heaven first, before the crowd gets there."

Sheila concurred and met Daria at the coffee pot. "Let me make you an espresso, you'll probably need it this morning." Her smile was full of knowledge and innuendos.

Daria saw Jo's eyes crinkle behind her coffee cup while Javier poured himself a giant bowl of Cookie Crisp cereal. When Pierre walked in, she knew there would be teasing.

Sheila went first. "I suggested Daria have an espresso to help get her through the day. Pierre, would you like one too?" Jo and Sheila exchanged smug looks, as though they'd been planning this ambush for hours. "Tell me Daria, do you sleep better with your bedroom door open all night?" Jo almost spat her coffee across the room in mirth.

Pierre kissed the top of Daria's head. "Good morning, Daria. Did you sleep well?" He flashed Sheila a reproachful look.

"I did," Daria said. "Just not enough of it."

"By 'it' do you mean sleep?" Jo was beside herself with the giggles.

Javier had gone to the next room to eat his cereal. "Both." Daria flashed a grin Pierre's way and he raised one eyebrow.

"The cat is out of the bag, as they say." Pierre looked so handsome, dashing, and delectable standing in Sheila's kitchen. He leaned against the counter without a care in the world. His aura's colors read peaceful and amused.

"Sheila and Jo are behaving like they're in high school." Daria poured herself a bowl of cereal and crossed to the fridge for milk, swatting Jo's shoulder on her way.

"Do I detect a trace of envy?" The twinkle in Pierre's eyes displayed his good sportsmanship. He stared down Sheila and she threw her hands up in surrender.

"Not me." Her aura was a light yellow, a color that usually meant happiness. "I have Jo."

Pierre drank the last of his coffee and set his mug in the dishwasher. He turned around, clapped his hands and spoke. "Are we going to stand around here talking all day about my infatuation with Daria, or shall we ski?"

Something fluttered in Daria's chest when he said that. Even though he'd told her last night that she was the sexiest thing he'd ever seen, something she wasn't quite sure she believed, it was thrilling to hear him say infatuation out loud. Especially for this worthy man who wore ski clothes like he was a Ralph Lauren runway model.

After conquering the easy green runs on Blackcomb Mountain that day, Daria and Pierre skied to the base to meet the others. They had a rendezvous point on the patio at Monk's Grill at three. As they clicked out of their skis and found a place to leave their gear, they talked about parties, then birthday parties and realized that they had the same birthday. In one week Pierre and Daria would both be another year older. Daria briefly thought about the candlelight aura's meaning. Aunt Beatrice hadn't elaborated on this phenomenon, only said that Uncle Art had the aura and she'd taken that to mean something very special in his case. Any way you looked at it, candlelight was a good sign.

"I'm pretty sure I'm much older than you," Pierre said.

"I don't think so." Daria guessed that they were close in age, but she didn't know.

"I'll be thirty-nine," Pierre said.

"Well, I'll be thirty-two and that isn't much older at all."

He kissed her and smiled. "It seems to be the perfect combination, Ma Cherie."

The sun shone brightly on the ski resort scene at the bottom of Blackcomb Mountain, making it look picture-perfect. Wooden patio tables and red umbrellas dotted the restaurant's cobblestone patio. They plunked down at a table and watched skiers come down the final stretch of snowy hillside. After a few minutes of searching, Pierre picked out Jo's neon gear, Sheila's graceful style, and Javier snowboarding. "Here they come."

Seeing the three glide to a halt not far off, Daria wondered if she'd ski with her daughters after this vacation. The thought of this magical week ending made her sad enough to push the thought away. She was exhausted. Two hours of sleep had not been enough. The temptation to stay awake the night before, to talk, to cuddle with this man, had been too great and tonight was not looking any different. As long as she and Pierre were in the same house, she wanted to spend every minute possible with him. Soon enough they'd go their separate ways and her Whistler love affair would be only a sweet memory.

As the women approached with Javier, Sheila announced that she had to get to the restaurant and left them sitting in the sunshine on the patio. When Jo and Javier went to the restroom, Daria turned to Pierre. "I'm exhausted. How will I make it through the evening? Damn you for being so irresistible." She looked into his twinkling eyes and wondered if she'd ever felt this excitement for anyone in her life. If so, she didn't remember ever feeling this wonderful. "I'm not used to all this exercise."

"I'll take that as a compliment." He grinned and drank his Canadian beer.

"You can take everything I say from now on as a compliment. But that doesn't change the fact that you wore me out last night and I need a nap."

They'd eaten turkey dinner left overs, loaded the dishwasher, and taken Scruffy for a walk when Jo asked if they'd be in charge of Javier. She wanted to go to town to wait out the last few hours at Sushi Yo with Sheila, and maybe help if she could.

"That's sweet, Jo," Daria said. "I'm not ignoring you, am I? We could play a board game or have a hot tub visit." She wasn't sure if Jo was feeling neglected.

"No. I just miss Sheila. I'll see you early tomorrow for Fresh Tracks." Jo hugged her and left the house.

Javier had gone into his room to play a new computer game and Daria was certain she'd fall asleep standing up if she didn't get to bed soon. When Pierre suggested they get in the hot tub to loosen their ski muscles, she said she hadn't brought a bathing suit.

The look he gave her almost melted her knees. "Darling, are you kidding? I've seen and kissed every inch of that body. You don't need to wear anything."

"But Javier may come out or want to join us," she whispered.

They compromised. Pierre wore his swim trunks and Daria wore a lacy blue bra and panties. When she dropped the towel and stepped into the steamy water, Pierre whistled. "Mon Dieu. Please say you will sleep with me tonight."

She settled in the water and purposely found a seat across from him. "I will." She'd become a temptress.

"I should rephrase that. Please tell me you will stay awake long enough to make love with me tonight." He moved over to her side and kissed her passionately, as if he wasn't sure she wanted him as much as he wanted her.

She straddled his lap and smoothed back his sandy-colored hair, cherishing his beautiful face. "Oh, Pierre." Her voice was a breathy whisper and she had to hold back the words that revealed she was falling for him. The two of them exchanged torturous looks of longing until he broke the silence.

"When we get to bed tonight, I'll give you a massage. Your shoulders feel tight." He kneaded her back and shoulders.

"That will be the end of me," she said as he slipped his hand inside her bra.

"Then we better make every moment count." He looked inside the house. "Have you ever done it in a hot tub, Cherie?"

She hadn't, but had a feeling she was going to.

Seven a.m. had come way too early but Daria felt more rested than the previous morning and looked forward to another day on the slopes. They'd managed to get at least six solid hours of sleep. One hour into skiing the perfectly groomed green runs, Daria released Pierre to go to the fresh powder on the backside of the mountain with Sheila and Javier. Jo would take a turn babysitting the newbie.

Jo led Daria to a new area of green runs and by the time they met the others for a late lunch, Daria was missing Pierre so badly that she almost cried when his gorgeousness came around the corner. He sat down beside her at the table and kissed the side of her head. The feeling of excitement and bliss reminded her of falling for another camp counselor one summer in Oregon. For the time being, Pierre was still hers and she tried to relax into that thought. The group talked excitedly about the adventure of skiing fresh powder on the backside.

"Tomorrow we will do fresh tracks again and head for the powder," Sheila announced.

When Pierre looked at Daria, she laughed. "No problem. I'll meet you for lunch."

Pierre stopped eating and gaged her mood. "You sure?"

"Yes, of course. I'll sleep in a bit and take Scruffy for a walk. Don't worry about me." Still, she felt slightly left out of the fun and told herself not to be so stupid. How would she ever leave this man in three days?

After another night of staying up late with Pierre, Daria slept in. She woke to his bare imprint in the half empty bed Pierre had abandoned two hours earlier, and the memory of them not being able to get enough of each other last night.

She'd needed the extra sleep and slid out of bed, feeling rested and like a woman in the process of falling in love. She'd had just enough time to walk Scruffy and get herself to the mountain before meeting the group for lunch on Blackcomb.

When Pierre said he wanted to ski with her that afternoon, she thanked him, saying she realized how boring the green slopes must be for an expert.

"Not boring. I like to stare at you," he joked. They spent the afternoon doing runs she hadn't tried yet. After the lifts closed, they met Jo and Sheila at the bottom and made plans for dinner. Javier was with his father, a real estate mogul who lived in the Blackcomb Benchlands so the adults were free to come back to the village for dinner and drinks.

"Did you have a nice sleep this morning?" Pierre asked her back at the house. She knew that the question actually was 'are you ready for another night of passion?'

"I had a wonderful sleep and I'm wondering why you aren't dropping from lack of it."

"I've never needed much sleep." He grinned as he watched her style her hair in the bathroom mirror. "I have other needs that make up for that."

Daria's insides turned to jelly. This man had such an effect on her, and she worried about the void she'd feel when he left the next day. "Are you leaving tomorrow for sure?"

His reflected image in the mirror grew somber. "That's the plan."

"Let's not talk about it tonight, and just enjoy ourselves." She didn't want to cry.

He kissed the side of her neck, just under her ear and then playfully pretended that he got her earring stuck in his mouth.

Pierre was so cute and he made her laugh, something she hadn't done nearly enough of recently. How would she ever go back to normal life after this? For her girls' sakes, she had to.

After a fabulous dinner of sushi and hot pots, they left Jo at Sushi Yo to help Sheila in the kitchen, and wandered around the snowy village, arm in arm. "It's so pretty here," Daria said, her breath vaporizing in frosty puffs.

"Let's plan to meet here every year at Christmas," Pierre said.

He probably didn't mean to make her cry with those words, but she had to fight to keep tears from forming. "Good plan," she managed.

When they got back to the house, Daria was trying to forget that Pierre would be gone tomorrow. She wanted their last night together to be as wonderful as all the others, not filled with sadness. But she also didn't want to wake up to find him gone. "Will you ski tomorrow?"

"Yes, I'll leave after that."

They brushed their teeth in his bathroom, getting ready for bed like an old married couple and Daria remarked how strange it was that they weren't ripping each other's clothes off at random.

"Oh, but I have very specific plans to get those clothes off you, Cherie." He grabbed her around the waist from behind and they silently stared at their reflection in the mirror for a few seconds. A feeling of sadness overcame her, though Daria tried to resist it. Pierre's aura had taken on a new glow, a darkness she hadn't seen before and she wondered what it meant. She tried to memorize what they looked like together, to always remember this man and what he'd meant to her.

In the bedroom, he undressed her slowly, kissing her between pieces of clothing. Throwing the clothes to hang from the overhead light, they joked that they shouldn't turn on the light or they might burn her only jeans. They made love slowly, almost carefully, and lying in each other's arms later, she bravely asked him his plan. "Are you driving straight to Portland or overnighting somewhere?" It would be a long drive.

"Scruffy will need the break so I'll probably stop just past the border, stay in a hotel."

Daria's heart ached, as though it was already breaking. She resisted asking Pierre anything more about his plan or himself, though she wanted to. She already knew too much.

Sunshine dictated the glorious day and when they stopped for lunch, Jo said she wanted to sit outside on the Chalet's deck and get some vitamin D. Daria agreed, pushing herself to engage in conversation even though her heart felt like a lead weight in her constricted chest. She knew it would be tough but not even when Robert asked for the divorce had she experienced such a profound sense of loss

"Just a moment, Daria." Pierre stopped her before getting a lunch tray and food. "I want to talk to you, Cherie. Privately."

They moved out of the lunch line to the window and sat on the ledge. "I have been trying to figure out my plan all morning so I can have more time with you. Leaving you in three hours doesn't feel right."

Daria held her breath and listened.

"If I drive straight through to Portland, tomorrow, I can stay here one more night but that would mean I might need a passenger to keep me awake. Eleven hours is a long stretch."

Her heart lifted.

He proceeded. "Are you leaving here tomorrow?"

She nodded.

"Will you drive with me as far as Seattle, skip the plane so we can have tonight together?'

She kissed him through her smile and threw her arms around him. "Yes, yes, stay one more night."

When they pulled apart, Pierre looked as happy as she felt. He said, "okay, but I'm a little worried about how much you're going to miss Scruffy when I go."

That night they joined Jo and Sheila at a French restaurant in the Village where Pierre translated the menu and ordered for Daria. "I hope you don't mind me taking control," he said, his aura glowing with a purplish tinge.

"No. If we were at McDonald's I would order for you," she joked.

Pierre kept his hand in her lap protectively throughout the meal. Sheila remarked that they couldn't keep their hands off each other, and Pierre responded with a nod and a smile.

"How will you say goodbye tomorrow?" Jo had no sense of timing.

Daria frowned and sent her friend a disapproving look. "Just eat your snails, Joanna."

The evening progressed until all four had ingested too much wine to drive and had to call a cab to get home. In the cab, Daria's emotions slipped just long enough to tell Jo how wonderful this whole trip had been and how much she loved her.

"I love you too," Jo cried, every bit as tipsy as Daria was. Before she confessed her feelings for Pierre, Daria mentally pinched her lips shut. Once inside Sheila's house, Daria grabbed a bottle of water from the fridge as she formulated a plan to sober up quickly.

Sheila and Jo had put on music and were dancing to Katy Perry, pretending to sing into microphones when Pierre came in from walking Scruffy. He removed his coat and boots and joined Daria by the fire.

She knew she had to come clean. "I know we have to," she slurred, "and I'm just postponing the inevitable, but my heart is breaking." She wished she'd sober up quickly and shut up.

He embraced her, his muscular arms tightening as though he'd never let her go. "Come on, slow dance with me. And then later we'll make love like it's the last night on earth."

Daria's cell phone rang at 5:52, waking them. Her heart leapt to her throat at the sight of Robert's name flashing on the screen. Early morning phone calls were never good.

"Sunny is in the emergency ward." Robert said before hello. "She's okay now," he said, "but she had an allergic reaction to Suzanne's cat, it seems, and her throat swelled up."

"Oh God!" Daria stood beside the bed and Pierre switched on the light. "She's breathing?"

"Yes, she's fine now."

"What hospital? Can I talk to her?"

"She's sleeping. Overlake Hospital. We're waiting for a room. They want to observe her so we'll stay today." He sounded shaken.

"Oh, my poor darling Sunny. Was she terrified?"

"I'd say frightened. She and Rose came to our room at three, Sunny complaining of her throat and shortness of breath. I called the ambulance and they transported her."

"When did Suzanne get a cat?"

"I gave her a Persian for Christmas, and it ended up sleeping with Sunny last night."

"So now we know it's not just rabbits and guinea pigs." Daria took a deep breath. "I'm coming home now. Tell her when she wakes up that Mommy will be there as fast as a plane can fly." Daria grabbed her suitcase with one hand and tried to open it. "Tell her I love her. And Rose too. Call me when she wakes." Pierre had flipped on the overhead light and was already dressing.

She hung up and looked at Pierre. "I need to get to the airport fast. Sunny had an allergic reaction and is in the hospital."

"Throw everything in your suitcase. Let's go."

Twenty minutes down the road, Daria sat silently, her mind running through every worst-case scenario at a dizzying pace, driving her crazy. Pierre spoke, jarring her from her frantic imaginations.

"Call the airport Cherie. See if there's a flight at 7:30. If not, it might be better to drive."

They'd said goodbye to Sheila and Jo in a rush from the bedroom door. Now they just had to get her to the airport. Daria called the airline and found that she'd miss the next flight and the one after that was too late. "WE might as well drive. Are you okay with that?"

Pierre grabbed her hand and kissed it. "Of course I am. Anything to help you."

Driving through Squamish, Daria received a text that said Sunny was awake. She called Robert.

"I didn't know if you'd gone back to bed so I didn't want to call." he said.

Back to bed!? "I'm on the road, Robert. I told you that I was coming. Can you put Sunny on?"

There was whispering and then Sunny's sweet voice lit up the line. "Hi, Mommy. I couldn't breathe but I'm okay now and I have a big hotel room with my own nurse."

"Oh, my darling girl." Tears fell from Daria's chin onto a sleeping Scruffy. "You can breathe fine now?"

"Yes, and I just ordered breakfast and I get to stay here and watch TV and order food today. Rosey is in bed with me, and she's taking all the covers. Can you tell her to stop pulling the blanket?"

Daria smiled. "Well, remember that Rosey wants to have some of the hotel fun too. Is Daddy there?"

Suddenly Robert was on the phone. "Honestly, Daria, she looks like it never happened. Back to normal."

"Thank God." Daria wondered if she'd have seen a black aura around her little Sunny, had she been there last night.

"Really Daria, don't worry. I know you want to be here but the girls are fine and even if you don't trust me now, there are nurses coming in and out."

"It's not that Robert. I just love them so much."

He was silent.

"Tell them I'll be there in time for lunch."

"Oh, wait. Rose wants to talk."

"Mommy, it was super scary to see Sunny like that. She went in an ambulance. And Daddy and Suzanne were fighting about the stupid cat." She lowered her voice to whisper. "And now Suzanne didn't come to the hospital. Didn't even drive me over. Daddy says he's done with her nonsense and I think they'll get a divorce."

"Rosey, don't you worry about that. Grownups fight when they're worried and then they make up. And don't worry about Sunny now. You're lying right beside your sister. She's doing fine." She'd always said Rose was her worrier, while Sunny was her warrior.

"Mommy, Suzanne had a black ring around her, like she was a bad Christmas tree."

Daria had suspected for a year that Rosey saw auras. Now she was sure. "That's okay sweetie. It means she was mad. We can talk about the rings around people when I come home. I'll be there soon." She looked over at Pierre and released the huge breath she didn't know she'd been holding. "Thank you."

"Du rien." He smiled at her tentatively. "It means for nothing."

"Can we stop for breakfast? I'm hung over and I need food." They smiled, from relief as much as humor.

At their table in the diner's corner, Pierre took her hand. "Sounds like she's doing well now?"

Daria nodded. "Yesterday, I saw this drive down the road going much differently. I thought it might be sad, but not overshadowed by an emergency."

"Why sad?" He looked as though he genuinely didn't know how horrible it would be to say goodbye to him—watch him drive off to Portland and eventually home to San Francisco.

Should she tell him the depth of her feelings? What did she have to lose? She knew he waited for her answer, and above all else, she owed him honesty. "This week in Whistler, and in particular with you, has been like a magical trip into a different dimension. One where I'm not just a mom, but a woman, and a sexy one who skis," she added. He smiled at her knowingly. "I haven't seen that side of myself in a long time. I've been lost in motherhood. I did a bad job of being a wife to Robert, I see that now. Especially once we had children. And after this time with you, I can see that I need to amend that."

"With Robert?" His eyes were wide.

"No, not with Robert. God, no. I just want to somehow merge those two parts of me. I want to be a wonderful mother first, but I also need to remember that I'm a woman and I need love. I didn't tell Robert any of that and we drifted apart." There, she'd said it. She needed a man like Pierre to love her and love her children and take her out on date nights and buy her popsicles at the grocery store when she was sick.

Pierre moved to sit beside her in the booth. "You are an amazing woman, Daria." He pulled her to him and kissed her cheek. "I'm lucky to know you."

She looked into his face and wondered why he didn't look sad, the way she felt. "I wish things could've been different with you and me. But I understand this was a one shot deal. That doesn't make it less difficult."

"Do you mean because I live in San Francisco and you live in Seattle?"

Had he thought about them, long term? "Yes." Their food came and they ignored it, thanking the waitress. "I knew going into this that it was a stolen moment with a man who I'd never see again. I knew that, but still it feels sad. Spending this holiday with you has been so wonderful."

"Ma Cherie, for me, too. I'm not ready to say goodbye to you and don't know when that would ever be. I fell in love with you that first night. The moment when you pretended with your daughters that I was your new boyfriend and I imagined that I was. I've never looked back. Did you think I would drop you off in Woodinville, never to be seen again?"

Yes, she did. Daria nodded. Did he truly think they could have a long distance relationship? From her viewpoint that wouldn't work at all, and meeting once a year in Whistler sounded lonelier than hell. "We live too far apart to make this work."

Pierre took her face in his hands and looked deep into her eyes. "No, we don't. This is worth fighting for, my darling. If you say the word, we are going to make this work."

"What's the word?"

"Love. As in I'm in falling in love with you, Daria. I can't imagine going back to San Francisco without knowing you are mine."

"I can't do long distance with no hope of eventually living together." Her heart pounded furiously in her chest. "I can't move to Napa with the girls, Pierre." Had he thought of that? "I have to live near Robert."

"I know that. But what you don't know is that I have partial ownership in a winery in Woodinville. Daria's mouth hung open. "That's partly what this trip was for. I spent some time in Woodinville on the way up and planned this extra day for a meeting tomorrow. I'm not expected in Portland until the first of January. For my birthday, our birthday," he added. "I lied about driving straight through to Portland because I wanted time in the car to tell you this."

What did this mean? That he'd be spending time just down the road from her?

"I didn't tell you that I'm opening this winery in your town because I didn't want you to feel pressured." He took a deep breath. "Up until a few minutes ago, I wasn't sure how you felt about me. Whether you wanted this to be something more than a fling."

Daria couldn't believe he didn't know. She hadn't said the words but hadn't she been making love to him for the last five nights? She shook her head. "I'm astounded that you don't know I'm crazy about you. Seriously, head over heels."

A smile crept across his face.

"And I didn't want to seem too needy. I thought at first, that you probably had your pick of women, and this was convenient and fun for you, and something you do all the time. I didn't know."

He looked hurt. "It most certainly is not. I haven't been interested in anyone in months and never like this. Once I started learning how to be a dad, my interest in playing the field died. I've been looking for someone like you for years." Pierre tucked a stray piece of hair behind her ear and trailed his finger down the side of her face. "I will do everything in my power to make this work, Ma Cherie."

Her happiness swelled to fill her heart.

"And I see now that I'm going to have to make a few demands on you before we go any further."

What? Here? Was he kidding?

"First, we will go to the hospital and you will introduce me to your girls as your boyfriend and this time there will be no white lie."

She nodded.

"Second, I'm a package deal. He paused. "With Scruffy."

Daria laughed. "Perfect. Luckily Sunny isn't allergic to dogs."

"Third, we go get your car at the airport after the hospital and plan on me staying at your house, on the couch tonight, and tomorrow you go to a New Year's party with me at Chateau Ste. Michelle."

She gave him a nod. "That's doable. I'm sure my next door neighbor will babysit."

"We'll be together on our birthday morning then I'll go to Portland, then to San Francisco and if you still love me after that, I'll come back in a few weeks with my toothbrush and razor."

She laughed again. "Yes Pierre. Yes to all but going to the airport today. I don't want to do mundane things when I have you only for one day."

"Darling." He leaned in and tenderly kissed her lips. "You have me for much longer than that. I'm already planning skiing with our daughters next year."

Pierre's aura glowed like candlelight with a touch of red that Daria interpreted as passionate love and she allowed herself to be deliriously happy. "Next year we'll have Christmas in Whistler."

She kissed him passionately, right there in the little diner. She knew her time away from the girls had made her a better person. As a huge bonus, it had given her Pierre. "I love you," she whispered against his lips. She knew he felt the same way. She'd seen the candlelight.

ABOUT THE AUTHOR

KIM HORNSBY once earned her rent money as a singer on Maui, performing at convention shows and opening for acts like Jay Leno and Jamie Foxx. Those were the days she rubbed shoulders with George Harrison and Alice Cooper at Maui parties, days when she drove a sports car and got asked for her autograph in the DMV lineup.

She now lives in the Seattle area where she's only known as her children's mother. Writing stories in the rainy months, Kim edits in the sunshiny months. A wife, mother, dog owner and adventurer, she loves to hike, waterski, camp, and avoid housework. Living vicariously through her character's exciting lives, she creates stories to fulfill her reader's need for adventure and the thrill of romance.

She's over the moon excited to have her first self-published novel up for Best Indie First Book by Indie Rom/Con this year. She lives for good reviews of her books and loves to hear from readers. When she gets a nice email, she prints it off and puts it in a file marked "Favorite Readers".

Visit Kim's Pinterest Page for Christmas in Whistler to see her vision of Daria and Pierre!

http://www.pinterest.com/kimberwrite/a-whistler-christmas/

If you liked this story, you may also enjoy Kim's Bachelor series, The Husband Hunt. The series is based on THE BACHELOR, ABC TV's Popular Reality show.

THE HUSBAND HUNT – Kat's Season

If you liked the paranormal twist in *Christmas in Whistler,* you'll probably like:

The Dream Jumper's Promise
Paranormal Romance
Nominated for Best Indie First Book

If you liked the romance in *Christmas in Whistler,* you'll probably like:

Necessary Detour
Romantic Suspense
Published by The Wild Rose Press

Visit Kim at

Kim Hornsby
Commercial Women's Fiction
You only journey if you dare to leave home
The Dream Jumper's Promise
Necessary Detour
http://www.kimhornsby.net
www.kimhornsby.blogspot.com
http://twitter.com/kimhornsby
http://www.goodreads.com/author/show/676385
Kim_Hornsby
www.facebook.com/kimhornsbyauthor

DEDICATION

This story is dedicated to my Canadian husband Roland, who took me to live in Whistler when we were first married and made me get a ski pass so I'd have something to do when he was at work. Love you, Honey!

Gift From the Heart
TRISH F. LEGER

Chapter 1

"**D**id you grab that last box?"

"Yep, it's done, one last one to worry about."

Simone Welter turned and took in the small warehouse that held all manner of decoration scattered around. It vaguely looked as if every holiday had vomited and coalesced in the small interior.

"Damn girl, we have way too much crap," Simone intoned to Alexa, the other half of NOSTALGIA, their joint venture into the business world.

Alexa huffed as she stumbled carefully around boxes strewn all over. "Tell me about it." She pushed a strand of curly blonde hair that Simone would kill for, over one ear. "Maybe we should put out extra stock?"

"There isn't enough?" Simone asked, gesturing to the doorway that led to the store. It was piled high with boxes spilling over with Christmas decorations.

Alexa shrugged, "I guess you're right."

"You know I am. Come on, I think Christmas has already passed with all the time we wasted in here."

"Bah humbug to you too, Grinch." Alexa quipped over her shoulder as they made their way into the store, which was closed for the night.

Simone didn't answer, she knew Alexa didn't expect one either. She followed her friend into the store and began to unload boxes one by one. The season began to take shape within minutes—large rotund Santa's with jolly faces and red cheeks, classic Norman Rockwell paintings depicting life during Americana Christmastide, and Simone's favorite, retro brightly colored decorations that would hang on the many trees in the store.

Humming invaded her thoughts. Simone glanced up and watched Alexa pushing the boxes out of the way as she placed different do-dads and ornaments around the store. Christmas was Alexa's favorite holiday. Simone was indifferent as a whole. She enjoyed collecting ornaments, but what would people think if they knew she felt neither here nor there about the Christmas holidays?

Paper crinkled under her hands, bringing her back to the here and now.

But, she knew she had no time for this. . Yes, life was crappy, but now that NOSTALGIA placed her directly in the public eye, she needed to get a grip and be real. In other words, she was lying—lying to her friend, her co-worker, and everyone around her.

Would she ever come clean with her true feelings about the holiday?

Shaking off her negativity, she smiled as she listened to Alexa's humming and realized that even though the worst part of the year was around the corner, she could enjoy a few things. Those things included her friend humming off-key Christmas tunes.

Lance Turner felt out of his element. An involuntary shiver started at his exposed neck and multiplied tenfold. This crisp mountain air would take some getting used to. And the smells were completely different. Pines, firs, and a generally woodsy northern scent infiltrated the truck, reminding him he wasn't in the south anymore.

Hard country poured from his speakers as he scoured the small mountain town of Broken Bow, Oregon. He could finally sit back and relax in his truck, just drive around, checking out his new part of the world. His new consulting job in Portland had taken all of his personal time so far, and this "getting to know Broken Bow" phase had seemed as if it would never happen. Lance had begun to think worry he would never see anything again but concrete and glass walls.

His phone's ringtone interrupted his thoughts. He accepted the call and his sister's voice filled the vehicle.

"You aren't going to believe this!"

Lance smiled at Chrissy's tone. She always had been the dramatic one. "What won't I believe?"

"I just found the one piece for my manger scene at a store in your 'new' hometown!"

His sister had collected rare and hard to find holiday decorations for years. Of course she'd check out Broken Bow now that he was here to act on her behalf as personal errand boy. He was only surprised it had taken over a month to get him involved.

"Really now?" Lance chuckled at his sister's over exuberance. "And I'm guessing that you want me to go pick it up for you?"

"Actually yes, but that's not the unbelievable part. You'll never guess who is working there!"

Lance gave her a few seconds of quiet before she practically burst at the seams from her excitement. "Well, go ahead and surprise me. I can't begin to imagine who the mystery person is."

"I can tell by the sarcasm in your voice that you're dying to know, but oh my God, it's just so amazing . . . "

"Chrissy . . . " Lance intoned, putting his "I'm older, don't jerk me around" voice to good use.

She huffed, "Okay, okay, it's Simone Welter."

The air in Lance's lungs practically crystallized. "Simone? Here, in Broken Bow?"

"Yep, in your new hometown, how awesome is that?" The excitement in Chrissy's voice had boiled over and was now reaching into the earsplitting decibel range.

Lance cleared his throat and tried to do everything BUT think of Simone. "Why do I even need to pick up this doohickey for you anyway? Doesn't her store have shipping?"

"It sure does, but apparently subtlety isn't your forte, older brother."

"What the hell does that mean?"

She huffed again, "It means that I'm giving you an excuse, the first in over ten years, to get Simone face to face and explain once and for all what happened."

Lance sighed, and realized he'd definitely lost the battle to put Simone out of his mind. He pictured her as he'd last seen her, solemn, her long, dark hair framing her delicate face. "I don't have time for this, Chrissy."

"Sure you don't, but the store is NOSTALGIA, when you change your mind."

And with that, she hung up, leaving Lance staring out of his windshield and praying for the past to stay buried.

It didn't, of course. Once the image of Simone had invaded his thoughts, she was stuck there, like peanut butter to the roof of his mouth..

Lance shook his head as he pulled onto Main Street, the charm of the small town breaking past thoughts of Simone and hitting him in the gut. It was picturesque, quaint, and there were even people milling about in the cold, smiling and waving.

All the comforts of home, minus the oppressive heat, sweeping magnolias, and people speaking in the relaxed southern drawls he was accustomed to.

What the hell was Simone doing here?

He remembered her leaving for college after high school, weeks after graduation, but nothing since. After that horrible night, he'd had no ties to her. No one and nothing to keep him updated on the lively, outgoing young woman he'd once known--very well, in fact. The young woman who'd changed, drastically.

Well, you screwed that up, Turner.

He'd done more than screwed up. The damage he'd inflicted on her was irreversible.

But he knew he needed to apologize. Damn, the image of her, staring at him with horror, was seared into his frontal lobe. It would never go away. No matter how many years passed, or miles between them, nothing had removed the memory.

But now he had a chance.

He could only hope she had forgotten him completely.

Chapter 2

Simone scraped her hair back and got down to business. This wasn't going to do itself, and the store had to be in tip-top shape by Monday. That was the mutual deadline she'd set with Alexa. Since they'd pulled the boxes into the main area of the store yesterday afternoon, they had all day today and tomorrow to get things squared away. Tim and Leah, their two main employees, were both there helping as well.

The work went by quickly. The store began to take shape as a Winter Wonderland breathed life into the once empty space. NOSTALGIA wasn't large, per se, but it was a good size. The building had begun as an old general store back in the day, and the multitude of hidden nooks and areas broken off from the main floor enabled them to have their own multicultural Christmas card, come to life.

Alexa had decided to decorate each area according to different traditions and nationalities. Their store catered to rare and hard to find objects, so for Simone, it was like stepping into heaven.

That's why she'd partnered with Alexa, in the first place. Her creative nature had been dormant for too many years. The artistic side that had once been so much a part of her that she used to fall asleep with her artwork in the bed beside her, had stirred to life when Alexa began to speak of opening this place. Sure, with the economy nearly at a standstill, they had taken a huge risk, but Alexa could charm the bristles off a brush when she put her mind to it. And it wasn't like Simone was hurting for money, considering she had her trust.

She'd believed her creativity had died years ago, along with everything else of importance in her life.

Protective paper crinkled in her hands as she pulled out another delicate and very rare box. Designed as part of a trio, it depicted the gifts of the Magi. Simone turned the beautifully painted and designed piece in her hands, and felt a shimmering inside of her that couldn't be contained.

It seemed her one true passion wasn't completely dead after all.

Monday rolled around bright and cold. Broken Bow was a small town, but it wasn't far from Portland, just a thirty or forty minute drive, depending on the weather. Considering the season and the weather—the first snow of the year had dropped a week ago—people were in a rollicking good mood. If their sales were anything to go by, they were salivating for Christmas to come.

"Honey, I need another coffee!" Tim exclaimed, bursting through the back door on his way to the small desk he shared with Leah.

Simone smiled at his remark. He and Alexa got along great because both were dramatic, full of flourish, and it took negativity of epic proportions to kill their good mood. Simone and Leah were more alike, with their unobtrusive, quiet nature.

"And, this is too important to forget, but did you see the ass on that guy that just left?" Tim fanned himself as he walked by Simone's desk.

At least they would never have a dull moment with Tim around.

"I must have missed that," Simone answered, grinning despite herself. There was a glass wall in front of the desk, so if she wanted to see, she would have been able to.

Tim stopped by her side, putting a hand on her shoulder. "I about passed out when he turned around after checking out. Whew!" He fanned himself again, and Simone couldn't help the giggle that came out.

Alexa poked her head around the doorway. "Did you see that guy's ass that just left?"

"Oh my God, really?" Simone questioned. "I think y'all need to pay more attention to everything else going on, and leave that poor guy's ass alone."

Tim walked towards Alexa, "See, I know we're really getting to her when she says 'y'all' in that southern drawl of hers."

Alexa laughed and left the doorway.

"I don't think that's funny!" Simone shouted back in retaliation.

"I'll get you another latte because I still love you, darling!" Tim's voice echoed back to her as he left the shop for Ruthie's down on the corner.

Minutes later, Alexa poked her head around again. "Okay, this is going to sound terrible but, the guy with the fantastic ass, well, he's back." She smirked as she whispered, "Just thought you'd like to know before you miss out again."

"Y'all are terrible, horrible people, you know that?"

But she must be included in the same damn group because she couldn't resist making her way into the main area of the store.

Just in time to see the man in question walking through the front entrance.

Well, I haven't even seen his ass yet, but the front is amazing enough . . .

She froze in her tracks, her thoughts congealing as he got close enough to get a good look at him.

Tall, dirty blond hair, perfectly groomed, massively wide linebacker shoulders, but with the lower half of a swimmer—a lean waist that tapered into narrow hips. The man had a built-in swagger that had made her heart thud in awareness—just as it had when she was a teenager.

She knew this man. She knew those ever changing grey eyes, that handsome smirk on his face, those damned dimples.

Oh God, she knew him.

And she wanted Lance Turner to walk right back out of her door and leave her alone, just as he'd promised he would when she was eighteen.

She looked older and wiser, but definitely not any happier to see him. Lance could tell she recognized him immediately.

He had no idea what had made him chicken out the first time he came in. He'd gotten Chrissy's darn manger addition and then he turned stupid and left. Halfway down the street he'd realized how much of a dumbass he was being by not saying *something* to her.

But how was she going to treat this situation? Would she ignore him? Turn around and go back behind that glass wall? Or would she politely exchange niceties while rage burned behind those brown eyes of hers.

He wouldn't want to be anywhere around Simone if she had access to a weapon.

"Lance, Lance Turner, how odd to see you in Broken Bow."

By way of pleasantries, that was pretty good, considering the steam that would erupt from her ears very soon.

"I could say the same for you, Simone."

There was a gasp from the blonde standing not far from her, but Lance ignored her and focused on Simone. Everything about her was so much the same, yet different, and he absorbed every detail. Glorious long, dark hair fell past her shoulders; her hair had always been long. She was tall for a woman, reaching him face to face, and he remembered that she'd hated being tall when she was younger because she always thought women were more attractive to men being short and curvy.

Well, she should have no issues with that anymore. This woman had curves, curves in every place a woman should. It was such a difference from his tomboyish teenage friend that it took Lance a second to realize Simone was gorgeous, beyond so.

His friend had grown up.

Huh, he mentally scoffed, she wasn't his friend anymore. He'd taken care of that personally. She wasn't *his* anything.

The silence became uncomfortable. In the past, they'd never had this problem.

"Did you find everything okay? Is something wrong with the item you purchased?" Simone questioned, and Lance could tell it took everything she had not to ask him one more time what in the hell he was doing here, disrupting her life.

He picked up the bag he was holding, "No, everything is fine. This is for Chrissy, she's the one who had me stop by. Apparently she saw this on the net and couldn't help herself."

A small smile tipped her lips, "How is she?" Those brown eyes of hers were genuinely curious.

Lance smiled, "She's just fine, married with one girl, Maggie."

"She still in Lafayette?"

"Ah, you know Chrissy. She'd never leave Cajun country."

And just that quickly, her eyes glazed over. Her easy going demeanor turned frigid.

Lance wanted to curse himself. Instead he cleared his throat, "Look, I just wanted to say 'hello', that's all." To make sure she understood his peace offering, he stared into those whiskey eyes of hers, "Maybe we should meet up sometime."

"Maybe."

Well, at least she hadn't flatly refused him. He nodded and left, before he really blew it and made things ten times worse.

Chapter 3

No, oh hell no! What in the hell was Lance Turner doing in her town? In her refuge? Her heart thudded with no relief in sight. Even being home, in her cozy bungalow, she still hadn't calmed down. Tremors shook her hands when she thought of that devilishly handsome man striding into her store as if he owned it.

Simone attempted to make sense of it all. She hadn't seen him since she was eighteen. Lance had been good-looking then, but damn, if he hadn't aged into a flipping Greek god.

Stop reminding yourself of how handsome he is! He's a liar, someone you should never trust! You of all people should know this!

Yes, she knew that. She'd been taught that harsh lesson, but she'd just been re-introduced to his overwhelming, in your face—maleness. No way on earth could she *not* think about it.

The man was every bit as stunning as the boy had always been. He'd been a friend, a very close friend, and by the time she'd turned fifteen, she finally realized what all the other girls in Lafayette were talking about when they spoke of Lance Turner. He was, in a word, *HOT*. Damn her for being a late bloomer and learning that lesson last, as always. Her friends had been jealous of their close friendship, and at first, she could never fathom why.

Back then Lance had it all—he was a jock, upperclassman, and son of the mayor. But even more important was the fact that he was friendly, down to earth, and so easy-going. That laid-back manner of his had easily caught Simone's eye.

That, and the fact her brother and Lance had been best buddies.

She squeezed her eyes shut as thoughts of Lance meshed with thoughts of Stephen.

A tear escaped from the corner of her eye and slipped down her cheek, and she palmed the mug of cocoa that had cooled to lukewarm. She cuddled on her couch while the TV lightly blared in the background.

What was she going to do? How could she stop her emotions from creating a mess out of this scenario?

"I'm not going to allow him to rule my life. He's just a man. That's all."

Simone wondered how many times she'd have to remind herself of that.

Lance leaned back in his enormous bed, his mind whirring with thoughts of Simone, Broken Bow, and work.

Simone won out. He was beginning to think she always had.

Raking his hands through his hair with enough strength to tear strands out wasn't helping, neither was Sports Center, which was on and not working to keep him occupied.

"You've gone over ten years without seeing her, is this really going to be a problem?"

He would not answer his own question. That would just prove his insanity.

He might not have seen her in a while, but he knew from one look that she'd changed. Her eyes, normally bright with laughter and friendliness, had been guarded, solemn.

And he'd been the one to add to her horrible past. It was mostly his fault that the life had literally been pulled out of her. He knew it. He felt it deep in his bones. His reaction so long ago had caused this beautiful, vibrant young woman to close in on herself. And if he hadn't come to that conclusion himself, his sister would surely have let him know over the years.

Simone as a teenager had been fun, easy going, much like himself. But back then she'd been a bothersome younger sister to his friend, Stephen. He'd pretty much ignored her, or tried to as Simone could grow on a person. After spending years around her, the time came when he could no more ignore her as he could stop breathing. They grew as close as brother and sister.

Until the afternoon of her graduation from high school, when everything had changed.

And damn him for being the immature, young, hot-headed dumbass he'd been. He'd added to her pain.

Now he'd have to make sure she knew why he'd left, why he'd walked away. Because now that Lance had seen her, had talked to her, there was no way he could go on living with the knowledge he'd put that storminess in Simone's eyes.

He wanted her, the *real* her, back in his life.

"He works in Portland for Lakeland Promotions as an upper consultant. And he's not married."

Simone didn't answer, just glared at Alexa and Tim. Leah laughed lightly in the background and added, "Did you find out if he was gay or straight? Because I'm sure Tim's just jumping up and down to get word on that."

Tim huffed and responded, "Honey, he's straighter than the road outside. I could tell that from a mile away."

"I wish I had that uncanny ability. Being single and dating sucks."

They all laughed at Leah's remark.

"Ain't that the truth?" Alexa agreed, then turned her gaze back to Simone. "You seem surprised that I could find that out."

"Not surprised, per say, but surprised you give a damn." She tried to stay busy, logging information on the computer, keeping her eyes downcast while her brain railed *he's not married*, over and over.

"This is a small town." Alexa supplied, wiping down a delicate ornament. "And he's deliciously sexy. It was easy to find out that information."

He *was* sexy. That was another thing bothering Simone. Lance Turner as a young man had been smoking hot, but with his friendly attitude, he had been a god among guys his age. Now, over ten years later, that boyish aura was gone, replaced with a man who was almost a stranger.

Simone shivered, remembering the intent in his smoky eyes as he stood before her. This was a man who was determined. And a determined Lance Turner always got what he wanted.

So, what in the hell did he want?

"What I want to know, sugar, is how do you know this walking, talking, fine specimen of manhood?" Tim intoned, dragging her attention up and towards the three of them who seemed to be patiently waiting for an answer.

"I knew him years ago." There, that should be good enough.

"Ha! Years ago?" Tim barked out.

Apparently it wasn't good enough.

"I guess that part could be right, but I'm thinking there is more to the term 'know' than what you're telling."

Damn. Simone looked back at the computer. "I don't see why any of this matters." She shook her head as the three of them stood waiting for more.

Out of the corner of her eye, she saw Alexa move closer. "Simone, I think we could all tell that you have obvious *history* with this man. Since we've never seen you give anyone such a cold reaction, we are curious, to say the least."

Cold reaction? Had she really been that cold to him? Would it matter?

"Yep, I agree with Alexa. But I also think that Simone will say more when she's ready. We should just give her some space."

Simone wanted to kiss Leah for being so insightful.

Tim hugged her from out of the blue, startling her so much she almost fell off of the chair.

"I'm here for you, darling. Just let me know if Mr. Sexy Ass does something wrong. I'll take care of him for you."

Simone laughed, "I'm sure you will."

That Friday afternoon, Lance strolled in the front door. Damn. Simone manned the front register while Alexa and Tim ran an errand and Leah was off.

"Good afternoon." She figured she had to speak to him. There was no way to ignore him and she couldn't turn away a potential customer.

"Good afternoon, Simone," he responded.

God, the way he spoke her name in his southern drawl was so familiar and yet so different from what her ears were now accustomed to. Her mind travelled back in time to humid days, hot nights, shrimp etouffee, and spicy boiled crawfish. She missed Louisiana, the friendly people so full of southern hospitality, the music, and dancing—God she loved dancing a quick jitterbug or a slow waltz to a good Cajun band. In general, she missed the joie de vivre way of life of southern Louisiana. She always had. But it hadn't hit her until then, how much she'd missed Lance.

She became the focus of his grey eyes, and a burn invaded her insides, not to mention her cheeks. She blushed like a schoolgirl.

This man left you. He walked away from you. He cannot be trusted. DON'T let his handsomeness suck you in!

Simone snapped out of that train of thought, like closing the lid tightly back on her past and emotions. "I'm not surprised you work in a place like this." The words sounded innocent enough. But the voice, ah, that voice was like music to her ears.

She cocked her head curious to know if he really believed that, or if he was just making small talk. "Really, why is that?"

He smiled and loosened his tie, worn with a blinding white shirt. His heavy trench coat covered what Simone speculated was a suit. "Because, you've always been interested in history and art," his hand encompassed the general area, "This is your forte, your haven, where you feel most comfortable."

Simone quirked a brow and tried to ignore the pounding in her heart, but failed miserably.

"I love every inch of this shop," she said, stopping just short of getting flustered in front of him.

He gave her a cursory glance, up, down, and back to her eyes. "I know. It's easy to see."

She swallowed a sudden urge to shout at him that he knew nothing. "Was there something else you needed? Maybe something else for Chrissy?"

Now his eyebrow hiked up. "Can't I say 'hello' to an old friend?"

Simone's nerves threatened to snap the pencil gripped in her hand. The anger at his gall coursed through her system, red hot and ready to explode. "We haven't seen each other in years. We aren't friends. Haven't been in a while.

You want to come in here and disrupt my life? Deal with me pissed off at you.

His eyes wavered for one second before settling back on hers. Simone swore there was something there, something pitying or regretful in his gaze. "Don't say that, Simone."

Sadness suddenly swamped her. "Why not, it's the truth." She couldn't bear his gaze on her anymore, so she lowered her gaze to his hands where they rested on the sales counter.

"It's not the truth, and you know it," he said. Simone watched his hands fist before her, gathering air within his grip as if to brace for a fight.

Why are you here? What makes you think I'd want you back in my life?

She would never voice those questions. Not if she wanted to remain cool and unaffected before him.

The ding of the door opening saved her, literally. She glanced up, seeing a regular customer walking in.

"Hello, Mrs. Winstead."

"Why, hello dear! I need to ask you a question about one of the sets of crystal I bought the other day, do you have time?"

Simone looked quickly at Lance, saw the determination in his eyes dim a bit, and replied, "Yes ma'am, I'll be with you in one second."

"Thank you, dear," Mrs. Winstead walked around a few decorations as she made her way towards the front desk.

"I guess I'll be seeing you," Lance said, giving her his trademark smile, showing off those killer dimples, "Don't think this conversation is over either," he quipped, walking backwards.

Simone's heart sunk as he turned and walked out the door.

"She wants nothing to do with me. You know better than to ask that."

Chrissy snorted at the other end of the phone. "Damn right, I know that. I wouldn't want anything to do with you either. For years now you know you've been wishing you could get within ten feet of her and apologize. Now you have your chance."

Lance looked towards his ceiling; waiting for the divine intervention he hoped would come. Nothing happened. "Look, she's not the same woman you remember."

"Lance, honey, how could she be? With everything she's gone through, I imagine you wouldn't be the same either."

"Of course, you're right."

Chrissy laughed loudly, "Paul, you've got to come get in on this conversation. Lance just admitted I'm right."

Lance grinned as he heard Paul mumbling in the background.

"Paul said you're lucky you're so far away."

"Ha! He knows how lucky he is, he just acts macho in front of all of y'all," Lance responded, feeling a little homesick at the sound of his sister laughing.

When the call ended, he grabbed a beer from the fridge and stood before the large windows in the spaciously empty condo he inhabited. The company he worked for had supplied the housing and the truck, all incentives to get him up here. He wasn't complaining, especially now that he'd discovered Simone, but the Northwest was completely different from the south. That was the best way to put it. The landscape and atmosphere was the most dramatic difference: No sweeping Live Oaks or Cypress trees with moss hanging like icicles from a Christmas tree, No winding bayous or wetlands at or close to sea level, no fishing in the Gulf of Mexico. Now he was chock full with a daily dose of majestic mountains, evergreens, and briskly frigid temps. Lance shook his head and turned around.

His condo was large, masculine and modern. He had managed to put a few of his own touches here and there, pictures from home and a few of his favorite paintings, but it still didn't ring true to him yet, and it sure as hell didn't feel like home.

Maybe he needed something fresh, something original. Something Simone had created.

That girl had been talented back in the day, making something glorious from anything she could get her hands on. She could paint, draw, sculpt, and create the most unusual and beautiful things. As far as he knew, there was only a few pieces of her creations left, his sister had one, the town hall back in Lafayette had one--and how could he have forgotten this? He had one, too.

Lance strode into his spare bedroom, glancing at all the boxes as he walked in. There weren't many, and he knew exactly where it was. Within minutes he had the box out and seconds later he was tearing through it. The hard edges of wood came into view, and seconds later his gaze landed on Simone's handiwork. It had been boxed up prior to his college days, and he hadn't seen it in a long time.

She'd made it after a conversation between the two of them about life, and the funny things that happen in it. Lance had thought the whole conversation amusing at the time because Simone had only been seventeen. To his knowledge, she'd been far too young to know anything of life. It wasn't much later that he'd learned she'd been more knowledgeable and stronger than anyone had given her credit for.

He passed his hand lovingly over the long, slim piece of wood. She'd used a dremel tool to carve designs into it, as well as her favorite quote:

A FRIEND IS SOMEONE WHO GIVES YOU
FREEDOM TO BE YOURSELF

Lance sat there for a moment, holding the cypress in his hands, feeling the weight of it, and the weight of the years that stretched out to that point where he no longer knew her. He recalled the one time they'd had a conversation about life. They'd also spoken of his family life, or lack thereof. Hers had been more of a family to him than his own parents had been. Chrissy and Lance had practically lived at Simone and Stephen's house while they'd been in school.

Later, while he was at LSU, he would go back as often as possible, but since he lived in a dorm, the trip was only on the weekends—until Chrissy and Simone's graduation, which also happened to be the night Simone's world fell apart.

He thought of her response to him just this afternoon in NOSTALGIA. She'd seemed shocked to see him, but he'd also seen a fierce blush stain her cheeks. Was that from anger? Or was it possible she was blushing for a different reason?

Now, that's an intriguing thought . . .

Not one that he'd actually had before. Sure, he'd known back then that Simone was decently pretty, but she'd also been Stephen's little sister. That was a glaring NO in his book. Not to mention, he would have had to choose between Stephen kicking his ass, or putting the moves on Simone.

He smiled as he remembered her long hair, dark eyes, and smiling mouth. She'd been such a tomboy. He'd never been able to get past that image . . . until now. She wasn't tomboyish anymore, that hair, those eyes . . . those curves. The woman was FINE.

For the first time, Lance felt something totally different for Simone Welter. The sudden realization gave him even more incentive to make things right between them.

Chapter 4

"Simone, phone for you," Alexa called cheerfully as she exited the office.

"Who is it?"

"Not sure."

Simone walked towards her desk and glared at the slim phone handle, the fierce feeling in her belly deepened as she picked up the receiver.

"Hello?"

"Simone, are you busy?"

Dang, she knew that voice like the back of her hand. "Not at the moment."

"I know that you're usually very busy, so I'll make this quick. Chrissy and her family are coming up to visit this weekend for an early Christmas. She really wants to see you. Are you free? Can you make it over?"

The ball in her belly felt like it weighed one hundred pounds. "I'm not sure . . . "

"It's only Chrissy, you haven't seen her in years."

Quit stating the obvious! Crap!

"I guess I could." She all but growled her displeasure into the phone.

He laughed, "Don't sound so convincing for me. I don't want to tell my sister I had to drag you here."

Simone almost smiled then caught herself, *none of that.* "What time and where do I need to meet y'all?"

"I can come pick you u—"

She cut him off. "No, that's fine, just tell me where and what time."

He sighed heavily, "1025 Gander Lane, it's the condo with windows facing the mountains. And you can come around 5 p.m. this Saturday. Is that okay?"

"That's fine."

"I'll see you then. Bye, Simone."

Her heart fluttered lightly as his accented tone pronounced her name. "Goodbye."

She hung up the phone, wondering what in the hell she was going to do now.

Lance retrieved Chrissy and her family from the Portland airport late Friday afternoon. After getting them settled in his condo, he, Paul and his sister sat around the large den, drinking wine and relaxing. "By the way, I've invited Simone over for supper. I knew you'd want to see her."

Chrissy's eyes brightened before narrowing suspiciously on her brother. "You aren't going to be an ass and bring up the past in front of us, are you?"

Nothing better than the bluntness of a little sister. "Give me some credit, will you? I'll talk to her, but not until she and I are alone. I just thought you'd want to spend a few hours with your long lost friend."

Chrissy didn't have to know that he had ulterior motives for having Simone over tonight. His strategy was to soften Simone up with his family.Lance checked the Beef Stew simmering on the stove. He stirred it one last time as Chrissy and Paul set the table. He glanced over at his niece as she sang along to one of her cartoons in the living room. It sure felt good to have family around.

The chime of the doorbell had Lance feeling like a gawky teenager about to go on his first date.

Calm it down, Turner.

He took a deep breath and hung back in the kitchen while his sister gently attacked Simone. He could hear their excited tones, and when he turned and watched them come around the corner, his heart sputtered at the look of genuine joy on Simone's face. Until she saw him, and that look disappeared.

Seems he would have to work on her and their friendship a bit more.

"Lance, doesn't she look amazing?" Chrissy exclaimed, after she introduced Simone to Paul.

Lance responded with a nod and an adamant, "She certainly does." He had a feeling the only person who heard him was Simone. Her cheeks reddened immediately. He took in the total package of a red sweater, dressy jeans, and heeled boots. She looked amazing. Her eyes were bright once again. He loved that the most.

"This is Maggie," Paul told Simone, as he picked his daughter up from the floor, her bouncing blond curls curtaining her dimpled face.

"She's a beauty, Chrissy." Simone smiled gently at the youngster, while Maggie gave her a gap toothed grin.

"She's a handful, is what she is," Paul said.

Lance agreed, "That little girl reminds me of another little girl." He gestured towards his sister as he spoke.

"You mean she's just like her momma?" Simone asked, avoiding looking at Lance.

"Exactly," Paul agreed with Lance. "We're going to have to watch for frogs in her pockets, dirt in her hair, and a sly smile on her face when we correct her."

"Maggie, don't listen to them. Your mother was an amazing child. Just as you are, my darling!"

Everyone laughed when Maggie answered with an adorable, "I know, momma!"

Supper was surprisingly good and Simone enjoyed herself immensely. From meeting Paul, the perfectly matched husband for Chrissy, to catching up with her old girl friend, things were going well.

But every time she looked at Lance, her stomach bottomed out. She wasn't sure if it was nerves, attraction, or just plain skittishness causing it.

He was gorgeous tonight. The dark green pullover shirt he wore fit him closely, highlighting all of his chest and arms, and apparently he worked out. The delineation of his body was on full display and his jeans hugged him everywhere they should. His exuberance at having family over was charming and he hadn't stopped smiling the entire time.

Simone caught herself smiling in return.

Sipping her glass of wine, she watched, heart in her throat, as Chrissy and Paul left the room to put Maggie to bed. Alone with Lance, she began to fidget, nervously twirling the wine in her glass. It was different from the old days. Being alone with Lance hadn't been a problem before.

But your past had never been the issue.

She took a deep breath and sent a cautious glance in his direction. Bold grey eyes met hers, nearly causing her to choke on her wine. She couldn't prevent the small cough that escaped, and he smiled slightly before glancing away. Damn it, he knew he was the reason for her nervous gestures.

"Thanks for inviting me." Her voice was clear and smooth. She couldn't believe she wasn't sputtering like a lunatic.

He turned back to her, smile in place. "You're quite welcome." He played with his wineglass, turning the stem around with long, masculine fingers. "I have to admit, I thought you'd find a way out of this."

Simone blushed at the slight reprimand. "It seems you can still read me, even after all these years."

"It's like riding a bike. You just never forget some things. You've always been easy to read, Simone."

"Yep, that's me, all right."

"Don't be so hard on yourself. You're a great person, always have been."

She smiled. "This must be compliment-your-guest-night."

He seemed shocked, or perhaps surprised, by her smile. He couldn't look away, and his hand had stopped spinning the glass. Simone's nervousness came back full force.

"How long have you been in Broken Bow?" He gulped at his wine, as though trying to gain back his composure.

She glanced around, looking anywhere but at him. "Since I was twenty-four. I came here with my coworker, Alexa, after we graduated from college. She grew up here and mentioned something about opening a store. The rest is history." She sipped at her own glass of wine. "What about you?"

He placed his empty glass before him on the coffee table and his eyes met hers again. "I accepted a consulting job in Portland. Since I refused to live in the city, they offered me this town instead." Leaning back against the couch, he sprawled, a man obviously comfortable in her presence. "I love it here. Of course, it isn't Louisiana, but it's my new home."

"The place does grow on you. So do the people."

"I'll admit I miss the accent the most. There's just something about hearing a thick southern accent that does wonders for your soul."

Simone did smile at that. "You're right."

There was a moment of silence and then, "I've missed that, Simone."

Her eyes slid to his, almost hesitantly, "What?"

His eyes were heavy on her face. "Your smile, the last few times I've seen you, it was in hiding."

She gulped deeply. It hit her that this was Lance. The same Lance she'd grown up with. The same Lance who had spent nights at her house, the same Lance she'd had her first crush on, the one that had also broken her heart. Somehow she managed to respond to him.

"I've had few reasons to smile." She freely admitted that. He knew those reasons.

"I'm glad I've given you one then."

Her breath escaped in a loud whoosh, leaving her agitated and breathless. She turned, looking around for something, anything else to focus on, rather than this man. Something on the far wall caught her attention.

A rough piece of wood hung there. The scrollwork was familiar, as was the quote sitting smack dab in the middle of the piece. Her heart began to thud in her chest. He still had it.

She stood on shaky legs, depositing her glass on the coffee table. It was time to go, past time.

"Simone, what is it?" He jumped up, closing in on her as she tried to ease her way from the room.

"I need to leave. Now." There were no other words. She just had to go. She made it to the foyer, grabbing her purse from the hall boy, when he caught up with her.

"You can't keep running. Eventually, we need to speak about our past."

Fury blossomed inside her. She spun to face him, surprised to find him so close. His unique scent teased her nose, reminding her. "Running? You think I'm running?"

Determination once again filled his eyes. "Yes, you're running."

She cocked her head. "You know what, maybe you're right. Maybe I am running." She swiped her keys from her purse, slinging the object on her shoulder with force. "You'd know, after all, you being the freaking expert."

"Simone . . . " He practically growled her name, and from the fire in his eyes, she could see that he was pissed.

"Goodbye, Lance." She didn't wait for him to say anything else, but walked out the door.hapter 5

Simone was a shaky bundle of nerves by the time she returned home. She was beyond the point of composing herself. That man still had the power to bring her to her knees. He'd always possessed that ability. But once he'd left her high and dry, it seems as though she should have formed some kind of protective barrier against him—against his words, his looks, his actions. She threw her keys on the side table in the foyer of her cottage home. She slung off her purse and stalked into the kitchen for a wine glass and some much-needed fortification. Nothing like a little liquid courage to build up the wallowing defenses, although the wine at *his* place hadn't seemed to help her at all.

Simone wasn't sure what surprised her more, the fact that he still had that plaque, or that he'd invited her to his home in the first place.

She pondered the thought as she sipped her wine, rather than gulped it, as she wanted to. The plaque had been hanging in the place of honor, right above the mantle. He was obviously proud of it, and her hard work, but how did she know he didn't hang that up just before she got there to get a reaction from her?

She shook her head. It didn't matter now. None of it did. She had managed to get out of there without having a breakdown in front of him. And she was reasonably certain that if they ever spoke of their past, a breakdown was sure to follow. Hell, she couldn't even think about that conversation without freaking a little.

She had just slipped off her shoes when someone knocked at her front door. Simone stopped immediately. It was past ten at night on a Friday night.

She stood and moved slowly in that direction. By the fourth knock, she prepared herself for what she somehow knew, just *knew*, she would see when she looked through the peephole. Seconds later she cursed her sixth sense for being correct.

"Let me in, Simone, I know you're in there. I followed you home."

"Shit." She wrung her hands and manned up, knowing there was no escape from this.

She opened the door and let Lance in.

Lance could tell she hadn't expected him to follow her. But damn it all to hell, he was tired of this. Now that he'd found her, he wanted, no *needed* to purge the past from his soul. And he wanted her to be his live audience. No matter how demeaning it would be for him.

"Thank you," He murmured to her back as she walked away, leading him toward a small, but cozy den. He saw signs of her, her character, in every nook and cranny of the room, even though it lacked even one single piece of art designed by her unique hand. The place was comfy, cozy and intimate, with bright jeweled tones bringing out the smaller dark corners of the cottage.

"Look, I know our past is causing some issues."

"Hmph, you can say that again."

Lance nearly smiled at her disgusted tone. "Then why haven't you tried to talk to me about it?"

No answer, but her face turned slightly downward as she stood by the sofa, her eyes drilling holes into the worn wooden floors.

"Simone, we need to get this done. We need it out of the way between us." He said that with all honesty. It pained him to put her through this. Yes, he knew he had caused some of the hurt she felt, while the rest was due to life, plain and simple. The urge to repair the damage on his part drove him to follow her.

She raised her face to his, and he could see her emotions at war with the results of a good upbringing in those beautiful brown eyes of hers. Manners won out eventually. "Would you like something to drink?" She sounded cordial enough, but Lance sensed she would sooner serve him arsenic in a glass than something refreshing.

"No, honey, but I would like to sit and talk this out with you."

She seemed awed slightly by his honesty. "Sure, have a seat." She sat on the sofa facing him, while he took the easy chair.

At some point during the uncomfortable silence that followed, Lance realized that it was up to him to break it.

"You know that I've missed you every day for a long time now, right?" He leveled his gaze on hers, refusing to back down. "You were under my feet, well, mine and Stephen's for years, and then suddenly, you weren't there anymore." Lance shook his head. "It was a shock to find out you were here, in the same town as me."

"It was also a shock for me to see you." She moistened her lips, sending a hesitant glance his way. "And I've missed you, too." A fiery blush tracked up her cheeks at that soft admission. Lance felt his heart begin to beat harder.

He cleared his throat. "I miss Stephen too, Simone. Awfully bad."

She nodded in acceptance, as tears pooled in her eyes. "God, I do, too." Clasping her hands, it seemed to Lance she was trying to hold her emotions in. "And, mom and dad."

Her soft voice cracked with emotion, tearing at Lance's heart. He was doing everything possible to keep his ass planted in the chair but damn, it was difficult when all he wanted to do was hold her in his arms and let her cry it out. If he'd allowed her to do that years ago, they wouldn't be in this fix.

"They were like *my* parents too, Simone. Both Chrissy and I lost a family that day also."

She took his admission like a punch to the gut, but she met his gaze, undaunted. "I lost more than my family, Lance. I lost my friend, too."

That hit him in the chest like a bullet. "I know, and I'm so very sorry for that."

It seemed the more emotional she became, the more fiercely her demeanor shined. His words added more fuel to her arsenal.

"You left me, Lance." Her fists clenched. "You left me alone, with no one else." She lowered her gaze for a second, before glancing at him again. The look in her eyes flayed him alive, telling him, for certain, how badly he'd broken Simone's heart that day.

He cleared his throat, thinking of ways to convince her to hear him out, even though he didn't think he deserved her forgiveness. "I have no fancy words of apology, Simone, none. All I can say is I'm sorry."

She exploded out of her seated position in a rush, startling him. "Sorry? You're sorry? I literally *begged* you to stay with me, to help me." Her chin began to tremble, and Lance's heart ached for her.

He stood, but didn't move, not knowing what her next move would be. Slowly, he lifted his arms, held his hands out to her.

She glared at him as though he was crap on the bottom of her shoe.

"Ah, I see. You're tired of the guilt, and knowing how you hurt me . . . but you know what? I don't care. Welcome to my world, Lance."

"I was a young, stupid, immature young man, I d—"

"Yes, yes you were," she railed at him. "I begged you, *begged* you, and you walked away. Left me with no family, no friends, literally, no one." She stumbled and sat back down. She sat there, hiding her face in her hands, until Lance had enough.

He approached her cautiously, and did his darnedest to pull her into his arms.

"Please, Simone. We've both hurt enough, haven't we?"

"You mean you haven't hurt me enough?"

He ran his hands up her arms and down again. "Shh, come here, that's enough for now. Let me hold you, Simone, please?"

That seemed to break her. She broke down in sobs, catching his arms and pulling herself into his space. Lance needed no further acceptance. He wrapped his arms around her and held on.

Eleven years earlier.

Lance tried, and failed, to shake off the emotions that had clogged his throat for the past couple of days. His best friend, Stephen Welter, and Stephen's parents, had perished in a violent car accident just a few nights ago. It had been the night of Stephen's sister, Simone, and his sister, Chrissy's graduation. Nothing since had been normal.

His sister, Chrissy, finally cornered him.

"You need to go talk to Simone. She's lost and so hurt." Chrissy's eyes had pleaded with him more than her voice. "She to know you're there for her."

He'd given in, but he still wasn't sure if he could handle being around Simone. They had always been close, given his relationship with her brother. Since the accident, Lance was having a hard enough time being civil to everyone, much less the young woman who would need so much more than

Minutes later he'd been welcomed into the Welter home by a distant cousin staying with Simone while everything was being settled. The funerals for all three members of the family had taken place two days ago, and he was sure a ton of paperwork and legal matters had to be settled before Simone could have true peace.

He knocked on her bedroom door. *What in the hell am I going to say to console her when I can't console myself?* "Simone, it's Lance."

She threw the door open and said his name as if he were some kind of God or angel to deliver her from the Hell she'd found herself in.

Seconds later he was in the room with her, his heart pounding a mile a minute. He attempted to step away, but she ignored that and barreled into his chest, hugging him tightly.

He tried, he really did, not to wrap her tightly in his arms, but this girl got to him. She always had, and he couldn't deny that.

She shifted, breathing deep against his chest. "I'm so glad you're here."

He mumbled something in response, something meaningless, just beyond glad she wasn't crying.

Way to make her feel better, Turner.

He saw their reflection in her dresser mirror. Suddenly a deep-seated fear pressed down on his chest, cutting off his air. He couldn't do this—she needed so much more than he could give right now. He slowly pushed Simone away from him. God, it hurt even to look into her eyes. He had no idea what he was doing and he had a horrible feeling that she was going to ask him for more than he could give her.

"The last few days have been hell, but I'm glad you're here." She pressed her palms into her eyes, as if to stave off tears. "You being here makes this place feel a little normal."

He shook his head. He couldn't be a band aid to cover the wound for her. Hell, he had no idea how to deal with any of this. How in hell could he help her to accept something he couldn't face yet? "I can't stay here, Simone." He waved his hand at her room. "Being here is hard, too hard. I can't be who you want me to be."

Shock eclipsed her features. Probably because he'd never turned her away for anything.

"What do you mean?"

Lance took a deep breath. "I'm heading back to LSU tomorrow." He turned away from her, trying not to notice the pain intensifying in the room. He could practically taste it.

"Heading back, already?" Her voice was throaty, high with emotions. "But you can't. I thought you had a week off."

He faced the opposite wall, too much of a coward to even look at her. "Yes, I can. I have to."

There was a short silence before her simple, but pitiful request reached his ears. "Please, don't leave me, Lance."

He shook his head, barely able to make her out in his peripheral vision. "You don't know what you're asking, Simone."

"I lost my family. You're all I have left."

The words were soft. She wasn't crying, but she made him want to. He had to go, like—yesterday. Then she hit him with the harsh truth, again.

"Please, Lance, you're all I have left. Don't go." Once again, her voice was pleading, but louder now.

He couldn't handle this. The emotions, the pain, it pounded through his body, hitting his heart with force. He had to show her she wasn't alone. She wasn't the only one who'd lost someone, something, a family. A fiery heat invaded his body. Fury-fueled sentiment bled from every pore. He rounded on her, "I lost someone too, Simone. You weren't the only one!"

His outburst sounded far too loud in the small bedroom. He'd even shocked himself. But the look on her face stiffened his resolve. Her eyes, brimming with tears, that was something he just couldn't deal with.

The slap came out of nowhere. Lance felt the sting instantly across his cheek. He rubbed the sore spot, glancing sideways at her.

Her eyes had narrowed to angry slits, but she didn't say a another word to him. Lance took that as his parting gift and left her.

Present day.

After a good ten minute cry, Simone's tears had diminished to quiet sniffles. The boulder that had held her emotions in check for so long had finally rolled away. She didn't know if it was the argument, or Lance's long needed apology, but she finally felt free of the anger.

"Oh crap, I've messed up your shirt." She clumsily tried to wipe away the tears and runny mascara from his shirt, but he stayed her hands.

"Leave it. It'll wash. I'm more worried about you."

The softness, the gentleness in his tone was enough to create a fresh run of tears, but she managed to keep those at bay. "Thank you," she said, embarrassed display of tears.

"Stop it, I know exactly what you're thinking." Lance pulled her back into his embrace with his strong arms.

Simone couldn't stop the shiver of awareness that covered her skin.

"We are going to have a nice long conversation. And you're going to stay right here."

Somehow she'd forgotten how Lance had always wanted control over a situation. Seemed things hadn't changed.

"Just to clarify, I was an extremely young, immature man at twenty." His finger tipped her chin upwards. Simone wanted to hide her face, considering half of her make-up was on the man's shirt. His next words killed that notion.

"But I'm no longer immature. What I did all those years ago was foolish and stupid. I caused you pain, more pain you didn't need on top of losing your entire family. That was certainly not my intention. I was just extremely overwhelmed. My best friend had died, and , I lost the truest parents I'd never known. You know my parent's liked their Grey Goose Martinis and Jack Daniel on the rocks more than Chrissy and me." He stopped, seeming to gather his thoughts. "Please say that you understand."

She nodded, still not believing the utter absurdness of this moment. She was in Lance Turner's arms. He had apologized for the single most destructive thing in her life that he'd caused. Was she dreaming? Hell no, the arms around her were real, the smell of his aftershave was real, and so was the entire length of him beside her.

"You are forgiven. I was blinded by the past, by the pain. I understand now."

He released his breath in a rush. Her body erupted in another round of shivers, for a different reason this time. The man she'd crushed on for nearly all of teenage life had her wrapped in his arms.

"Thank you, Simone." His massive hands slid down her arms, stopping to cover hers.

Her heart pounded with excitement. *No need to freak out. Just play it cool.*

"I saw my plaque on your wall. I didn't know you still had it." Now why had she brought that up? Her mind was warped with Lance's nearness.

His thumb began to stroke her hand with deliberateness and Simone was about to melt into the sofa cushions.

"Why would it not be there?" His voice was deep and she could feel the vibration of his deep voice against her side.

She shrugged her shoulders, not knowing quite what to say.

He tapped her shoulder with his. "What, you at a loss for words?"

She could hear the smile in his voice, and that seemed to make her more nervous.

"Never," she said with false bravado. Obviously, their recent conversation had only been a minor hurdle for him, whereas it had been life altering for her. Now that the barrier had been obliterated between them, they were friends again. But could they ever be more?.

The air grew thick with silence, until she finally broke it. "I haven't created a piece since they died." Lance didn't say anything, but she felt the solidness and comfort of his weight beside hr. It gave her the strength to continue.t. "I was so depressed after the accident and funeral, and then you left." She shook her head. "It was almost as if the sadness consumed me. My need to create died with them."

Within seconds she was plastered to his side. He held her tightly, but didn't cloud her confession with words of apology. He allowed her the freedom to continue as she desired.

"Seeing that plaque, well, it gave me the itch again. To be honest, I've been having the itch quite a lot lately."

He released a low chuckle. "I'm glad to hear that. These people are totally unaware of your talents. Your creations are truly extraordinary."

Simone beamed inside from his praise. He had always been her supporter, always encouraging her to do more, dream bigger, to go farther. She'd lost more than a friend all those years ago. She'd lost her mentor, her champion.

"Thank you, Lance."

He brushed the hair back from her face and tipped her chin until their gazes locked. She felt the intensity of his scrutiny deep in her bones. Everything, every moment with this man felt so right, no matter if they were romantically involved or not. He was that much a part of her life even though he'd missed the past few years.

He passed his fingertips lightly over her face before stunning her senseless with his next move. Out of nowhere, he leaned forward and captured her lips with his. Simone sat there in shock, until he gently adjusted the position of her face. From that point the kiss went from gentle, to exploratory, to downright lethal.

She had no warning to guard against this kind of attack, no protection from him and his skilled mouth, nipping at hers, his tongue rubbing sensually at the seam of her lips, silently begging her to open.

And Simone did what any woman in her right mind would do. She let him in.

Lance had no plan formulated to kiss her, but he couldn't have stopped it from happening. He simply knew it was foolproof. They were closer than they'd ever been, even more than all those years ago, when he would have never gotten this close to her. Now, he knew he'd never get enough of her.

He had reasoned, told himself as he'd leaned forward to kiss her , don't go too fast, don't rush her. But one touch of her sweet mouth against his, and his plans had been shot to hell and back.

He knew he shouldn't rush her and the thought had him pulling back. He sure as hell didn't want to make her run, again.

"I'm sorry." He whispered the words against her lips, not willing to move away from her any farther than that.

She moistened her lips, accidently touching her tongue to his mouth and he groaned. When she spoke, he wanted to shut her up with another kiss. The nearness of her mouth drugged him.

"I wasn't expecting that, Lance. After all these years I didn't think you could do anything to surprise me." She was breathless as she said it. Lance found he liked that. The rush of feelings coalescing in his chest exploded through him like a bomb.

"I've wanted to do that ever since I saw you in the store." He huffed out a laugh, "I just didn't know it until now."

She laughed in response, and it was so light, so full of joy that Lance's heart began to pound even harder in his chest.

He wanted more, so much more from her. He stroked her chin with the palm of his hand, catching her attention. "When can I do it again?"

Her fingers chased the words against his lips. "Right now."

Chapter 6

D ays later Simone walked into Lance's house, still overwhelmed and surprised at how the night had ended during their "conversation". He'd left late, or rather early, Saturday morning after they'd spent every available minute talking about everything under the sun and stealing kisses that managed to shake her to her core.

She was still in shock. Not only that he had finally kissed her but that she had survived it. Why they hadn't progressed to anything more than that still mystified her. Now that he'd been the one to cross the line, she wanted it crossed all the way.

Here it was, the evening of Christmas Eve, and she'd have the chance to spend another Christmas with Lance.

"Hey, brown eyes, you made it."

She blushed at his nickname for her. "Yep, wouldn't miss it."

He invited her inside and led the way to his spare room. "What am I doing here?" They stopped in the hallway.

He turned to her, giving her a comical grin. "What, seeing me isn't enough? Oh, wait, I know what it is. I forgot to give you something when you walked in."

Simone backed away slightly, not knowing what he had in mind.

His grin morphed into a lusty smile, moving toward her like a predator, until she felt as though he was stalking her.

"You mean like a Christmas gift? I wasn't expecting anything when I walked in."

He caught her against the wall. "Then I'll give you something you least expected."

She gasped and instant before his mouth captured hers in a kiss. But instead of gentle and exploratory, this kiss felt more possessive, as though it was Lance laying claim to her. His body brushed up against hers, the heat of his chest and hips pressed fully against her, reminding her that he was all man, as though she could ever forget the obvious.

Simone melted into him, her knees weak with need. She looped her arms around his neck, pulling her body up and fully against his.

He pulled away the slightest bit and growled her name against her lips. "I'm never going to let you go again. You do realize that, don't you?" He was breathless in his need, his words savage, and exactly what she wanted to hear.

She brushed her lips against his and whispered, "I won't let you."

He attacked once more, and within minutes Simone wondered how 'd ever lived from day to day without knowing how Lance Turner felt and how he tasted. She was completely addicted to this man.

Minutes later they finally came up for air, both smiling like idiots.

Lance was the first to break the kiss-emblazoned silence. "Follow me." He opened the door to the spare room and stood aside to let her in.

Simone stood in the doorway, her heart pounding with excitement. ."What is this?" Candles of several shapes and sizes burned in the room, filling it with a gentle glow.

Lance turned to her, his eyes shining with unbridled excitement. "This is your Christmas present."

Simone was speechless. She opened then closed it, but no, nothing would come out.

Lance's thumb slid along her lower lip. "I want us to have something together, something for our future. Not from our past." He hesitated a moment, before continuing, "It's blank, ready and waiting for you."

Simone shook her head. "I don't know what to say." Emotions clogged her vocal chords. A deep yearning flared to life, encompassing everything within her. She faced Lance, grabbed his hands with her own, leaving the gift in the background. She felt helpless to do anything but pour out her soul to him. "I love you. I think I always have."

He froze as the endearing smile vanished from his face. Simone felt genuine fear creep up inside her. *Oh God, this was going south too fast.*

She opened her mouth to apologize, but his blinding smile reappeared, keeping her from saying the words. That charming dimple of his came back in full force.

"I have no idea how I made it this far without you, Simone."

She whimpered and threw herself against him.

"I love you so much," he whispered against her ear, nestling his chin in her hair.

Simone cleared her eyes of happy tears until she could focus on Lance's Christmas gift to her. She finally recognized it for the message it was. Candlelight blazed in the darkened room, highlighting the rough edges of a blank piece of wood. The Dremel tool and equipment beside it made perfect sense.

Christmas morning dawned clear and bright, the view of the snow covered mountains looming gloriously through Lance's large, picturesque windows. The tree he'd managed to find and decorate the night before sparkled and shined from the corner of the room, while candles burned brightly from strategic positions around the room.

She hadn't partaken in the tree decorating festivities. She'd been locked up in the spare room, too busy reacquainting herself with the various crafting tools he'd seen her use in previous years. It had all come back to her so easily, the grips and handles fitting her hands as smoothly as hand tailored gloves. After a long night of working into the early morning hours, she'd completed her gift to him.

By the time she'd perfected the piece, she discovered Lance had gone to bed after decorating the tree. He'd somehow known she needed the privacy and space.

So, she'd tiptoed around the apartment until she'd found a burgundy towel to wrap around the gift, and placed it under the tree. It was the only gift there, but some gifts couldn't be wrapped.

She'd laid down on his large comfy couch and fallen asleep easily, watching the twinkling tree lights.

He'd woken her with a kiss, and a mug of warm cocoa, with three large marshmallows, just the way she liked it.

And now the two of them sat on the plushly carpeted floor before the tree.

"Go ahead. Open it. I made it for you," she said, tilting her head toward the solitary gift.

His smile reached clear to his eyes as he reached for it. "Whatever this is, it's for both of us. The beginning of our new life together." One eyebrow arched adorably. "Agreed?"

She thought of the message she'd lovingly carved into the piece of wood, knowing how well it fit the situation. After a brief nod, she smiled. "Agreed."

He pulled away the towel, revealing the magnificently carved creation, and sat back. "Oh God. I'm in awe of your talent, babe. I mean you've always been good but this . . ."

She leaned against him and studied the piece. "Yeah, I think it's my best, by far."

He kissed the top of her head and lifted the carving so they could both see it. "It's perfection. Just like you, Simone."

"Just like you," she whispered.

He put his cocoa down to lean over and kiss her. "Just like us. This is . . . *us*."

She beamed at him as she looped her arms around his neck. "Yes it is." She wasn't alone anymore. Her other half was with her. Just as her creation stated:

"No Longer Alone—
We Two Halves Created by God
Complete Each Other"

ABOUT THE AUTHOR

Trish Leger lives in South Louisiana, and other than writing, also has a full time job. She is married, and from a loving, boisterous family. Since food is so important in the south, it is also important to her, ranking right up there with writing, reading and watching movies.

Writing with a strong sensual bent, intent on capturing the growing relationship between a couple falling in love, Trish adds warmth and emotion to her stories.

She is a fan of everything from Drama to Historical Romance.

OTHER **SWEET** NOVELLAS BY
TRISH F LEGER:

Seasons Of Love Anthology-Hearts, Hearths & Holidays:
Three Weeks Before Christmas
Seasons Of Love Anthology-Spring Promise: His For One
Night.
Available on Amazon and CreateSpace!

SPICY, SENSUAL PARANORMALS
BY TRISH F LEGER:

Her Druid Temptation-Prequel to the Amber Druid Series
Her Druid Desire-BOOK ONE of the Amber Druid Series
Her Druid Fantasy-BOOK TWO of the Amber Druid Series-
Coming Soon!!
Available on Amazon and Createspace!

DEDICATION

To those who have lost loved ones to the effects of
Alcoholism, and drunk drivers.

I would like to thank Lori for this chance to have another
novella in her wonderful Anthology series, along with these
other authors.

Also a BIG THANK YOU to Kathy P, Melissa, and a few
others on FB who helped me make this story what it is.

A Heart Awakens

By Karen Sue Burns

Chapter 1
Dating? No Way

Nervous excitement bubbled in her chest as Cara Allen ran her fingers through her blonde curls and took a deep breath. Her fingers clenched then opened as she muttered, "I can do this." She exited her SUV and nearly stumbled while stepping onto the sidewalk but managed to cross it without her usual display of slips, trips, and falls.

She secured her purse strap over her shoulder and pushed open the glass door decorated top to bottom with rainbow colored paw prints. The pungent aroma of rose potpourri floated through a door open to the interior of Sammy's Small Dog Rescue. Barking followed the scent through the opening.

Her eyes scanned the stacked display of pet food and the bulletin board of notices as she approached the reception desk. A young woman with bright red curls and white cat-eye glasses pounded on a keyboard.

Cara waited a moment to catch the woman's attention then finally spoke. "Please . . . excuse me; I'm here to adopt a dog."

"Why didn't you say so?" The young woman stood so quickly her chair pushed backward, she stuck out her hand. "I'm Amber, part-time proprietress of this pet establishment. How may I help you?"

Cara sucked in a breath. Why the hell was she so anxious about taking home a little dog? "Like I said, I'm here to adopt a dog."

Amber pushed the glasses down her nose and narrowed her eyes. "Are you sure about that?"

"Um, yes, of course I'm sure. I've done my research and Sammy's seems like the perfect place to find my dog."

"Okay, great." Amber realigned her glasses. "Have you completed an application?"

"I did it online a few days ago and received an adoption confirmation."

"What's the name and address?"

Cara recited the requested information and began to tap her foot. Although her nerves were on high alert, she was eager to start her search. She'd waited too many years. Her husband had been allergic to dogs yet when he'd died three years ago from a heart attack she still couldn't bring herself to adopt one. But the months had passed and she'd made a vow to add a puppy to her lonely household of one before her next birthday, the big 3-6.

Amber waved a hand. "You're right here on our listed of approved adopters. Let's go find your little darling. I'll get a volunteer to help you." She spoke into a walkie-talkie.

Less than a minute later, a tall man walked through the door. Amber pointed towards Cara and the volunteer stopped in front of her. Cara twisted her hands together. She'd imagined a teenager or a little old lady helping her, not this hunk with deep blue eyes and sandy colored hair that curled over his collar.

He smiled and nodded toward the kennels. "I'm Jake. Ready?"

Hell, yes, she was ready—ready for those biceps and that killer grin. Oops, spontaneous girl reaction.

"Nice to meet you, I'm Cara."

"Okay, Cara, let's find your baby. I understand you want a female less than a year old."

"Uh-huh." She followed him through the door and unfortunately noticed his jeans molded to his backside. It had been a long while since she'd noticed a man's butt in a pair a jeans.

Once in the kennel, he made a quick turn to the right and stopped.

"This is the section holding the young ones. Take a quick look around and then we can discuss the individual dogs." Jake motioned for her to go down the walk between the cages. "Take your time. I need to check on something and I'll be back in a couple of minutes."

Cara waved her hand at him, "No problem."

She preferred to look at the dogs alone. That way she wouldn't be influenced by anyone else's opinion as to the right dog. Actually she didn't need the perfect dog, just the dog that was perfect for her. The plan was to walk down the right side and then the left. She took a deep breath, slowly released it, and moved in front of the first stack of cages.

Ugh. She hated the word "cage." She'd think of them as kennels instead, or even better, a doggie hotel. Regardless, the kennels were stacked vertically in three's, with four stacks on either side of the walkway. And every kennel was full. Her hand automatically gripped her purse. How in the world would she choose the right dog?

Once she took her first step, pandemonium erupted. The dogs barked, whimpered, jumped on the door of the cage, or huddled in a corner. It was as though they had been waiting for her to declare her intent.

She took another deep breath before pushing out her hands and mimicked a quiet down motion. "Come on guys, settle down. Yes, I'm here to find a dog and I can only take one of you home. Okay? Hopefully, y'all can understand." She glanced at a few cages and noticed the dogs had moved to the center or a back corner and were either sitting quietly or lying down. Good, they did understand.

She made a quick survey, taking note of the kennels with small dogs. There were three. The first dog had a pointy muzzle she didn't like and the second one turned around with its back to her. Huh? She walked to the last kennel and viewed the dog, her name was Gracie. Cara liked what she saw.

Gracie's head was cocked to the side as her dark brown eyes watched Cara. She stood and stroked her paw on the floor, then she barked as though saying "hello." Jake arrived just as Cara debated whether to open the kennel herself.

"How's it going? Any of these fine animals strike your fancy?"

Cara turned at the sound of his voice or was it the scent of his musk after-shave? "Actually, yes, I'd like to get to know Gracie."

"Ah, good choice, she's a sweetheart." He opened the door, pulled out a hopeful-looking Gracie, and plunked her in Cara's arms. "Cara, this is Miss Gracie, cutest dog on the block."

Cara nestled the half-pint dog in her arms, surprised at how light she felt and the softness of her wiry hair. *So far so good.* She re-positioned the dog in her arms and looked at her face. She had a shiny black nose, a square muzzle, brown hair with patches of black here and there, and those soulful brown eyes. Yes, this might be her dog.

"Do y'all have an area where Gracie and I can get to know each other?"

Jake led them down a hall to a scratched door leading to the back of the building. Cara managed to step over the doorjamb without tripping and entered the small yard. She leaned over and set Gracie on the patch of grass. "Just in case you need to pee."

Gracie licked Cara's hand then performed one of those head rolls that the cool girls do and pranced off, swinging her little stub tail.

Cara crossed her arms over her chest and watched the pup move from one section of the yard to another, sniffing bushes and flowers. She glanced at Jake standing next to her. "Tell me about Gracie."

"She was found on the street, in downtown Houston, no tags and no chip. She's a well-mannered dog and seems intelligent. I think she got a rough deal from someone, some asshole. She'll make a fine addition to a family."

Cara watched her squat to pee then continue to check out the smells in the yard. For a small dog she had a big presence. Cara had a good feeling about her. Gracie stopped and turned her head towards Cara. Her left ear hitched up and she barked. Cara hunched down and Gracie ran over to her, placed her front paws on Cara's knees, barked almost a whisper, and winked at Cara.

That was the sign. Cara scooped Gracie into her arms, kissed her head, and rose. "Okay. I've made my decision. Do I need to sign something?"

Thirty minutes later, at her local pet store, Cara pushed a shopping cart through the aisles with Gracie sitting in the upper basket. The goal was to get accoutrements fitting a doggy princess. Cara knew without a doubt she had made the right decision in adopting Gracie. She talked in the car nearly non-stop, telling Gracie all about her house and her friends. Gracie had the good manners to simply nod and wag her tail.

The cart was soon full of an oval bed, a pink blanket, a variety of dog toys, snacks, and bags of food. They were almost at the check-out register when Cara remembered a leash. She fully expected to lose a pound or two walking Gracie around the neighborhood. She tossed two in the cart, one for the house and one for the car, and retraced her steps to the front of the store.

Once she'd stowed everything in the back of her SUV, Cara headed home. She turned to a country station on the radio. Gracie seemed to approve of the music as her head bopped up and down, almost in time to the beat of the song.

Cara grinned. Having Gracie in the house was going to be just what she needed.

"Stop by for a glass of wine after work," Cara said to her best friend Susan. "I want you to meet Gracie."

"She's a dog. You don't meet dogs." Susan chuckled over the phone. "But I will accept your happy hour offer."

"Good. I'll see you around five-thirty."

Cara clicked off and reviewed her to-do list for the day. Gracie slept on the pink blanket in a corner of the sofa. Today was a test of sorts. She would leave Gracie alone in the house for the first time. She hadn't bought a crate so Gracie would have free reign of every room. Cara didn't like the idea of penning up her dog even though the experts said it was a good idea.

Gracie was different. Cara *knew* she wouldn't get into any trouble. She gathered her purse and a stack of mail, and rattled her keys to wake Gracie. "I'm going to the post office and then the grocery store. You mind your manners while I'm gone, okay?"

Gracie yawned and rolled over on the blanket, burying her head against the sofa.

"Good, she understood me," Cara said as she walked to the garage.

First stop was the post office. She had thank you cards for clients plus a signed contract for another. Naturally, she had to wait in a long line for certified mail, which meant she could jot down a grocery list while she inched forward.

After digging a small notebook and pen from her purse, she concentrated on what she needed to buy for happy hour, or dinner in Susan terms. It was late-October and that translated to casserole weather. "Hmm, which recipe?" she muttered, chewing on the end of the pen.

"Recipe? You cook?"

Cara turned at the male voice behind her. Well, of all the post offices in Texas, who would have imagined she'd run into Jake, in the line from hell, at this particular one in Sugar Land.

"Jake, hi."

"I was on my way to a job and need to mail some cards." He raised a stack of envelopes in his hand.

"I didn't know you worked around here."

"Yep, both my office and house are in Sugar Land. You, too?"

Cara nodded, "I work out of my house." She stepped forward as the line moved closer to the counters. "I'm a freelance writer."

"I guess we have something in common, I own a business, too."

"What do you do?"

"Landscaping and pools, decks, all that outdoor stuff."

"I could use you at my house. I'm not much of a gardener."

They both shuffled forward as the line shortened. Jake leaned toward her. "Anything in particular you need help with?"

"How about everything?"

"Everything? Hmm, that sounds interesting." He cocked an eyebrow as he spoke.

"I didn't mean everything, everything. I was talking about my yard."

"Oh," he said with a mischievous grin. "Do you have time for lunch? There's a sandwich shop down the block and you'd save me from getting fast food. We could talk about gardening."

Cara snuck a glance at her watch. She hated getting off schedule but she could swing a quick lunch. She calculated forty-five minutes for it and she'd still have plenty of time for the grocery store.

"I'd love to have lunch with you."

"Good. We shouldn't be here all that much longer," he said.

The line moved again and Cara stepped to the busy counter. She turned back to Jake. "I'll meet you out front."

A few minutes later they entered the sandwich shop and shortly slid into opposite sides of a shiny blue booth, each carrying a sandwich basket and a soft drink.

Cara soon wondered if Jake regretted his impromptu lunch invitation. He dove into his turkey and cheddar on whole-wheat and kept his head down or directed toward the wide retail window bordering the oh-so interesting parking lot.

After another minute, she couldn't stand the silence. It reminded her of her husband and his refusal to talk before he had a cup of coffee in the morning. She said the first thing that came to mind.

"How long have you volunteered for Sammy's?"

Jake's head turned slowly toward her, his blue eyes glittering in the sun light streaming through the window. "Hmm, I guess it's seven or eight years now. I started a couple of years after my divorce."

"Oh, you're divorced."

"Almost ten years now, college sweethearts who didn't marry for the right reason. What about you?"

"My husband died three years ago, heart attack." She stuffed a pickle in her mouth to refrain from revealing anything else. She didn't feel comfortable talking about Justin with another man. Three years was not enough time to heal the hole in her heart.

"I'm sorry to hear that. Were you married long?" Jake seemed genuinely interested.

"That's old news." She was not talking about her marriage. Losing a spouse who had just turned thirty-six was an absolutely horrific experience. The subject was off-limits to Jake or anyone else. "How did you decide to go into landscaping as a business?"

His face froze for a mere second then he recovered. "That's easy, my grandfather, David "Green Thumb"

Martin. He's a master gardener and loves to grow vegetables and flowers."

"Sounds like a cool guy. Does he live close by?"

"Oh yeah, he retired a couple of years ago from the Rosenberg police force. He was chief for over twenty years." He sucked on the straw of his drink. "I spent a lot of time with him growing up."

"Working in the garden?"

"Right, mowing a huge lawn and weeding a ton of flowerbeds. Gramps believed in the old adage that children were to be seen and working their asses off."

"And with all that ass working you fell in love with green things?"

He laughed, a rolling carnival erupting from his chest. "That sums it up."

"That's a wonderful story. Do you see him often?"

"Oh yeah, he's my number one consultant on large jobs."

"That's wonderful. My grandparents live in Florida and I only see them once a year."

"He is a good guy, just too opinionated sometimes."

"I know what you mean. My Nana loves giving me advice, usually about clothes or cooking."

"You really do like to cook?"

"It's a hobby for me and I blog about recipes I try. One of these days I'll write a cookbook from all my blogs."

"You said you're a freelance writer. Do you ever work on advertising copy?"

She nodded. "I've had a few assignments."

"Good." Jake pushed his basket to the side and placed his elbows on the table, leaning forward a bit. "You're hired. This is what I need."

Cara relaxed against the back of the booth and simply watched. As he talked, there was something about Jake that invited her scrutiny. His hands orchestrated the ebb and flow of his words while the planes of his face reflected the knowledge behind the words. It was easy to see his passion for landscaping and building backyards for families. She liked that.

They talked about flowers and patios for another two hours. Cara finally checked her watched and realized she was way behind schedule. As they exited the shop, Jake asked her to a high school football game and dinner on Friday night. She quickly said yes, concerned about not being ready for the happy hour with Susan. Once she thanked Jake for lunch and headed to the grocery store, she realized what she'd agreed to. Holy crap, she had a date.

Cara hurried to answer the door, wiping her hands on a dishtowel.

"Come on in." She held open the door for Susan. "I was just about to open the wine."

"Good, I'm thirsty."

"I have snacks, too."

Susan took her usual spot at the granite counter across from the sink. "I'm glad I came for happy hour. Much appreciate the buffet."

Cara chuckled and placed two trays on the counter. She poured the wine, a delicate chardonnay. "This is from a new vineyard near College Station. I think you'll like it."

Susan sipped and smiled. "Yum, I do like it." She turned her head from side to side, her gaze directed at the kitchen floor. "Didn't you tell me about a new roommate? Where's the puppy?"

"She's in time out."

"Time out," Susan spit out. "A dog can't be in time out, that's for toddlers."

"Gracie acted like a toddler this afternoon and deserves her punishment."

Susan swung a foot back and forth. "Oh boy, this is gonna be good. What did poor little Gracie do that made her momma angry?"

"She chewed through the strap on my favorite designer purse. It was totally uncalled for."

"I see. You left her at home alone, right?"

"Yes."

"She had free reign of the house?"

"Yes, it was the first time I didn't keep her in the utility room."

"And you left the door to your closet open." Susan pumped her arm with an "ah-ha" movement. "It's like you sent her an invitation to chomp on some tasty leather."

Cara popped a bacon wrapped shrimp in her mouth. Chewing it gave her a few seconds to think about how not to sound like a complete idiot when she explained her logic for not locking up Gracie. She knew without a doubt that whatever she said would sound lame.

"I don't agree with putting dogs in kennels, owners need to train them properly. I accidentally left the purse on my bed and—"

"Oh, oh, it's your fault. That's too funny." Susan rose from the stool, walked to the utility room door. "I think it's time I bust Gracie out of doggie-jail."

Before Cara uttered a word, the door opened and Susan stood looking down at Gracie who sat just inside the doorway. Gracie's head was cocked to the side and she had a "what the hell" look on her face, er, muzzle. After a moment she nodded, stood, stepped around Susan, and walked to Cara. She sat again and extended her left paw, her sweet face looking up to her owner.

Susan grabbed her wine glass and stood behind Gracie. "This is one talented dog. Interesting, she has the same eye color as you."

Gracie barked, just one woof. Cara was a goner, all over again. She knelt in front of the pup, patted her head, and scratched a floppy ear. "Okay, you're forgiven."

Gracie rose and wiggled her back end. She barked again.

"I believe your dog understands human speak," Susan said with a sloppy smile.

"Yes, she does," Cara agreed. "But I need to be more consistent with my training. This can't happen again." She rose and shooed Gracie to the living room. "Go lay on your blanket while I talk to Susan."

Gracie woofed, turned her head to Susan, then sashayed out of the kitchen.

"Did you see that? She just winked at me," Susan said.

"Right," Cara said. "Have more wine."

Susan returned to the stool and surveyed the tray of appetizers. "She'll grow out of the chewing phase. What do you call these bread things?" She popped a snack in her mouth.

"That's crostini with dried tomatoes, basil, Greek olives, and feta cheese. I tweaked a recipe I found online. Try the spiced almonds. I may give jars of them to my clients this Christmas."

"You are so nice to the people who pay you."

"That reminds me, I think have a new client and a date."

"A date? Shut the front door . . . finally." Susan playfully pounded her fist on the counter. "Tell me everything and don't leave out one detail."

Cara sipped her wine and took a deep breath, blowing it out slowly. This conversation was truly a first during the past three years. All of their talk about dating had revolved around Susan's escapades, although she had dated her current boyfriend for six months. That, too, was a first. Usually they didn't last longer than two or three months.

"Remember the man who helped me when I adopted Gracie?"

"Uh-huh, you said he was a volunteer at the shelter and on the hunky side."

"I met him today at the post office and we had lunch and then he asked me out for Friday night, a high school football game and dinner—"

"Hold on a second. You met this volunteer guy at the Sugar Land post office? He lives around here?"

"He owns a local landscaping business and lives over in the Commonwealth subdivision. He's divorced, no kids."

"You learned a lot at the post office." Susan said.

"We went to lunch, nothing special, the sandwich shop down the street."

"He invited you to a high school football game? That's interesting with no kids."

"It's his sister's son who's playing. Apparently he's the star quarterback and only a junior so that's a big deal. Jake goes to all of his games, being a supportive uncle."

"He sounds like a nice guy. How long has he been divorced?"

"I think he said ten years, not sure. He said they didn't get married for the right reasons in college. No clue about the divorce"

"Hmm, she probably got pregnant. Why don't people use birth control?"

Cara threw up her hands. "Who knows? College students are known for doing dumb things. I remember a time or two you used lousy judgment."

"And more times than not, you were right next to me."

"True, except for that time you decided to cook soup in the pot thing for heating scented candle pieces. You almost burned down our apartment."

"Whatever. So you're going out with Jake, the hunky dog shelter volunteer, landscape business owner. Cool. I'm happy for you." Susan topped off their wine glasses. "Notice I haven't said it's about damn time you had a date."

"I did notice that. Good restraint." Cara laughed and stuffed a couple of almonds in her mouth.

"You said client. Has he hired you?"

She nodded. "He's asked me to revamp the marketing program for his business including a new logo, copy for TV and print advertising, and a couple other things. It's a great opportunity for me."

"Do you think it's a good idea dating a client?"

"I hadn't even thought about that." Cara leaned against the edge of the counter across from Susan. How could she be so stupid? Of course she couldn't date a client. "I need to call him and cancel the date. You're right, this is totally unprofessional."

Susan raised her hand. "Hold on, I didn't say it was unprofessional. Let's think about this. If you do work for him it will be a job with a set beginning and an agreed to end date. Right? Freelance work doesn't go on forever."

"I see what you're saying. He won't be a client for more than a couple of months." Cara pressed her palm over her heart and briefly closed her eyes. Things would be okay. "If Friday night goes well then I'll plan my work for him to be completed as quickly as practical."

"There you go. Problem solved."

Gracie barked in the living room. She must have agreed with Susan. The only problem was the fact Cara hadn't touched a man in over three years and had no clue how to prepare for a date as a thirty-five year old widow.

Jake drove his sedan to Cara's rather than his truck as it was habitually dusted with soil and grass. Not good for taking a lady on a first date. He turned into her neighborhood, knowing exactly where to go. His company had several lawn maintenance clients in the area. He'd always liked the houses, mostly one story with well-tended lawns and kids' toys strewn over the front walks.

He turned into Cara's driveway and rang the doorbell. He tugged at the waistband of his jeans. He hoped the white shirt and cowboy boots looked okay. First dates always made him nervous.

The front door opened. Cara stood in the doorway like a yellow daisy gracing a spring garden. Uh-huh, she looked hot. Her top exposed a bit of cleavage, very nice.

"Come on in and you can see Gracie."

She moved to the side and he walked past her into the foyer. It wasn't big but had a side table with a tall vase of silk flowers. He hated silk flowers. He'd bring her real flowers next time.

Cara walked beside him. "Gracie's in the living room. We just had a little talk about being good while I'm gone. Had a problem last time I left her alone."

Gracie was indeed in the living room, sitting like a princess on a pink blanket on the sofa. Jake bent over to rub her ears. "How ya doing, Gracie? Looks like you've settled into your new home."

She licked his hand then woofed.

"I think she remembers me." He gave Gracie a final scratch on her tummy and turned to Cara. "Are you ready? We don't want to miss kick off."

"Let's go." She grabbed her purse off a chair and off they went.

Within ten minutes they entered the parking lot next to Mercer Stadium. Jake hadn't said much other than comment on the weather and mention that Cara would meet his sister. She always got to the games early and would be saving seats for them in a prime location.

The band played a rendition of *We Are the Champions* as they got their tickets and walked up the ramp to the stadium's seating area. The lower section was individual seats in boxes and the upper section was bleacher seating.

He led Cara to the box where the family usually sat and sure enough, his sister was there, holding her cowbell, ready to cheer. They went down the steps and Jake made the introductions.

"Janet, this is my friend, Cara Allen." He watched the two women shake hands and say hello. Janet, defying her usual standoffishness, surprised him by shaking Cara's hand and smiling. For some reason, she seemed genuinely pleased to meet her.

"Where's the rest of the crew?" Jake said as they took their seats. Janet's husband and their daughter were usually at the games.

"It's just me tonight. Bob had an emergency at the hospital and Julie has a slumber party that she couldn't miss. I'm glad you two are here to help me cheer on the Wildcats."

The band marched to the sidelines as the cheerleaders ran to the middle of the field. The opposing team ran out first, followed by the Wildcats. Both side of the stadium went nuts with cheering and ringing their cowbells. *Gotta love Texas high school football.* Within minutes, the Wildcats had won the toss and elected to receive the ball. Jake rubbed his hands together; this should be a good game.

"Here we go." He patted Cara's knee as the ball soared into the air headed toward the waiting Wildcats. The ball was caught at the fifteen yard line and carried to almost twenty yards before the player was tackled.

"That's a good start," Cara said.

"Sure is," Janet said, addressing her remark to Cara. "My son, Carter, is the quarterback, number 6. He's a greater player."

By the time halftime rolled around, Carter had thrown two touchdown passes to put the Wildcats ahead 17-3.

"I need to stretch my legs. You want to come with me to the concession stand?" He rose at Cara's nod and pulled her up by her hands, enjoying the way they fit in his. It felt right. They headed to the ramp, but it was slow going. He didn't mind a bit, since he took the opportunity to hold his hand against her back.

When they finally reached the bottom, Cara headed to the restroom and he headed to the long line at the concession stand for soft drinks. After shuffling forward for several minutes, he winced as an all-too-familiar voice called out his name. Oh, crap. This was all he needed. He turned reluctantly as his ex-wife sashayed up to him as though auditioning for a runway modeling job.

"Oh, Jake, it's so good to see you." Meagan wrapped her clinging arms around his neck, and squeezed like she wanted to choke the life out of him.

He removed them quickly and stepped back to put some distance between them. "I don't remember you liking football."

"Oh, silly, you have the worst memory. Of course I love football. Janet asked me to come and watch Carter." She swung her hair back and grinned liked a small child. "And as usual, I'm late." She stepped toward him and reached out to encircle his waist. "It's so good to see you."

"Jake, I'm back."

He turned, seeing the puzzled look on Cara's face and separated himself from his ex-wife's death grip. It was impossible to miss the smug look on Meagan's face. Damn.

"Cara," he said and stepped close to her side. "This is my ex-wife, who came to watch the game with Janet."

"Nice to meet you." Cara politely offered her hand which Meagan had no choice but to shake.

"Right, same here." She scrutinized Cara like a python stalking a pig, and smiled at Jake like sex on a stick. "Sweetie, I didn't know you'd started dating again, especially after that last disaster. Didn't you make a vow or something?"

Thankfully, the line moved forward bringing Jake to the order counter. "See ya." He turned Cara toward the counter, hoping Meagan would take the hint and go home. He spoke softly near Cara's ear. "Sorry about that. What would you like?" From his peripheral vision, he saw Meagan stomping childishly toward the ramp.

Soft drinks in hand, they headed back to the stands. As soon as they rounded the corner of the bleachers, Jake realized that Meagan was in the box with Janet. Damn it. Why the hell had Janet invited her?

Cara went down the steps to their seats first and noticed Meagan. "Oh, you're here."

Janet waved. "Hi, y'all, the second half is about to start. Meagan came by to watch Carter."

Something strange flashed on Cara's face before she sat next to Janet. Jake could only imagine what she was thinking. He checked his watch. If things got too weird they could always leave early, claiming a dinner reservation. Yep, that would work. The teams trotted back on the field and the crowd stood and roared.

The Wildcats kicked the ball, chased it like a battering ram, and tackled the receiver at the five yard line. The spectators cheered like crazy as Jake gave Cara a one-armed hug. "Now that's a football team."

Cara leaned into him and wrapped an arm around his waist. "I agree. Thanks for inviting me to the game."

"My pleasure." He planted a kiss on her cheek, amazed at how good and how right it felt.

"I love this restaurant," Cara said, placing her fork across her plate. She was stuffed with excellent food. "I can't believe I've never come in here before." The décor reminded her of a bistro she'd visited in Rome many years ago. She had no idea why it stood out in her mind, other than a fantastic meal.

"I'm glad we came. David Lombardo, the owner, and I went to high school together. I went to A&M and he enlisted in the army."

"Not only is he an excellent chef, but this ambiance is fabulous. I like the Coliseum theme."

"His wife Jenny is the decorator. I'd introduce you but they're not here tonight, family emergency."

"I hope everything's okay."

"David's mother broke her leg and had surgery this morning."

"Sounds painful."

"She's a cool lady, and tough. I'm sure she's ordering the nurses around, and keeping everyone on their toes."

"Are you close to them?"

"They're like family. Mrs. Lombardo was my mother's best friend. She was almost a second mother to me after my parents died in a car accident."

Cara placed her hand over his and rubbed her thumb along the side. "I'm so sorry. I know it must still hurt."

Jake nodded. "It's something that's always with me—a big hole in my gut that I've learned to live with."

"Believe me, I understand. I lost my parents almost ten years ago."

"What happened?"

"It wasn't long after my wedding. They took a long-awaited European vacation and were on the train that was bombed in Madrid. It was awful." Cara didn't like to talk about that time.

"Crap. I hate that we have the loss of our parents in common."

A resigned sadness touched Cara's smile. "I know, but sometimes two people can draw strength from a shared experience."

Jake pursed his lips, and then smiled, thinking maybe Cara was on to something. Commonality of human emotion—an excellent reason the two of them should spend time together.

"I agree. Not everyone understands the sudden loss of parents."

The waiter returned after the last dish was cleared and they declined coffee or Italian liquor.

Cara tried, but couldn't quite manage to stifle a yawn.t.

"Are you ready to head out?"

At her nod, he rose and stepped back for her to exit in front of him. He did like the looks of her from the rear, especially in a tight pair of jeans.

Within a few minutes he'd pulled into her driveway. "I'll walk you to the door." He debated with himself on whether or not to kiss her, which in itself was stupid and lame. Jesus, he was thirty-eight years old, not some middle school kid.

They stopped on the small porch and Cara offered her hand. "Thanks so much for the game and dinner. I had a good time."

He took her hand and brought it to his lips, kissing the top. "Me, too. Perhaps we can do this again. Do you like professional football?"

"Sure, totally rooting for the Texans."

"Good. I have tickets for the home game two weeks from Sunday. Would you like to go with me?"

He loved that her face brightened at his suggestion. She seemed to show her emotions for all the word to witness.

"I'd love to. I've not seen them play in person."

"It's a date then." He leaned toward her planning only a quick kiss, but the spark of excitement in her eyes made him rethink his strategy. Instead, he wrapped his arms around her waist and she snuggled into his embrace. The deep, soul searing kiss he gave her, as well as her response, told him everything he needed to know. Mm, this had all the makings of something very, very good.

Chapter 2

This Could Work

Cara closed the door behind her and floated to her kitchen. After that kiss she was suddenly wide awake and in need of something—something to drink or something to do. Not a chance could she get to sleep. Gracie came running after her and skidded on the tile in the kitchen before plopping on her butt, her head cocked to one side as she released a single bark.

"Yes, I had a good time with Jake. The Wildcats won the game and dinner was delicious."

Gracie's head bobbed and she patted her right paw on the floor.

"I guess you're happy for me." She bent over and gave Gracie a good ear scratch. "In honor of your support, I'm going to make those dog biscuits I told you about."

Gracie barked, ran in a circle a couple of times, then headed for the living room.

Cara chuckled as she pulled on her apron and grabbed the recipe off the refrigerator. Maybe she'd have a glass of wine while she baked.

A few minutes later she had poured a chardonnay and assembled all of the ingredients for the biscuits. Her plan was to take several dozen to the shelter before Christmas. It was the least she could do to thank them for letting her adopt Gracie. This was the test of the recipe.

As she mixed the ingredients in her favorite yellow bowl, Jake came to mind. He had such a nice smile and well, he looked great in a pair of jeans and cowboy boots. She'd always been partial to men who wore jeans and a white shirt. That image made her think of George Strait, her all-time favorite country artist. Justin had hated country music and refused to attend any of George's Houston concerts.

"I wonder if Jake likes George?' she muttered as she began to spoon out pieces of dough and roll it in her hands into small balls. She quickly had a cookie sheet full of the balls and popped it in the oven.

Then again, so what if Jake does enjoy country music? It doesn't mean anything. Even though she'd enjoyed their date, the Texan game would be the last one. She wasn't ready to devote her time and energy toward dating Jake or anyone else. That kiss had proven to her she simply wasn't ready to date. She'd enjoyed it way too much and she wasn't ready to deal with the emotional toll of a relationship with Jake. Frankly, he scared the hell out of her,

Even if she did have a great time with him, was she really ready to date another man? Was she ready to push Justin's memory aside? He'd been her first love and the man she had hoped to raise children with. How could she date someone else when Justin still filled her heart?

Perhaps she should back out of the Texan game date. But she'd never been to a game in person. She laughed out loud, disgusted with her own inability to make a solid decision. Well, she'd already said yes to Jake and she did have a job to do for him. *That's it.* The game wouldn't be a date but business entertainment. That happened all the time. Problem solved.

It was well after midnight before a batch of biscuits had cooled enough to try. Cara bit into one of the super hard creations, the first requirement of any decent dog biscuit.

She nodded, deciding the flavor wasn't half bad. She took one into the living room for Gracie who was the official taste tester.

Cara found her in the usual spot on the sofa. The pup rubbed her eyes with her paws then rolled over.

"Hey sweetie, I have a treat for you."

Gracie accepted the small round biscuit. Her eyes focused on Cara as she chewed. Cara held her breath, waiting for a reaction.

"If you like the biscuit bark three times."

Gracie's head wobbled and she sat up. After a beat she barked, "Woof, woof, woof."

"Excellent. They've passed the taste test. Thanks, sweetie. You can go back to sleep."

Gracie lifted a paw then stretched out on her pink blanket and closed her eyes.

Cara went back to the kitchen to take the last batch out of the oven. These dog treats would be perfect for the shelter. She stowed the cooled biscuits in a storage container to save for her sweet dog. Actually Gracie was more than a dog. She had almost human mannerisms and seemed to understand everything Cara said. That was ridiculous, of course. Dogs learned from their humans based on repetition of the same words. She had no special powers. Gracie was simply a very smart puppy.

Monday morning came much too fast and Cara had to get to work. After a long dog walk, she headed to her office. Gracie kept guard of the street from a footstool by the front window in the dining room. All of the Halloween trick or treaters ringing the doorbell last night had brought out a protective streak in her.

Cara entered her office, once again amazed at how much she loved the space. Justin had helped her decorate and they had combined two opposite styles—she was country chic and he was wood and leather—into a new style they called "country meets downtown." The desk was an old door from his parents' farm they had sanded smooth and then clear varnished.

She opened the electronic calendar on her computer. She had plenty to keep her busy this week and all the drop-dead due dates were next week. Excellent, she could start working on Jake's project. The quicker she had the first draft for him, the quicker their meetings would be over.

She reviewed the notes she'd written at lunch. He wanted a complete overhaul to his website, brochures, print advertising, and all the associated branding materials. The first task was to think about his brand and how it compared to his local competitors. She opened her internet search engine and began to work.

The phone rang and Susan's office number displayed on the caller ID. "Hope you're having a good Monday."

"So far so good," Susan said. "Sorry I didn't call you yesterday. My friend and I had our first overnight date and it lasted until after dinner yesterday."

Apparently Susan was smitten. Smitten enough to rush one of her own rules about what she would do with a man and when. Overnight dates were at the bottom of the list, even after six months of dating.

"You sure took your time getting to this step. Hope you had fun."

"Sure did. What about you and Jake? How did everything go?"

"It was good. He's a very nice man. I met his sister and his ex-wife and—"

"You're kidding, the ex-wife already. What was she like?"

"She and his sister are still good friends. She's pretty but seems on the high-maintenance side. Don't know if she works or re-married. Jake doesn't have a lot of patience with her."

"He probably has good reason for that. Are you seeing him again?" Susan said.

"Probably this week, I'll have a first draft of branding and marketing material. We're going to the Texans game a week from Sunday."

"Aren't you the lucky girl? Sounds fun."

"I'm looking forward to watching a game in person but it will be the last date. I'm not ready for a relationship," Cara admitted. "I haven't put Justin's death behind me and it's not fair to Jake or anyone else."

Surprisingly, Susan agreed. "You know best."

"Wait, no argument from you? I expected some push back from you."

Susan laughed. "Sorry! Gotta go, my other line is ringing."

Cara turned back to Jake's project and continued to research landscape companies, broadening the search from Sugar Land to the state of Texas. She jotted notes in a spiral notebook as she clicked on links and viewed dozens of websites. She loved doing projects like this where her imagination could run the gamut. Much of her freelance work focused on producing work according to specific guidelines from her clients.

This project for Jake was feeding her creative juices.

She heard a bark followed by Gracie running into the room and jumping on the leather loveseat. Cara had laid down an old throw to keep Gracie's nails off the leather. So far she had been a good dog.

Cara laughed as the pup wiggled her butt to get settled just right. "I guess you chased away all the bad guys on the street."

Gracie nodded and barked, then dramatically flopped on her side and closed her eyes.

"Being a watchdog is tough work," Cara commented before turning her attention back to her computer.

By Thursday afternoon, she had a good draft of new branding along with print and media suggestions for Jake. The document was ready for primetime. Should she call him or email him? After thirty minutes of debate and drinking a homemade cappuccino, she made her decision and sent him an email, suggesting he drop by her house for dinner on Saturday evening. After all, she owed him a meal after he'd bought her lunch and then dinner. Fair was fair, right?

Over the years, Cara had prepared countless homemade dinners. Her only rule was to fit the menu to the occasion and to the guests. This dinner involved one guest to discuss a business assignment. She concluded that meant easy and no fuss—beef stroganoff, a green salad, and garlic bread. And she'd throw in her Love Drop cookies and coffee as a bonus.

Even though it was a business dinner, Cara added a nice cabernet sauvignon to the menu along with her favorite recipe for cheese sticks. Having something to munch on kept her guests busy and calm. Who didn't like finger food?

She surveyed the kitchen, everything was ready. She'd prepare the stroganoff once Jake arrived. After dinner they'd go over his changes and set a date for the final submission. A car door slammed outside. Gracie ran into the kitchen and barked. Jake had arrived.

He walked in the door wearing a large smile and carrying a vase of yellow daisies, which hit Cara's top-ten list of sweet things a man could do. He said hello to Gracie who barked in response then sped off back to the living room. Cara had tuned the television to Animal Planet and the pup seemed to enjoy the channel.

"I hope you like flowers," Jake said as he handed her the vase in the kitchen. "Daisies suit you."

"Why do you say that?" She settled the vase on the end of the island counter.

"I often assign plants and flowers to people I meet, guess it's a hazard of being a landscape artist. You strike me as a happy person and a daisy is one of the happiest flowers in the garden."

"I see," she said, not seeing at all. She hadn't truly been happy since Justin died. Obviously she was good at hiding her feelings. "Have a seat and I'll pour a glass of wine."

"Thanks, I've been going non-stop since seven this morning. Spending down-time with you will be a treat."

His last remark surprised her and pleased her at the same time. She placed a glass in front of him. "I hope you like cabernet."

He raised the glass to his lips and smiled. "Yes, ma'am, I do." He sipped the wine. "I like your taste in reds."

She set a basket of the cheese sticks on the counter. "Nibble on these while I get things started." She first set the burner under a pot of water to boil the noodles then retrieved the beef from the refrigerator.

"Do you mind me asking what you're making?"

"It's beef stroganoff." She turned to him, praying he didn't have a problem with it. "I hope you like it."

"I love it. My mom used to make it on Saturday evenings. She'd use hamburger when times were tough and then sirloin when things were better."

"That's so odd. My mother did the same thing. I'm using her recipe." Cara wondered how many other things they had in common.

Jake snacked on a cheese stick. "Anything I can do to help?"

"No, you sit back and relax since you had a busy day. This won't take but a few minutes."

They chit-chatted while Cara prepared the stroganoff. She'd cooked the dish so many times that she was on autopilot. While the sauce thickened, she grabbed the salad and checked the bread in the oven.

"Would you like to eat here at the counter?" she asked.

"Sure," he said. "No need to go to any trouble."

Ten minutes later they had their plates full and sat beside each other at the counter.

Cara realized too late that sitting at the island put her in close proximity to Jake. There wasn't a table between them. She could smell the musk of his aftershave, one of her favorite scents. Damn, why hadn't she set the dining room table?

She picked at her food while Jake cleaned his plate.

"Would you like more?" His enthusiasm hadn't helped matters. It thrilled her that he liked her cooking.

He nodded with a sheepish grin on his face. "This reminds me of my mother's stroganoff."

"I'm sure it was a popular recipe back in the day." She refilled his plate at the stove. "I bet it was in one of the women's magazines."

"Along with articles on how to keep your man and maintain big hair all at the same time."

"I bet articles on men and colored polyester pants on the golf course were equally popular."

He raised his wine glass in salute. "I do believe you're correct about that."

"Thank God we're past big hair and green polyester."

"Think so? Let me tell you a story about one of my clients." Jake had an amused expression on his face as he relayed the tale.

Cara studied his hands as he talked. In high school she'd taken several art classes and had concentrated on human hands for all of her projects. Jake had nicely shaped hands, broad palms, long and thick fingers. His palms were callused yet his nails were clean and manicured. A man who worked with dirt and yard tools had such beautiful strong hands—what a contradiction.

". . . and then she shut the door and drove off."

He finished his saga and she hadn't heard a single word he said. "That's quite a story," she said, hopefully covering her rudeness. "Would you like coffee while we discuss your project?"

"Sure." He rose and grabbed his plate and hers. "Let me help with the dishes while you make it."

"You don't need to do that."

"I've been trained well by my sister." He turned on the faucet and opened the dishwasher door.

"Okay." A man who volunteered to do the dishes and volunteered at an animal shelter surely had to be one-of-a-kind. And that was why she needed to stay clear of him.

They met back at the island counter after Cara retrieved her folder of printed material for Jake's project. She placed it on the counter then added two red mugs of coffee and a plate of cookies.

Jake placed his hands around the mug. "Hmm, that feels good. Seems like it's getting cold early this year."

"I was telling Gracie the same thing yesterday. I hope we don't have a harsh winter."

"You talk to your dog about the weather?"

"I talk with Gracie about everything. She's a very good listener."

He munched on a cookie. "These are really good. What are they called?"

"I call them Love Drops."

He raised his eyebrows, "Love Drops?"

"I thought it was catchy." She opened the folder and fanned several papers on the counter in front of him. "Let's talk about the new brand for your business."

The coffee pot was empty along with the plate of cookies. Cara and Jake thoroughly discussed every aspect of her proposal. She jotted notes from Jake's suggestions and marked the items he approved of "as is." It was a good meeting.

"We've covered the entire project," Cara said, thrilled that he liked her proposal. "Another cup of coffee?"

"No, thanks, I'll be up all night as it is." He rose and placed his hands on the top of the stool's back. "I very much appreciate all the work you've done for my company. You really have a gift with this stuff."

"Thank you, I do enjoy my work."

"I better get going," Jake said as he walked out of the kitchen.

She followed him to the front door.

He turned to her. "Thanks for dinner, and the conversation." He smiled and stroked his hand along her upper arm.

"It's nice to cook for someone other than myself."

"Perhaps we can do it again, my treat though." He leaned toward her, his head lowering slowly.

She was certain he would kiss her, like he did before. This man knew how to kiss a woman. She closed her eyes, waiting for the touch of his lips on hers.

She waited. No touch. She opened her eyes as he kissed her cheek. What the hell?

"Thanks again." He opened the door and stepped to the porch. "I'll call you." He walked to the driveway. "Don't forget about the Texan's game in a week." He saluted, then climbed in his truck.

Cara closed the door and leaned against it pondering the non-kiss. What had changed from the football game to tonight?

Jake wrapped up his project by the end of the next week, three days before the Texans game. Cara sent the final email to Jake and leaned back in her desk chair. No matter how confused she was over Jake, she couldn't deny her pride in this assignment. She'd done a great job; in an area where she didn't have much experience. Of course, she'd never tell Jake that. A girl had to have a few secrets.

Her shoulders slumped. If truth be told, she had too many secrets. Like her wishy-washy attitude about dating. Jake had no idea she felt so conflicted—her loyalty to Justin versus her belief that she needed to go forward with her life. Why couldn't she let Justin go? Why did everything have to be so damn complicated?

It was at times like this, the crossroads in her life, that she especially missed her mother. Talking about a problem had been so easy. They had shared so much, almost like sisters. Yet while growing up in Sugar Land, Cara had never made the mistake of assuming that her mother was a friend rather than a parent—a parent who believed in tough love, boundaries, and discipline.

She had loved her mother unconditionally, her father as well. They weren't perfect, but had worked hard at being good parents. The gift of hindsight and adulthood allowed

Cara to understand them now. She avoided most everything on March 11, the date of their deaths. Perhaps, someday, she would be able to find peace. That day had yet to arrive.

The house phone rang and Cara let it go to voice mail. She didn't feel like talking to anyone until she'd decided about going to the Texans game. She was at odds with herself about which way to go—unprofessional to date a client versus she'd never been to a Texans game. In the end, she didn't have to make the decision.

On Saturday afternoon, she went to bed with a stomach virus after hours of horrendously painful cramping. She called Jake and he understood completely. To make up for her missing the game, he invited her to Thanksgiving dinner at his sister's house. She agreed, simply to be able to lay her head on the pillow. She later learned from a voice mail that Susan planned to go with her boyfriend to his parents' house for the holiday. Yep, everyone had holiday plans.

The sky was overcast, not a snow sky, but steel colored and flat. The forecast predicted rain in the late afternoon, but that didn't hamper the outdoor frying of a turkey. Cara had not yet experienced this particular Thanksgiving tradition, now demonstrated at the home of Jake's sister and her husband.

They had arrived two hours ago; an early start on the holiday was another tradition. Jake explained there was much to do for their dinner so they always began their preparations promptly after breakfast. Cara figured the real deal was to get the heavy lifting done before the football games started.

After watching the turkey slide into the bucket of oil, she waved to the slew of males standing around the pot and went back to the kitchen. She'd volunteered for peeling-vegetables-duty. Janet greeted her and pointed to the sink.

"You can peel there. There's plastic on the bottom of one sink. I don't use the garbage disposal for the peelings."

"Okay," Cara eyed the mountain of potatoes and carrots on the counter and totally understood. "I'll get started."

"There's an apron on the stool by the desk," Janet said, a tight smile slicing her face. "Don't want you to get that pretty sweater dirty. I expect you don't spend much time in a kitchen."

Although Cara didn't understand her comment at all, she ignored it. "Not to worry. I enjoy cooking." She wrapped the apron strings around her waist and returned to the sink.

Janet stirred something on the stove. "Really? Like Chinese take-out and pizza?"

What the hell should she say? She didn't want to antagonize Jake's sister but she didn't appreciate the snippy attitude. What a change from the football game. She peeled a potato, watching the brown peel drop to the bottom of the sink. She'd take the high road.

"You're right, I do love Chinese food and pizza." Cara patted herself on the back for her diplomacy. But she was a girl after all and added. "I have a fantastic recipe for Szechuan Beef. Maybe I'll make it for Jake one of these days."

The pot lid slammed behind her and heels clicked on the slate floor. She turned around and Janet had disappeared. Damn. Not good. But why had Janet been so catty? Perhaps she was being a protective sister and looking out for her brother. Cara shrugged and continued to peel; she'd play it by ear.

A few minutes later, Jake and the other men came in through the back door. They talked and laughed over each other, something about a bet on a college game. Jake moseyed over to Cara while the rest of them headed toward the huge television set in the family room.

"Why are you in here by yourself?" he asked, before sneaking a quick kiss to her neck.

"I'm on veggie duty," Cara said lightly. "Your sister left a minute ago. I'm sure she has a dozen details to look after."

Feminine laughter floated into the kitchen from the front of the house.

"Oh, crap," Jake said, his jaw flexing.

"What's wrong?"

He briefly put his head on her shoulder then straightened up. "Just wait."

The laughter became louder and Janet and Meagan strolled into the kitchen, arm-in-arm, and grinning like squirrels with a winter's supply of nuts in their back pockets.

They stopped next to the long island counter, two southern belles who appeared to be two peas in a very comfortable pod. Meagan stepped forward.

"Jake, darling, I didn't realize you'd be here today." She wiggled over to him and kissed his cheek, wrapping her hands around his bulging bicep. She gazed at Cara. "Oh, and you're here, too. I forgot, what was your name again?"

Jake pulled away from her clinging hands. "Meagan, aren't you missing a party or a happy hour somewhere?"

She flicked her hand in front of her ample chest. "You are such a comedian. Why don't you run along to the family room so we girls can do the cookin'."

Jake stepped in front of Cara, his back to Meagan, and threw her a pleading "help me escape" look.

"Go ahead, sweet pea," Cara said before grinding her lips on Jake's, enjoying the confused surprise in his eyes as she pulled back. Touchdown.

Nearly five hours later, the Thanksgiving dinner had been consumed along with Cara's apple pie. Dishes were stacked on the kitchen counters as everyone transitioned to the family room to watch the kickoff of the Texans game. Jake helped Bob make Irish coffee at the bar tucked into a corner of the room. Megan volunteered to serve the drinks while Cara relaxed on a loveseat not too far from the bar.

The room was large and comfortably furnished with a variety of sofas and chairs in either tan leather or a golden herringbone fabric. Sturdy oak tables were scattered about to hold drinks and decorative accessories and family photos in thick frames. One long wall of floor-to-ceiling windows looked out to the patio and a swimming pool. Cara like the space as it had a homey and family feel.

"Here darlin', I have a coffee for you." Megan handed Cara a glass coffee mug. "I told Jake to go easy on the whiskey as I figure you're a light weight."

"Thanks, Meagan," Cara said. "Compared to you, I probably am a light weight."

Meagan screwed her mouth into a witch's scowl and stomped off. *Good riddance.*

Someone turned up the volume of the television as the Texans lined up for the kickoff, drowning out any conversation. Jake joined Cara on the loveseat and patted her knee.

"Here we go. Finally we get to watch a Texans game together."

"You're right," Cara said, squeezing his hand on her leg. "Thanks for inviting me. It's been a great holiday."

"I'm glad you came," He said, planting a quick kiss on her temple.

The room erupted in clapping and yelling as the Texans kick returner ran the ball to their forty-seven yard line.

Janet hurried over to them and whispered in Jake's ear. Cara couldn't hear a word she said.

He rose and touched her shoulder. "I'll be right back." He followed his sister out of the family room.

She turned her attention back to the game. The Texans had scored a touchdown in the few moments she'd been distracted. She tuned out the cheers and focused her thoughts on Jake instead. Her feelings about dating him ricocheted from still-loyal-to-Justin to let's-go-for-it. She had to make a decision. The time had arrived to throw off her wishy-washy cloak and go forward with life, at warp speed. She wasn't getting any younger.

Coming to a resolution about this made her feel better. In fact, the idea of seriously dating Jake or another man was exciting. What was that saying about the rest of a life started with one step?

She realized she'd just taken that one step, all by herself and it felt good.

She needed to use the restroom and looked around for Jake. She didn't see him and headed for the hallway next to the kitchen.

A few steps out of the family room she heard Jake's voice. It came from the study she'd toured earlier that day. She walked to the half-open door, intending to say hello, but stopped at the tone of Jake's voice. Janet spoke.

"I'm asking you one more time. Why in the hell are you seeing that woman? She's a loser."

Cara hadn't realized Janet disliked her so much. Sure, she got the sister-is-friends-with-the ex-wife thing, but this sounded personal.

"I told you before; it's none of your damned business who I date."

"Right. And this one will be just like the last one, and the one before that. It'll end in a huge disaster and I'll have to soothe your damaged ego. When are you going to do the right thing?"

"You are going too far, Janet." Jake's voice had lowered and he enunciated his words.

"No. You need to face reality and admit you should have never divorced Meagan. You two are meant for—"

Cara eased back from the door and hurried to the bathroom, tears in her eyes. She looked in the mirror and splashed cold water on her face. Well, so much for her first attempt at dating. It wasn't in the cards for her, at least not with Jake.

She refused to let this happen to her again. Justin had walked away from his family to be with her. She'd ended up with feelings of terrible guilt over the years he'd missed with them. She had no desire to put herself, Jake, or anyone else through something like that again. She dried her face with a hand towel. She knew what she had to do.

Jake drove Cara home during half-time. She declared a major headache and Jake being a gentleman, catered to her claim. She kissed his cheek quickly in the truck so he wouldn't walk her to the door.

Tears sliced down her cheeks as she watched his car back out of the driveway and race down the street. Well, that was that. She turned away from the dining room window and noticed Gracie sitting in the wide doorway with her head cocked to one side. She had a "what's wrong" look in her eyes.

Cara scooped the pup into her arms and buried her face in Gracie's soft fur. She loved her dog. "It's just you and me from now on."

Chapter 3
Dogs Rule

The calendar on the refrigerator didn't lie. It was less than two weeks until Christmas Eve and Cara had fallen into an alien vortex. She hadn't purchased a single gift, which was so unlike her normal holiday preparation. Not being in the mood for the upcoming holiday didn't even cover the essence of her situation.

Jake had called several times and she'd let it go to voice mail each time. She hadn't returned a call or responded to one of his emails. Not answering his calls was childish but she didn't know what to say.

She couldn't see herself embroiled in a family feud between him and his sister. That was entirely too much drama and unfair to Jake.

She did manage to make a triple batch of the dog biscuits and take them to the shelter. Naturally, she'd almost run into Jake in a hallway but turned a corner before he saw her.

Typically, during this time of the year, her business slowed down and she had extra time on her hands. This year she planned to use the time wisely—to outline the cookbook she'd been mulling over for months. She planned to publish it herself. Everyone was self-publishing these days. Why couldn't she?

It would serve a double purpose as well. Planning the book and researching alternatives might keep her occupied just long enough to forget him. She pictured him as she'd last seen him—filling out his jeans to perfection, mesmerizing her with that sexy smile of his, and those deep, blue eyes. Cara groaned and shook her head. Who was she kidding? Publishing a cookbook may keep her busy for a short while but it wouldn't keep her mind off Jake permanently. But damn, she had to try. It'd be best if he never contacted her again.

Cara had just added nonfat creamer to a freshly brewed cup of coffee when the doorbell rang. She peeked out the window beside the front door. Her breath caught in her throat as she caught sight of Jake standing on her porch.

Locusts swarmed inside her body, leaving her incapable of moving. What should she do? He didn't know she was at home so she could do nothing and he'd go away. The doorbell rang again. Gracie came running and skidded to the door.

Oh, what the hell, she opened the door.

"Jake, this is a surprise."

"Do you have a minute to talk?" His face looked pinched. "Hi, Gracie."

She barked once, then took off running for the living room. Her favorite Animal Planet show was on.

"Come on in, I just made a pot of coffee." He followed her to the kitchen, his boots slapping on the floor.

Cara grabbed a mug and poured Jake's coffee. "Here you go," she said, sliding the cup across the island counter to where he stood next to a stool.

"Thanks." He lifted the mug to his lips while his gaze never left her face.

Cara wanted to get this over with, and quickly. Jake's closeness sent goose bumps along her arms and caused her breath to feel shaky.

"What do you want to talk about?" she said, getting the ball rolling.

He set the mug down and placed both hands flat on the counter, leaning slightly forward. "What happened between us? You haven't answered my calls or replied to my emails.

"I've been busy."

"Really? If I'm not mistaken, you told me on Thanksgiving that December was your slow time."

She did tell him that. Damn. Cara sipped her coffee, stalling for time. "Okay . . . I'm not ready to date yet. I realized I haven't gotten over Justin's death. I need more time."

Jake stepped back from the counter, rubbed a hand over the stubble on his face. "I can accept that. But it sure as hell contradicts that mind-blowing kiss you gave me in Janet's kitchen."

Damn, again. They were going in circles and she'd soon spill her guts if she didn't get him to leave. She braced herself.

"Not really. I was just showing off in front of your ex-wife. It was a girl thing, had nothing to do with you."

His eyes briefly rounded then he smiled, real slow. "If that's the case, I'm sorry I bothered you today. It won't happen again." He turned and headed to the front door.

Why had she said such a nasty thing? She hurried after him, mentally wringing her hands. Could she be any more of an idiot in dealing with men? She should tell him the truth about Justin being estranged from his family because of her.

Jake had his hand on the doorknob and turned back to her, his face grim.

"I'm real sorry about everything, Cara. You're a nice lady. Take care of yourself." He opened the door and strode to his truck, his boots silent on the concrete. He jumped in and within seconds, shot down the street.

Cara stared at the empty driveway, tears welling in her eyes. Why had she driven him away? Because she didn't have the guts to open up to another man and tell him the truth. She'd given her heart to Justin and he'd died so young. It was better to end things with Jake before she opened herself up to the possibility of being hurt again.

She shut the door and turned away, rubbing her eyes. On her way back to the foyer, she tripped over the fringed Santa rug and down she went. Wrenching pain tore through her leg as her right foot slid and she hit the floor hard on her right side. Her head followed with a loud whack an instant before she sank into darkness.

Gracie raced into the foyer, circled Cara with head down, sniffing and nudging at her. She licked at her face but nothing happened.

She ran through her doggie door to the backyard, around the corner of the house and to the front fence. Running straight to the loose slat in the fence, she nudged it aside with her nose and belly crawled through the opening. She raced down the street, hoping to find the one person she instinctively knew could help her mistress.

Jake couldn't believe Cara had acted like that. What the hell was wrong with that woman? He turned the corner and swung into a drive-in. He needed to think and a cheeseburger and fries would help the process move along. He parked in a slot and shouted his request via the order station out the window.

He slumped against the seat and the door, and looked through the windshield at a park across the street. It had a variety of outdoor equipment built for kids; mostly empty this time of day. Wouldn't it be fun to take a child of his to a park like that?

As he waited for his lunch, he purposely didn't think about Cara. He needed time to get past the lost opportunity. He knew in his heart they had a chance for a good relationship.

His thoughts were interrupted by barking, very loud barking.

He straightened up and glanced out the window. What the hell?

Gracie stood next to the truck, bouncing on the pavement and barking like crazy.

He opened the door, and patted his leg. "Come on girl, jump up." Without missing a beat, Gracie jumped onto his lap. Jake wrapped his arms round her and rubbed her back. "What are you doing here? Did you get out by accident?"

Gracie licked his face, her rear end moving from side to side.

"Okay, I get it. You're a runaway and I need to take you home." Jake cancelled his order then backed out and retraced his route to Cara's house.

He scratched Gracie's ears as he drove. "Your mom won't be happy you snuck out. But she'll be very glad you're home safe and sound."

Gracie barked and snuggled against Jake.

He pulled into the driveway then carried Gracie to the front door. He rang the doorbell once, then twice. Gracie began to bark. She wriggled until he lowered her to the ground. Her barking grew more excited as she jumped repeatedly against the door.

Jake stared at the dog, his chest tightening with a bad feeling of foreboding. He tried the doorknob. When it turned, he pushed the door open and stepped into the foyer, calling Cara's name.

He paused briefly before rushing forward to kneel beside Cara. Gracie remained at his side, silent as a stone.

He touched Cara's shoulder and said her name. She didn't stir.

"Gracie, I need to take Cara to the hospital. You stay here and guard the house, okay." The dog seemed to nod in agreement as he patted her head. "Promise me you won't leave the house."

She danced on her hind legs.

Jake bent over and scooped Cara up in his arms. He looked down at Gracie. "I'll be back as soon as I can."

He closed the front door of the house and quickly settled Cara in the passenger seat of his truck. He noticed her right foot was swollen over her shoe. That wasn't good. The nearest hospital was ten minutes away and he lost no time in getting there. He parked in the emergency room parking lot and lifted Cara back into his arms. He rushed through the doors to the front desk.

"Please help. She's unconscious and she hurt her foot."

A nurse came around the desk and motioned to him to follow her. They came to a treatment room and Jake carefully laid Cara on the bed. She moaned as he released her.

"Do you know what happened to her?" The nurse said while wrapping a blood pressure cuff around her forearm.

"I think she must have fallen, maybe tripped on a rug." He remembered the crumpled rug under her.

"Are you her husband?"

"No, a friend."

"Do you know if she's allergic to anything?"

"No."

A woman in a white coat walked in the room and bent over Cara with a stethoscope.

"Sir, why don't you go to the waiting room and we'll call you once we know what's going on." The nurse gave him the evil eye. "The doctor will do what's best for your friend."

He provided his name, Cara's name and left the room, eyes scanning for the exit to the waiting room. He found the right door and staked out a spot on a row of chairs near the television.

Someone switched television channels, knocking Jake out of the zone he'd been in for over an hour. His mind had circled the facts several times, hopping from the image of Cara lying on the floor, to thoughts of how Gracie must have known that something was wrong. The dog was clever as hell, that's for sure. How had she known to go searching for him, and how the hell did she know his truck? He shook his head. Some dogs have almost human-like instincts and Gracie seemed to be one of those dogs. He checked his watch and two hours had passed since he'd entered the ER. He ran his hand over his hair. What was taking so damned long?

A young woman in navy blue scrubs approached him. "Are you Jake?"

He nodded and she continued. "Mrs. Allen is asking for you. Please come with me."

That was good, right? His heart nearly leapt out of his chest. He jumped up and followed her back to the original treatment room.

Cara's eyes were closed when he entered the small space. He prayed she was okay, resting comfortably and not in a coma. She seemed so thin under the blanket. He'd never thought of her as petite but now the term fit her perfectly. He stepped closer and took her hand. Her eyes opened immediately.

"Jake, you're here," she whispered. "Thank you."

"How are you doing?" He brushed hair off her forehead.

"Okay, I guess." She licked her lips. "I hit my head and broke my ankle. They put a splint on it, the ankle, I mean."

"I'm not surprised. It looked swollen. Does your head hurt?"

"Not really. How did you find me? I don't remember."

Jake told her the story and she thinned her lips, slowly shaking her head.

"What are you thinking?" he said.

"That I have an amazing dog. But how did she get out of the yard?"

"I'll check the fence for you."

"You don't have to do that. I'll get my yard guy to look at it."

"I am a yard guy." He patted his chest. "It's not a problem."

"Okay. But still, how amazing that Gracie found you."

"She's a smart dog."

"She's more than smart. I think she's . . . um, gifted in a people-type way."

He narrowed his eyes; it *was strange* how Gracie found his truck. "I'm beginning to think you're right."

A nurse entered the room the room with a stack of papers in her hand. "Mrs. Allen I have your release orders. Since you refused to stay the night for observation, we won't send you home unless someone stays with you tonight."

"Well, I—"

Jake interrupted Cara. "I'll make sure she's not alone."

"You don't need to do that," Cara countered.

He squeezed her hand. "Shh, listen to the rest of your orders."

The nurse gave her two prescriptions for pain and inflammation, and the name of an orthopedist who would cast the ankle once the swelling went down. An aid came in with a pair of crutches and leaned them against the end of the bed.

"Have you used these before?" the nurse said, pointing to the pair.

Cara shook her head and grimaced. "I'm notoriously klutzy. This will not be fun."

Actually, Cara hadn't worried about not having fun the last three days. Jake played the role of male nurse to a Hollywood, Oscar-level degree. Hiring him on a regular basis had crossed her mind, but that was probably the pain meds talking. Regardless, he had been a blessing.

Today she'd finally get her walking cast. It would be the last day he'd have to help her and occupy her guest room. She figured she'd be able to move on her own and get back to normal. Thank heavens she hadn't required surgery.

Right then he was at the grocery store, stocking her pantry so she'd be set for at least a week. He'd easily accepted her list and didn't squawk at its length. The man walked on water—which made her life so much harder because she knew they could never have any sort of a relationship in the future.

She would not be the cause of a family fight between Jake and his sister. Been there done that, period. But she would enjoy the time she had with him even though her heart would break when she had to say good-bye.

She leaned her head against the back of the chair for a moment, and closed her eyes. Her foot rested on a matching ottoman. She intended to refresh the ice bag in a minute.

She awoke to find Jake bending over her leg. "How long have you been back?"

"Long enough to stow the groceries, how's the pain? I'll get more ice."

"The drugs are good."

He chuckled as he scooped cubes into the ice pack that sat on top of her ankle. "Would you like a sandwich for lunch? We should leave for the doctor's office in an hour."

Yep, the man was a saint.

Nearly four hours later, she had a yellow walking cast and a special plastic bag that slipped over the leg and cast so she could take a shower. Walking was more painful than she'd expected. Thus, Jake had convinced her he would stay one more night and then leave her on her own the next day.

She again rested in the chair with her leg on the ottoman. Gracie sat next to her, keeping her company. Jake had been in the kitchen ever since they'd returned, starting on dinner. He said he'd prepare his specialty. A man who had a special dish that didn't involve barbequing on an outdoor grill? Wow.

He came into the living room carrying a wine glass and wearing a dish towel over his shoulder. "Everything okay out here?"

"Enjoying my yellow leg. How's it going in the kitchen?"

"Under control." Jake grinned, and sipped his wine.

"I haven't had a pain pill in hours. May I have a glass of wine?"

"Under the circumstances, that's a fine idea. I'll be right back."

He quickly returned with a glass.

"Thanks. Sit with me," Cara said. "This is our last night together."

The hard planes of his face softened. "Why? I'll be checking up on you every other day."

"That's sweet but not necessary. I'll do okay." She caught a whiff of an aroma from the kitchen. "Mm, something smells good."

"It'll be worth the wait." He planted himself on the sofa and Gracie joined him, stretching out against his thigh.

"I hope you'll give me your recipe."

"Maybe . . . probably."

"That's a definite yes."

"I'm curious," he said. "Did you learn to cook with your mother?"

"Uh-huh, the first thing I made by myself was apple crisp. I remember my hands shaking so bad slicing the apples. I was using my mom's favorite utility knife. I managed to keep all my fingers."

"I bet you were a cute little girl."

"Nothing special." She shook her head yet a tingle of pleasure canoed across her stomach. "How about you? What were you like as a kid?"

"Just like you, nothing special."

She laughed. "Guess we both turned out pretty good then considering with started out so non-special."

Jake had a ball serving Cara dinner at the dining room table. He'd gone all out with flowers and candles along with his specialty, chicken spaghetti with a green salad and rolls. Her eyes glowed when she hobbled into the room.

"Look at this beautiful table. You have out done yourself."

He knew he blushed at the comment. Meagan never appreciated his efforts when it came to meals. "Thanks, sit down and I'll make you a plate."

Their conversation ping-ponged from favorite authors to favorite basketball teams to the best vacation to take. He liked that they both favored mystery novels and preferred the beach to the mountains. They had so many things in common. Why couldn't she understand they could have a future together? Or, at least admit it was worth a try to find out.

What the hell—he wanted to know the truth.

"Cara, you said you don't feel comfortable dating because of your husband."

"Yes, that's right."

"Are you sure it's not something else?"

She set her goblet on the table in a rush and water dotted the tablecloth. "How can you even ask me that?"

He was going all the way. "What you said about the kiss, that it didn't have anything to do with me. That's the kind of silly logic my sister would use when we were kids . . . to deflect the real issue."

"Silly?"

"It doesn't make sense so I know there's another reason. Did I offend you?"

"No, of course not."

"Then what is it?"

She turned her head away from him. After a long moment she turned back to him with her eyes looking glassy. "I didn't want to tell you."

He parked his hand over hers on the table, hoped his silly grin would encourage her. "Tell me anyway."

"Okay," she said, brushing both eyes with her fingers. "Remember at Thanksgiving when you left the game to talk with your sister?"

"I remember. I missed a Texans touchdown."

"I heard you arguing with Janet, about me." She played with the stem of her wine glass. "I don't want to be the cause of a family feud. That happened with Justin's parents and I'm not going through it again."

"What happened?" His gut told him if she got this out, he would have a fighting chance. His bluntness was worth the chance of pissing her off.

She looked at him, her eyes round and trusting. "Okay. I'll give you the short version."

"Go ahead."

"Justin and I met in college. We were crazy about each other, the perfect match . . . except for one thing." She sipped her wine and took a long breath. "I wasn't a debutante."

"A what?"

"Justin's parents are old Houston with money going back a hundred years. All of the women were debutantes with many invited to this big International Ball in New York City. Me, I'm middle class and could care less about that kind of thing."

"His parents didn't approve of you and that created a major family issue."

"Bingo. We ended up eloping to avoid the eventual family confrontation. After three or four years Justin and his parents resolved their differences. We'd actually attended a couple of Christmas dinners before he died. His folks were very supportive during the funeral."

"Sounds like the original problem was resolved."

"But look at all the years that were wasted," she cried. "I'm not going through that again."

"You don't have to. I guess you didn't hear me telling Janet that I'll pick my own girlfriend and to give up her notion that Megan and I will get back together. We should never have gotten married."

"You've said that before. Why did you get married?"

"Junior year at A&M, first time we had sex, she gets pregnant. We tell our parents and boom, we're married by the nearest justice of the peace, and away we go. Months later she had a third trimester miscarriage." He rubbed his hand of his stubble. "I miss not having that child."

"I'm sorry," Cara said. "Yet you stayed married."

"Dumb, I know. I didn't want to admit to myself I'd been a fool."

"Yeah, I get that."

"Glad you understand. Will you reconsider going out with me?"

"No."

Cara loved to bake. Today she was making a batch of her Love Drops cookies for Susan to take to her boyfriend's brother's house on Christmas day. She sat on the stool most of the time, giving her ankle a time out. She'd had the cast for nearly a week and managed to stay upright without tripping over herself.

It was two days until Christmas Eve and she had yet to make the final decision for her holiday menu. Although she and Gracie would be alone, she still enjoyed making a big deal out of the food. Why not? Being alone on a holiday wasn't a crime.

The doorbell rang and Gracie started barking. Cara shuffled to the front door with the dog behind her and peeked out the side window—hmm, a delivery person.

She opened the door and greeted a cute teenage boy.

"Cara Allen?"

She nodded and he shoved a clipboard in her hands. "Sign on the last line."

She signed and he placed a vase of red tulips in her hands. "Merry Christmas."

Cara was perplexed. Who in the world would send her tulips, gorgeous red tulips? She sat the vase on the kitchen counter and retrieved the card. They were probably from Susan to say thank you for making the cookies.

She tore open the envelope and read the message on the card: "Please reconsider dating— I'd be honored if you'd spend Christmas Eve with me, I'll cook. Bring Gracie with you. –Jake"

She slipped onto a stool and hugged the card to her chest. Oh my, Jake had touched her heart with the tulips and his request. Her heart ached to be open to him and what he represented. But could they actually work as a couple? She knew exactly what to do, once Susan's cookies were cooled and boxed.

Two hours later, Cara drove into Forest Lawn Cemetery. Yes, she was driving with her left foot on the accelerator, and she was careful. It took several minutes to park and walk to the large Allen section of memorials. Justin's was on the right side, below his grandmother.

Although it was December, the day was clear with temperatures in the low seventies, perfect Texas Gulf Coast weather. She stepped to her husband's grave.

Usually Cara sat on the grass but this time she stood, not sure she'd be able to get up with the cast on her foot. She placed her hand on the top of the charcoal granite headstone, feeling its warmth in her palm. It gave her comfort. Justin had a way of doing that for her without even trying.

"Hey, sweetie, I need your help with something." She rubbed her fingers along the smooth top of the marker. "I've been thinking about starting to date, uh, get on with my life. What do you think about that?"

She closed her eyes and listened to the sounds of the cemetery. She heard the crunch of car tires on the gravel road, a distant cry of grief, and the mottled voice of someone long since departed. Rubbing her arms against a sudden chill, she opened her eyes and noticed a hot air balloon rise above the trees.

Stepping away from Justin's grave, she watched the balloon float slowly in the western sky. It had the University of Texas longhorn emblem on the side facing her with cream and orange vertical stripes. How strange. Justin had graduated from UT and he'd been a dedicated football fan. She turned in a full circle, wondering if something else would appear. Nothing out of the ordinary caught her eye. She turned back to Justin's gravestone. It was glowing silver in the late afternoon light.

Cara wasn't a fool and she understood Justin's sense of humor. She had her answer.

Sure she had a broken ankle, but that didn't make Cara helpless. Yesterday, she'd phoned Jake and accepted his invitation for Christmas Eve. And she offered to bring the dessert, the least she could do considering he was cooking dinner. She'd gone through dozens of her recipes, searching for the right one to wow Jake.

Finally she found the perfect dish, tiramisu, and thankfully she had all the ingredients at home—no trip to the grocery store on Christmas Eve—that was a blessing. She'd put the dessert together; rest her ankle and get her beauty rest all at the same time.

On her way to Jake's house, Cara gave Gracie a mini-lecture on how to behave in someone else's home. The talk included the major good-dog points—don't pee inside the house, no chewing on anything that's not identifiable dog food, and don't jump on furniture without permission. Yeah, the usual stuff for a guest dog with manners.

Jake's huge house graced the end of a street with a circular driveway, wide lawns, and spectacular holiday lighting. She drove slowly along the drive, enjoying the looks of a yard maintained by a professional.

She heard barking as soon as she pushed the button for the doorbell. Jake answered the door with an adorable white dog by his side.

"Merry Christmas," he said and leaned over to kiss her cheek. "Come in and we'll get this party started."

"Merry Christmas, you never told me you had a dog."

"I adopted her a month ago. You inspired me. Ernie, say hello to Cara and Gracie."

Ernie bounced on her hind paws and barked twice. Then she and Gracie touched noses, ran across the foyer, and scooted into another room.

"They made friends fast," Cara said. "Is her name really Ernie?"

"Earnestine. They were bunk mates for a while at the shelter. Let's go to the kitchen."

She walked behind him and once again ogled his butt encased in faded jeans. This time her heart felt no guilt while she enjoyed the view.

One step into the kitchen and she stopped, her mouth surely mopping the travertine floor. "Holy moly, I could sleep in here, it's fabulous." Between the stainless steel, the concrete counter tops, and the rich oak cabinets, her dream gourmet kitchen had materialized.

"I'm glad you like it. I plan on begging for cooking lessons down the road."

"No problem as long as the lessons are here."

He laughed and took the tote bag she'd been holding. "Have a seat at the counter and we can start with a snack and a glass of wine. Once your foot is rested, we can tour the house."

"Sounds like a plan to me." She sat in a wide leather chair and watched Jake fuss with the trifle dish she'd brought. "That goes in the refrigerator and the plastic bag is doggie treats. I thought I might need them to coerce Gracie into good behavior."

"So far so good, I haven't heard any crashes."

"The night is young," she said with a silent prayer that Gracie wouldn't create a problem.

"Have faith, they're good dogs." He busied himself for a minute before pouring a glass of wine. "Try this out. I hope you like it."

She did as instructed and wanted to smack her lips. "Love it."

"Try these." He held a stoneware dish holding black and green olives, feta cheese, and grated carrots. He handed her a small fork.

She scooped a bite and tasted his appetizer. "Mm, nice, is balsamic vinegar in the dressing?"

"Yes, ma'am, it's my secret weapon."

Barking and the clicking of doggy nails on the floor caused Cara to turn in the stool. Gracie and Ernie ran into the room and around the corner of the cabinet, no doubt to Jake.

"They must want something," she said.

"It's called dog biscuits." He winked and tossed two treats in the air.

The dogs ran out of the kitchen, biscuits in their mouths.

"Those two are like kids," she said, shaking her head. "Sure makes it easier they get along so well."

"I agree." Jake leaned across the counter and kissed her, sending soothing warmth straight through her. She returned his kiss as his hand stroked her arm. Then he pulled back.

"Don't want to get distracted too early in the evening," he said. "Your red sweater looks nice on you."

"Thanks." She decided she liked hearing a man give her a compliment. It had been too long.

"Are you up to a house tour?"

"I think so, as long as it's not a race."

Cara didn't know, but she was the first woman Jake had invited into his home, ever. His sister or grandmother didn't count. Yes, sir, it was a special occasion for him. He had high hopes this was the beginning of many visits to come and eventually, something more. He was a patient man and willing to start at the beginning to woo the woman with whom he hoped to build a strong friendship and then, well, make it permanent.

She seemed to like his house—complimented him on the décor and the size of the rooms and the backyard deck and pool. He'd almost suggested they get in the Jacuzzi later but didn't. The spa shower in the master bath was a big hit, along with the potting sink and storage cabinets in the utility room. Women, he'd never truly understood what floated their boat.

The tour ended in the dining room. He liked the room but didn't use it enough. Guess he should do more entertaining.

Cara pointed to the crystal chandelier over the long table. "That's beautiful. Look how the prisms sparkle on the ceiling and walls. Where'd you find it?"

"At a store on Royal Street in New Orleans," he said, pleased she approved of his selection. "I was there for a flower and shrub conference and walked into this hole-in-the wall store one day at lunch. And there it was, smiling down at me in a corner. I had it shipped home and loaded every crystal myself."

"I love it."

"Thank you for approving of my taste in chandeliers." He bowed to her. "You look like you're ready to fall over. Let's go back to the kitchen and you can put your foot on a stool while I get dinner together."

He turned two stools facing each other so her right foot rested easily. "Do you mind if we eat in here? That way you can keep your foot elevated."

"I like that idea. What can I do to help?"

"Nothing, just relax. Tell me what you do for fun."

Cara talked about her love for travelling and a trip to Rome when she got out of college. Jake prepared their dinner while he listened. He soon set a long casserole dish on the counter, along with bowls of charro beans, and tortilla chips and queso.

"My mother made this for Christmas Eve when we were kids. I've made it every year I've been in this house." He set out placemats, plates, and silverware.

"I love Mexican food. The enchiladas smell delicious," she said and moved bowls of beans close to their plates. "You cooked your own beans, didn't you? I'd love the recipe."

"No problem." He set a covered dish on the counter and settled into the stool next to her. "That's my grandmother's rice recipe."

She smiled and touched his arm. "This is my kind of holiday food."

"Hope you don't mind, I always say a quick blessing." He placed his hand over hers. "Dear Lord, we have gathered together to share good times, good conversation, good friends, and good food. Cara and I thank you for all. Amen." He squeezed her hand then stood. "I forgot the wine. I always drink chardonnay with enchiladas and queso."

Cara needed to stretch her leg after their dinner and volunteered to load the dishwasher. Jake reluctantly agreed and said he'd take the dogs out to the backyard for a pee break. They'd been well mannered dogs. He must have been a psychic in a former life as he was spot on concerning them—no chewed shoes, no exploding sofa cushions, and no sneaking food off a plate.

Every minute of dinner had been enjoyable. They'd shared cooking stories, primarily the disasters and she marveled at the ease of their conversation. Surely that had to be beginners luck.

In quick order, she had the leftovers in the refrigerator, a pot of coffee dripping, and the concrete counter cleaned by the time Jake walked back in the kitchen.

"Dogs are ready to take a nap," he said, ruffling her curly hair. He stroked his hand over her back. "How about you, ready to relax on a comfy couch?"

"I like that idea."

"Let's go to the TV room. The dogs are in there already."

She didn't remember a TV room on the tour. He led her down a short hallway to a wide archway. She stopped and her hand automatically fanned over her chest.

"Oh. My. God. This is . . . it's fantastic."

She stepped into the room, taking in the flickering white candles covering almost every surface. Their glow added exactly the right touch, framed against the Christmas tree in the corner and fresh evergreen garland with red bows draping the wide mantel. A low fire burned beneath it, filling the room with a woodsy, winter scent.

"Jake," she said, wrapping her arms tight around his waist. "This is wonderful. It's Christmas by candlelight."

He kissed her cheek. "I'm glad you like it. I thought we might watch a movie." He led her to a light green tweed sofa with a Christmas throw across the back.

"This is perfect," she said. She placed her right foot on the matching ottoman and he laid the throw across her lap.

"Let me get the coffee and I'll be right back."

She noticed the two dogs sleeping side-by-side in a wide chair near the window. How did that work out so well? It seemed almost too good to be true. Would she soon snap out of a dream with this perfect man as the hero?

Jake returned carrying a small tray with coffee mugs. He placed it on a side table by the sofa then sat on the edge of the sofa next to her.

"Before I start the movie, there's something I've wanted to do all day."

Cara had no clue what he meant. "Okay, go for it."

He took her hand, kissed it, and leaned toward her.

Her heart thumped as he moved closer, and closer. She could see gold specks in his blue eyes. She swallowed as his mouth moved just above hers, and he stopped.

He wouldn't do this to her again, would he? She wanted his kiss. "What's wrong?"

He gave her an irresistible look that said "come and get it, if you dare," before his mouth twisted in a sexy-as-hell grin. "I'm just enjoying the view."

She wrapped her hand around his neck and played with the hair curling over his collar.

His mouth conquered hers. Lust. Longing. Crashing need. His hands ran up her sides, brushing against her breasts. She pressed against his chest, sinking into the luxury of the moment.

Jake finally broke the kiss and spoke in a voice raspy with desire. "Holy . . ."

She rested her forehead against his. "Oh God, I know, right?" she gasped, her breathing every bit as heavy as his—their hearts pounding their mutual need in perfect synchronization. *Now that's what you call romance by candlelight.*

She pulled back from him, giving herself a minute to catch her breath. "You know I'm a mess when it comes to this dating stuff. Totally out of practice."

"I can handle it." His finger nudged a strand of hair behind her ear. "It'll be an adventure."

"Mm, I like adventures." She reached up to brush his hair back from his forehead, unable to fight the urge to touch him. "Are you really as patient as you seem?"

He caught her fingers in his hand and brushed a kiss lightly upon her knuckles. "Most of the time, it's my tried and true, no stress method for dealing with problems.

"I see—patience equals no stress."

"Uh-huh. And in case you're wondering, this thing we have going here, it's gonna be good. But if you're not ready to jump in yet, I'm willing to wait."

He slipped his hand to the back of her head and pulled her close for another kiss before wrapping her in his arms for a huge hug.

Cara closed her eyes and breathed in his masculine scent. Could any man be this damn perfect, or was this a classic case of too good to be true? She glanced at the chair with the two dogs and saw Gracie watching her. After a moment, the pup nodded and tucked her head against Ernie. The corners of Cara's mouth lifted in a slow smile. The only assurance she needed was the steady beat of Jake's heart and his willingness to take it slow. Of course, she had a hunch she'd be itching to speed things up in no time at all.

Jingle Paws
(Bacon-Cheese Dog Biscuits)

- 2 cups rolled oats
- 1/2 cup unbleached flour
- 2 teaspoons baking powder
- 1/2 cup natural Cheddar cheese, finely grated
- 2 tablespoon Parmesan or Romano cheese,
- freshly grated
- 2 pieces bacon, cooked and crumbled
- 2 tablespoons canola oil
- 1/4 cup water

1. Preheat the oven to 325°F.
2. Combine oats, flour, and baking powder in a mixing bowl. Add cheeses and bacon, and stir until well mixed.
3. Make a well in the flour, and add canola oil. Mix by hand or with a mixer until crumbly.
4. Add the water all at once and mix until dough forms, and the ingredients are combined.
5. Turn the dough out onto a slightly floured surface and gently knead until smooth and soft. Spoon out the dough in pieces and roll into 1-inch balls.
6. Place the balls on a parchment-lined cookie sheet and press down with a fork. Bake 12–15 minutes until dry and firm to the touch. Turn the oven off and leave the biscuits in another 20–30 minutes.
7. Remove from the oven, cool on a baking rack, and store the biscuits in a plastic container.

Makes 30 biscuits

Love Drops
(Shortbread-Pecan People Cookies)

- 2 sticks butter, softened
- 3/4 cup confectioners' sugar
- 2 cups sifted all-purpose flour
- 1 teaspoon good quality vanilla
- 1 cup pecans, finely chopped

1. Preheat the oven to 325°F.

2. Beat butter until fluffy.

3. Gradually add confectioners' sugar, flour, and vanilla.

4. Mix well and blend in pecans.

5. Shape dough into 1-inch balls. Place on ungreased cookie sheets about an inch apart.

6. Bake 25 minutes or until pale golden-brown.

7. Roll cookies in additional confectioners' sugar while still warm. Roll in sugar again. Cool.

Makes 4 dozen cookies

ABOUT THE AUTHOR

Karen Sue Burns has been a writer since 8th grade. Her day job as a CPA has provided interesting experiences: travel to Rio de Janeiro, London, and Oslo, auditing wine bottle glass molds in California, and taking a helicopter to a drillship off the Texas Gulf Coast. Accounting has been good to her, but writing romance and mystery novels is her passion. She enjoys cooking and creating recipes so her heroines do the same. All of her indie anthologies and novels include one of her favorite recipes. *In Hot Pursuit* is her debut romantic suspense novel and *The Liberation of Mr. Delaney* is her first indie published novel. She is also a contributor to the sweet and sensual romance anthology series *Seasons of Love* with the books *Hearts, Hearths and Holidays; Spring Promise; and Sweet Summertime Love*. Readers may contact Karen via the Bio/Contact tab on her website. Check out the Recipe tab while you're there!

Find Karen Here:

Website: http://karensueburns.com

Facebook: http://facebook.com/KarenSueBurns

Twitter: http://twitter.com/karensueburns

Blog: http://karensueburns.com/blog

Pinterest: http://pinterest.com/KarenSueBurns

DEDICATION

This story is dedicated to all the animal lovers who also enjoy reading romance novels. All of our lives are richer for the loyalty and unwavering love from our family pets. A special shout-out goes to Carolyn Ross, who is my BFF dog-lover friend and to Ellen Watkins, who is my BFF cat-lover friend. Merry Christmas, ladies.

ONE STEP OVER THE
MISTLETOE LINE

ID NO 243325   DATE 25 DECEMBER

By CARMINE VALENTINE

Chapter 1

There would be snow in Seattle for Christmas. The first snowflakes floated and swirled outside the window, covering the sidewalk and the park across the road. Those inside enjoyed the comfort of a crackling fireplace.

"Kiss-my-eggnog!" Claire said, trying to sound like she meant it. With only a few days left before her Christmas rebellion, she had to make the most of her last assertive behavior session.

"That was pathetic," her neighbor, RJ, said from behind the Sunday paper. "Remember," he paused while he turned the page, "this may be your last time to vent. to take it out on me because the point is not to ruin your mom's Christmas, just stand up for your own choice of how you want to spend the holiday."

RJ Saint George had his bare feet on the coffee table amongst the bachelor disarray of Money magazine and newspapers from the last few days, Christmas cards he'd yet to open and his second mug of steaming coffee this morning. His home was devoid of all Christmas decorations with the exception of the advent calendar from his mother. He'd kept up with opening the little paper doors right up to the current date. All the little foil covered chocolates behind each door were gone.

Claire sat in the contemporary style leather armchair by the fireplace. A large, nicely framed black and white photograph of a sailboat navigating rough seas hung above the fireplace. The mantle displayed various shots of RJ in family photos with his parents and brother, as well as group shots of RJ and his friends. Claire had yet to see a photo on display of RJ and his girlfriend. As if the universe felt it necessary to remind her that her handsome neighbor had a significant other, RJ's cell phone lit up with the model's caller ID, a photo of her posing on a beach. The phone was on vibration mode. Without lowering the newspaper, RJ used his foot to nudge the phone under the pile of mail. Claire felt drawn to glance down into her open handbag to see if she'd missed any calls or text messages. Her phone was particularly quiet lately, in its absence of Brian communication. She hadn't seen him since their lunch date last week where he'd seemed preoccupied. She felt herself tense as she speculated what might be on his mind, the same thing on his mind the previous two Christmases when he had gotten down on one knee – and she'd replied "I'm not ready."

She zipped her handbag and focused on her session.

"Come on, let's hear it again," said RJ from the leather sofa where he sat across from her.

Comfortable in slender jeans tucked into knee-high boots and a cream sweater, Claire leaned forward, her long blond hair falling over one shoulder to brush across her knee.

"Kiss - my – rum balls!" She waited for his approval.

Claire lived just a few doors down from RJ in a lakeside community across from the larger metropolis of Seattle. From RJ's living room window, the tree-covered hilly landscape of Seattle, with its mix of condos, mansions, and both contemporary and craftsman style homes, were barely visible through the haze of snow over the lake.

The area they lived in, although considered the Eastside and consisting of several smaller cities of Bellevue, Kirkland and Redmond, to name the three clustered together off the main traffic fair connecting to Seattle, many of the life-long locals tended to generalize when they travelled and when asked "where are you from?" simply replied "the Seattle area."

RJ was one of the Seattle area's most eligible bachelors, having agreed to pose for a fundraising calendar to help raise money and bring awareness to a cause he believed in: the gap in the education system where standardized learning methods did not meet the needs of all learning types. Both RJ and his brother struggled through their school years with a learning disability. Because their parents had tutored them at home on top of their regular schooling, and with the assistance of professionals, they'd both learned tools to successfully overcome their disability and gone on to earn a higher education. Both RJ and his brother held PhD's in their specialized areas and both were also co-owners of their family's successful yacht building business.

Held over from his first professional career, RJ continued to practice as a licensed psychologist specializing in both assertive behavior and coaching kids and teenagers with learning disabilities. As for the calendar showing RJ tanned and fit in surfer shorts grinning from the bow of his sailboat on a sunny summer day, Claire had one in her office.

Apparently, RJ didn't think so much of her second attempt. She received a disapproving glance over the top of the newspaper. From beneath his neatly trimmed sandy hair with the exception of the unruly cowlick at his hairline, a pair of hazel eyes gave her a serious look. "My dog can do better than that."

In the corner sat a basket of dog toys that hadn't been played with in a long time.

"You mean your dead dog."

The newspaper went back up.

"It's been six months, RJ."

The newspaper remained motionless. She waited another moment, wondering if he'd soon be informing her that his hourly rate had increased.

Claire had tactics galore from her years in dealing with her rich and pampered interior design clients. Not that RJ was anywhere close to behaving like someone who might easily be mollified if something newer or more expensive were placed before them. Still, it wouldn't hurt to try her special tone of voice.

"Maybe you should get another dog. I saw an advertisement at the coffee shop for bulldog puppies."

"Not ready." The newspaper held stubbornly steady.

"Maybe I'm not the only one who needs a therapist." Claire sat back with one leg over the other, her foot gently swinging. She reached for the latte she'd brought to her 10am "stop by if you feel like it" session offered by RJ at the mere cost of a pot roast. She felt a bit special knowing that she was the only client that RJ invited over on a Sunday. Everyone else had to wait for week-day hours at his leased office space in a professional building.

"Brandy doesn't like dogs," he said, finally.

"Who cares what Brandy wants?" Claire blurted. Then remembered how much trouble she got in the last time she made a Brandy comment.

RJ was very respectful of others even if they didn't always deserve that respect, in Claire's opinion. She, on the other hand, was respectful up until someone's behavior warranted her opinion of that behavior. As for her past Brandy comments, they resulted in a clear drawing of a boundary line. But it was how RJ drew this boundary line that created a bit of friction between them.

He was very smooth, first complimenting her on her new dress with a casual look at her slender legs, a technique of his that always pulled her into his charm. Then he came in for the kill. He'd flat out told her not to criticize someone who'd had a tough life, the same woman who'd insulted Claire's volleyball techniques before purposely spiking a ball at her head during a game at the community center.

Claire and RJ were back on good terms now with RJ making a peace offering; his cabin up in the mountains if she still wanted to avoid her family for the holidays. A nice offer, but the sting remained. Lesson one: keep your opinion of a nice man's girlfriend to yourself.

She breathed a sigh of relief as it was apparent RJ chose to ignore her remark. He set the newspaper aside to take a sip of his coffee.

"Let's hear it again," he said. Did she imagine it, or had he winked at her with a smile in his eye before the newspaper shield went back up?

The newspaper was not for RJ's benefit but for hers. She couldn't look into his eyes and say what she had to say to people who loved her but didn't know how to show it any differently than to try and orchestrate her life. RJ's prescription for her problems with her mother? Set boundaries. Well, she might as well listen to the expert.

"Kiss my royal rum balls!" She jumped to her feet, with fists clenched and cheeks flushed with not-so-feigned anger. She took a deep breath, surprised at the force of her words. "Good enough?" She added with a roll of her shoulders and taking on a tough-chick stance with hands on her hips.

RJ set the newspaper aside. "Congratulations." His eyes were warm with amusement as he folded his muscular arms across his broad chest. "There's one more thing," he said.

"What's that?" Claire felt flushed, not only from her practiced performance, but from the manner in which RJ always scanned her body, as if he was considering ordering dessert.

This morning she was more aware of the chemistry between them than ever before. Perhaps it was due to her declining attraction to her boyfriend of two years who felt that Claire could find a more serious profession rather than that of cluttering up people's homes with furniture and artwork on their walls.

She reached for the caramel-colored wool wrap on the back of the chair and picked up her leather handbag to sling over her shoulder.

"I still don't think this is the best way to handle your mother when she starts insisting on how and where you plant your sweet ass during the holidays," RJ said.

"How about the next time she arranges a romantic opportunity for Brian to pop the big question?"

"Oh, yeah. That."

This was RJ's same response every time she mentioned her boyfriend's many attempts to arrange a romantic "pop the question" moment with her mother in on the plan. Claire had managed to avoid these close calls, so far, using the excuse of a last-minute phony client. The one thing she didn't have to worry about was RJ trying to draw more out of her as to why she was reluctant to receive Brian's proposal. Boundary lines again. Where he didn't want anyone to go, he didn't go.

"Claire?"

"What?" She slipped the wrap over her shoulders.

RJ watched her as she pulled the matching knit hat onto her head. "You've had your chance to vent. My advice in dealing with your mother is to keep it simple and be firm. If she gets upset, remember what else we practiced."

"Don't worry; I plan on being very diplomatic. I would never swear at my mom. Like you said, it just feels good to vent. Is your fee the same?"

"Yes. This time I'll take a pot roast with roasted red potatoes." He glanced to the dive watch on his wrist. "You do have another fifteen minutes."

She was done discussing her issues for the day. Instead she looked about the room and its minimal furnishings.

"Okay, out with it." RJ sat back wearing an expression of good humor. "I can tell when you're holding back. Come on, let's have it. What do you think this room really needs?"

Although a bachelor pad, RJ did have a woman in his life and that necessitated that Claire go about this carefully. "Brandy probably has her own ideas."

He gave one firm shake of his head. "I want to know what you would do. What would it take to make my home as inviting as yours?"

She hesitated only a moment longer. "Chocolate colored drapes at the windows and I saw a beautiful Asian style cabinet down at the import store that would fill up that wall in your dining room. Plus, you need bookshelves for all your books." She pointed to the stacks of books in the corner. "A few more pieces of art on the wall, toss the plant you never water and add an area rug in the dining room. Oh, and of course, a dining room table and chairs might come in handy." She smiled. "You should add a headboard to your bed. I'd go with one covered in linen. And you can never have enough lamps for ambience." Too late and she realized what she'd admitted to.

RJ wore a crooked smile. "How do you know I don't have a headboard on my bed?"

Her face warmed at his teasing. *Busted.* She grinned.

"I'm an interior designer. I can't help myself and I'm not apologizing for taking a peek." She just had to add. "I even took measurements for the headboard."

He looked slightly stunned. "You're kidding."

"Yes."

"You had me there, for a second."

"I know."

The steady manner in which he watched her made her weaker in the knees than she would ever admit to, or should be feeling. Brian never made her feel like that when he looked at her, not to mention that he would never let her lay an interior-design hand on his own home. She'd offered once and he'd reacted like it was the most horrific thought he could have imagined.

"You eye-balled it, didn't you?" RJ said.

She gave in. "You have a king sized bed and you even have room for an armoire to hide the big TV that's taking up all the room on your dresser."

"Anything else?" he said dryly.

"That's it for now." She realized she didn't know him well enough to know how far she should go with this cheeky banter. Besides, his girlfriend was territorial. She'd likely veto all of Claire's ideas. She had a hunch she wouldn't like what Brandy might do to his place. She felt her face heat up, again. "I should be going."

RJ was at the door. He gave her shoulders a brotherly squeeze, a gesture of affection she in fact she enjoyed the pressure of his arm around her. RJ smelled of clean laundry and warm cotton with a hint of cologne.

"You can do this," he said. "We've been practicing for several weeks now."

Grateful to him for helping her build the courage to face off with her mother, she did something she'd never done before. She stood on tiptoe to kiss RJ on the cheek.

But just as she did so, he moved his head to look down at her and she ended up planting one on his mouth.

Instantly, she reminded herself that RJ was just a friend, even though his lips were warm and firm. He was a friend, with a mean girlfriend. Holy Christmas cactus!

Claire immediately pulled away.

"I didn't mean to do that," she said.

"No worries." He took a careful step away from her.

Oh, great, there goes another boundary line.

She opened the door before she could make the uncomfortable situation any worse.

"Wait."

Okay, here it comes - Claire winced inwardly - *the boat builder with the PhD and great abs has finally figured out the obvious, that I have a crush on him.* Why hadn't she left a good ten minutes ago instead of staying to make small talk?

"What's the real reason you don't want to spend Christmas with your family?" RJ said.

"I told you." Well, she'd told him what she wanted him to know, having learned something from his own practice of keeping people at a safe distance.

Determined to carry it off like he was just any other guy, she kept her eyes glued to the faint white scar just to the left of the modest cleft. It might be too much temptation to look up at those steady eyes, at least not in such close proximity. That would be dangerous.

"While you're on your Christmas break from your family, you should think about the real reason you're playing the avoidance game."

Her face burned. "I'm just starting a new tradition."

"By yourself?"

"Sure." She shrugged indifferently. "Why not?"

"That's the only reason?"

If Claire didn't know him better, actually she didn't know RJ that well at all, she might have thought he was breaking his own rule about minding one's own business. Hey, if he wasn't opening up to her about his personal life, she wasn't opening up to him.

"It's the only reason."

"Claire."

His tone rubbed her the wrong way. "Don't you 'Claire' me, Mr. Closed-Up-About-Your-Own-Life."

A red stain darkened RJ's cheekbones.

Claire's tendency to say more than she wanted revved up. "That's right. You get people to open up and talk about their issues but I seriously doubt you've ever shared with anyone when there was something you needed to get off your chest or had an issue to work through. I think you just go sailing or hammer away on a boat to get away from your problems. You isolate yourself. Being a therapist, you should know that closing yourself off makes things more difficult to get past."

She'd seen his look of warning before, but that didn't stop her. "Your dog died, yet you refuse to talk about it."

"So."

"Let me back up a bit. Your dad died two years ago and now your dog died. You work with your brother and you get along with him but you never hang out with him. You have a lot of friends and like to hang out in a big group but you don't spend one-on-one time with anyone.

"I spend time with Brandy."

She rolled her eyes.

"I spend time with you."

"Right. When we spend time together, you always call it therapy."

"No," he said. "You always call it therapy."

The conversation was getting off track. "Let's get back to what I'm trying to tell you."

"Claire, you're not my therapist and you are leaving."

Well, that was a bit harsh.

She knew that she was close to losing the invitation to use his cabin, yet she drove right over his biggest boundary line. "I don't think you want to bond too closely with one person because you are afraid to lose someone close to you, again."

The door was wide open and RJ had angry sparks in his eyes. "My next appointment is here."

What? His next appointment? She was supposed to be his only Sunday patient.

A red sports car pulled to the curb. Brandy climbed out of the car, skinny legs and all, and blonde waist-length hair extensions and all. Wearing a long gold-lame puffy down coat and suede winter boots up past her knees, the former athlete turned swimsuit model wore dark glasses over her eyes and glossy red lipstick on her amended lips. Those lips lifted in a snarl as soon as she saw Claire.

"Do you get the feeling she wants to put me in a basement and forget about me?" Claire said.

"She's dealing with a lot right now," RJ said. "Don't take it personally."

"Dealing with what? Lack of social skills?"

"Her last plastic surgery didn't go as planned and it could mean future modeling contracts. Give her a break, okay? She supports her grandmother and younger brother."

Brandy stopped at the bottom step. Her flawless face was as unmoving as a store mannequin. It was hard to tell if the model looked at Claire or RJ. The sunglasses were round like a bug's eyes and just as black.

Brandy always sounded like she was bored. "I hope you're done fixing what can't be fixed. I have stupid presents to buy and I want you to drive me." She spun around and walked back to climb into the passenger seat. "Sometime this year," she said sarcastically before she slammed the car door shut.

"She's got a way of putting me in the Christmas spirit, how about you?" Claire said in a low voice.

Was she imagining it or was RJ slowly counting to ten? Whether she was the cause of his simmering temper or if clarity had finally revealed to him what everyone else saw in his girlfriend, she wasn't about to stick around and find out. She had the cabin key in her purse and her bags were packed even though her escape was two days way. As for informing her mother of her plans, well, timing was everything. She also needed to stop by Brian's house and explain that she needed some time to herself. She would find him at home today because, in all the time that she'd known him, Brian liked to spend his Sundays at home vacuuming while keeping an eye on the sports channel.

But at Brian's house, the blinds were pulled and the morning newspaper still sat on the welcome mat.

Chapter 2

"*O**h, the weather outside is frightful, but the fire is so delightful*," Claire sang as she shifted her BMW sports car into third gear and accelerated onto the freeway. A dusting of snow covered the four-lane freeway that would take her over the Cascade Mountains to the town of Cle Elum. If she timed it right, she should arrive by 2pm, well before sunset. She'd left early on this Christmas Eve Tuesday to avoid the holiday traffic of those making a last dash to the mall before heading to their holiday obligations, or making their own rebellious escape.

In truth, she'd left early before Brian came looking for her asking for an explanation of the Starbucks bag with coffee beans left on his doorstep and the brief note inside. There were two text messages from him asking her to call. But she hadn't. Since her Sunday session with RJ, she'd lost some of her holiday rebel momentum. What she had left she had to reserve for dealing with her mom. Brian would have to wait.

She'd belted out her third Christmas carol since leaving the lake-front community of Kirkland and quickly made the first leg of her escape that involved heavy use of the gas pedal as she ripped past the eastside city of Bellevue. She'd held up her hand like blinders so that she could not see the exit to her parent's home.

Jingle Bells. *Oh Little Town of Bethlehem* and now *Let it Snow*. Okay, enough of the avoidance tactics. Her speed was such that mother-guilt forces would not slow her down. In fact, she was going fast enough that the exits that otherwise might provide an opportunity to turn around, were just a blur.

She hit auto dial on her blue tooth and took in a slow and steadying breath.

"McNaughton residence where Santa knows who's naughty or nice," sang the cheery voice that answered.

"Hi, mom." Claire tightened her hands on the steering wheel.

"Oh, good, Claire. I need you to pick up some eggnog and a bag of those green and red M&M's on your way over. And tell me that you didn't forget to make Auntie Mame's rum balls. Your grandfather will be real disappointed if you forgot again. Also, you and Brian need to wear those pale green sweaters I left at your place. Our family Christmas photo is going to be lovely this year."

"Mom," she began.

"Dinner is at seven. We need to leave early for church services tonight because your dad does not want to park on the street again this year."

"Mom, I—"

"I may need you to wrap a few presents when you get here and I'll need you to run interference if your cousin and his girlfriend start bickering again, which reminds me, I need to hide the good scotch."

"Stop! Mom, stop!"

"Hold on, dear. Your father says that Brian called here earlier looking for you, saying that you were not answering your phone and he needed to talk to you." Her mother paused. "Are you two fighting?"

"No. Mom… I'm not coming to Christmas Eve dinner nor will I be there in the morning to open my stocking."

A heavy sigh broke from her mother. "Claire Marie don't you dare start in on this silly nonsense again. Where else would you go on Christmas Eve? You get your butt over here because the McNaughton's do not break tradition."

"I've made other plans."

The silence on the phone was long enough to get in a few lines of *Silent Night*. But her mother did not always have the best sense of humor.

"Claire Marie. What on earth—"

"I love you, Mom. I just need to be alone this Christmas."

"Oh, God! It's that bad Santa isn't it? He's taken you hostage."

"What bad Santa?"

"The one on the news breaking into homes and taking presents right out from under the Christmas tree. Oh, Claire," her mom's agitation level increased, "please tell me that you haven't been kidnapped."

"I have not been kidnapped." Claire knew it was going to take more than that to calm her mom. In order to keep her from calling out the National Guard, Claire gave up a little information on her plan. "I'm using a friend's cabin in Cle Elum. Don't worry about me. I'll be back in a few days. Love you."

Claire quickly ended the call and set her cell phone to vibrate mode.

It was really happening. The city landscape fell behind her in the rearview mirror and the highway into the mountain range opened before her like freedom's door. Her Christmas. Her way. Didn't mean it was guilt-free. She was almost angry at her mother for this lingering bad taste. She lowered the window for some fresh air and repeated some of RJ's coaching in her head as the miles sped by. "*This is your life, Claire, live it the way you want to.*"

She turned up the volume on the radio station playing Christmas carols.

Run, Run Rudolph blasted through the speakers. She urged the BMW on faster.

As the snowy hills drew closer, she had the strangest thought that maybe she didn't want to be completely alone this Christmas. Those thoughts strayed to RJ and whether he had plans to cozy up to his girlfriend tonight and if he would be handing her a fancy wrapped box from a jewelry store. She bit down on her lip. She should be thinking of Brian and her explanation to him when she returned. She wasn't good at this break up business. Claire would be the first to admit she could talk a crystal chandelier into taking up residency over a dining table made of old wormy barn wood, but when it came to discussing a difficult subject matter with a live person, she sucked. She didn't like to hurt people's feelings.

She concentrated on following the directions to the cabin unaware that her cell phone flashed repeatedly with an incoming call.

Claire had no idea that isolation could be so blissful. A fire crackled in the river rock fireplace. She wore her Frosty the Snowman Christmas socks and a red ceramic mug of hot chocolate warmed her hands. The chill was beginning to leave her bones after trudging one mile up a road closed to vehicles except those of the off-road and snowmobile variety. RJ had informed her that the road would be closed this time of the year.

She had followed his instructions to the Pine Loch Sun neighborhood lodge and parked in one of the guest parking spots alongside two unoccupied sheriff vehicles with their engines still warm and snow melting off their bumpers.

She'd declined RJ's offer to use his snowmobile to get up to the cabin. Even so, there was no snowmobile in the third parking space from the lodge.

Thankfully it was still daylight when she had arrived. And she didn't have to hike in alone. A couple loading their gear onto a toboggan came alongside of her as she skirted around the steel barrier that kept vehicles off the impassable road. Both were dressed in warm winter attire. The woman, wearing a leopard print headband with matching gloves and winter boots, introduced herself as Judy. Her tall boyfriend, named Earl, wore a ski cap and a red down vest over a plaid shirt with several layers underneath. They kindly offered to add her suitcase and small soft-sided cooler onto the toboggan and the three set off up the snow-covered road with Earl pulling the toboggan. Earl had looked back over his shoulder to the sheriff vehicles and commented curiously as to what their presence was all about.

RJ's cabin had surprised her. It wasn't as rustic as she had feared. The two-story, cedar-sided home with a green pitched roof was trimmed with a string of white Christmas lights. A Christmas wreath of fresh cedar boughs adorned the carved front door. The porch leading to the front door extended to the back of the cabin and provided a view through the pine trees of a lake in the distance with snow-covered foothills on the opposite shore. On the hike in, Judy had pointed out the glacier-fed body of water, named Lake Cle Elum. Earl added that elk and wild turkeys frequented the area and not too far off was the town of Roland, a former mining town, now with only abandoned mine shafts.

Claire left the drapes open as night descended, watching the falling snow, visible beneath the white Christmas lights. She looked around the room with appreciation and a bit of envy. This wasn't a cabin but a house with several guest rooms and baths. It was lovely and she couldn't imagine why RJ's girlfriend wanted to spend Christmas elsewhere.

In comparing RJ's home to this cabin, his home was decorated as if he wasn't planning on staying long. The cabin looked like someone had lived here for many years. It was eclectically furnished with an overstuffed red sofa and matching armchairs, antique cabinets and side tables, modern lamps, a chandelier made from deer antlers, and an old rotary style telephone that actually had a dial tone when she lifted the handset.

She had just set the handset back down when the phone rang with a loud jingle that made her jump. The phone rang and rang while she tried to decide if she should answer it. She even had this crazy thought that her mother might actually have a crystal ball and had found her. Or worse, what if it was Brandy who found out that RJ had offered her the use of the cabin and that meant war?

The old rotary wasn't connected to an answering machine. The ringing was going to drive her nuts. She quickly lifted the handset and set it back down again, hoping it was simply a solicitor.

Not two seconds later, the phone rang again. Okay. This was just too creepy. Who else would be calling?

Claire lifted up the phone and unplugged the phone line.

The silence was beautiful and she'd returned to exploring RJ's second home.

A faux fur black bear skin rug covered the hardwood floor in front of the river rock fireplace. The plush-looking rug beckoned an invitation. Even as she considered removing her socks and curling her bare toes into the softness, the thought popped into her head that the rug was purposely big enough for two. She pulled her eyes away from the rug, tried not to think about how often the cabin owner might have used the rug, and continued her admiration of the cabin's furnishings.

Table lamps of bronze retro style skiers and softly lit sconces on the walls provided a romantic golden light. An antique cabinet held the sound system for the large flat-screen television mounted on the wall above. Another antique near the kitchen held a full bar.

Upon her arrival, the cabin air felt chilled so she'd kept her ski hat on and down vest while the baseboard heaters and fire in the fireplace worked to warm the room.

She sank onto the sofa and pulled one of the soft cream-colored knit throw across her lap. The cabin leaned more toward a masculine theme and yet here on the sofa were a pair of needlepoint pillows that completely surprised her. The floral designs were handmade and skillfully done. Not something she imagined Brandy would take the time to do. Perhaps a girlfriend from Christmases past?

Fifteen minutes later with her feet propped on the leather ottoman, staring at the flames in the fireplace between her sock-clad feet and the empty hot chocolate mug on the table beside her, the isolation began to lose its appeal.

She grabbed up her phone and wasn't too surprised to see how many times her mother had called. Nor how many times Brian had called. What she hadn't expected to see was RJ's number on the call log. That was odd. If he was with Brandy on this special evening, why call her?

It was so tempting to call him back. But the message at the top of her phone displayed that there was no cellular service at present. RJ had warned her that the service was hit and miss in the foothills. She wasn't about to plug the rotary style phone back in. She tossed the cell phone on the side table and thought about what she should have for her dinner.

Suddenly she heard heavy footsteps on the front steps. Her imagination went into overdrive. Foremost was her mother's fear that she'd been kidnapped by the bad Santa. Her heart stopped in her throat as someone inserted a key into the lock!

She jumped to her feet, stifling a scream as the front door swept open. Cold snow billowed into the room, momentarily disguising the figure on the threshold.

RJ stomped the snow off his hiking boots then stepping inside and slammed the door shut. "Why the hell are you not answering your cell phone or the cabin phone?" he demanded. RJ carried a flashlight. Snow clung to his black ski jacket, snow pants and hiking boots.

She stared at her neighbor, not believing that he was here and not home with his girlfriend.

It took her a moment to recover. "Holy, freak'n eggnog! What's with scaring me like that?" She gestured toward the hot cocoa down the front of her down vest. "Look what you made me do!"

He grinned sheepishly. "I tried to call and warn you that I was on my way." He shrugged off the backpack and dropped it onto the bench that ran along the wall between the door and the staircase. His ski jacket went on the coat hook next to hers. His boots went next to hers as well before he unzipped the sides of the ski pants to hang them on the coat hook. Looking like he belonged in this cabin in his jeans and forest green flannel shirt with gray t-shirt beneath, RJ rubbed his hands together briskly and headed for the galley kitchen. "I'll make you a coffee nudge to make up for it. I could sure use one."

RJ was no stranger to his kitchen. He went about plugging in the coffee maker and searching in the liquor cabinet to pull out an assortment of bottles.

"I'm sorry," she said, shaking her head to clear it. "Did I get the dates mixed up? Am I not supposed to be here?" Then a really bad thought entered her mind. "Please tell me that Brandy isn't about to come through that door?"

With his head in the pantry, she could barely hear his muffled reply. "No Brandy. I can promise you that."

"No brandy for the coffee nudges or no girlfriend-Brandy?"

He came out of the pantry with his arms loaded. "No girlfriend-Brandy. Got plenty of the good kind, I mean, other kind."

She joined him in the kitchen and began to wipe the spilled hot chocolate from the front of her vest using a wetted dishtowel. "What happened?" she said.

RJ put coffee grounds into the coffee maker and handed her the carafe to fill at the sink. "What do you mean?"

"You were going to spend a glamorous Christmas with your girlfriend."

He back was to her as he opened a can of tuna fish. The granite countertop held ingredients for a meal that Claire eyed suspiciously: box of saltine crackers, jar of dill pickles, can of tuna fish, mayonnaise, a tin of smoked oysters and a jar of green olives.

"Hungry?" she asked.

"Starved."

She poured the carafe of water into the coffee maker and pressed the start button.

"See if there is a can of whipped cream in the refrigerator, will you?" RJ said.

"So what happened?" she said.

"Her idea of glamorous wasn't what I wanted."

"So…that's why you're here? To boot me out 'cause you want the cabin instead?"

He loaded a large plate with an arrangement of crackers, sliced pickles, a small bowl with the tuna and mayonnaise mixture, a pile of green olives and another pile of smoked oysters. The coffee maker hissed as it finished its cycle. He pulled two mugs from a cupboard and expertly prepared their coffee nudges with big dollops of whipped cream on top.

"You grab those." He picked up the platter and some napkins.

She followed him into the front room where they sat before the fireplace with their snacks on the large ottoman.

"RJ," she said, trying again to get a straight answer from him. "What's going on? If you're not here to be with Brandy, then why are you here? Not that you can't visit your own cabin."

"I'm here to make sure you're all right."

This surprised her. "Well of course I'm all right. Why wouldn't I be?"

"There's a manhunt on for a phony Santa who robbed several Seattle homes. He was last seen at the grocery store in Cle Elum."

"A manhunt?" Claire couldn't believe this. "Here on the mountain?" Then she remembered the sheriff vehicles in the parking lot and mentioned this to RJ.

"They weren't there when I arrived. Could be they're searching another neighborhood. But I did see plenty of sheriff's vehicles coming over the pass."

"My mom mentioned something about this bad Santa." She frowned in puzzlement. "All that fuss over a Santa who stole Christmas presents from a few homes?"

"Apparently, one of those presents was a gun with ammo. The homeowner tried to stop him and the Santa hit him over the head with a heavy candy cane decoration in the front yard. This Santa on the run is considered armed and dangerous."

"So you came all this way to warn me?"

RJ focused on loading tuna fish onto his cracker and adding a slice of pickle before putting another cracker on top and putting the entire sandwich into his mouth.

"I'm likely not in any danger, RJ," she continued. "This guy will probably just keep on running."

"Let's hope so or at least they catch him soon."

It warmed her heart that he was here to check on her. "You really didn't have to drive all this way to warn me."

"If you'd answered the phone, maybe I wouldn't have had to," he said with a teasing wink.

It was her turn to smile sheepishly.

He held up his mug to toast her. "Merry Christmas."

Still nervous about the girlfriend, she said, "Does Brandy know you are here?"

"She doesn't need to know I'm here."

Knowing that the volleyball spiker wouldn't be walking through that door tonight was enough to help Claire relax, some, but not completely.

She tapped her mug against his. "Merry Christmas."

"I'll leave in the morning," he said, no doubt to reassure her that his intentions were good. "Just wanted to make sure you were okay."

RJ propped his feet up on the ottoman, looking like a man perfectly content to be nowhere else but here.

She wasn't so comfortable. She'd yet to break up with Brian and here she was in a romantic and secluded cabin with a handsome man that she was attracted to. In her case: a highly dangerous situation.

The fire crackled cheerily away and warmed the room. With her heart beating a rhythm faster than the clock over the mantle, she drained the last of the heavily imbrued warm drink and curled back into the cushions of the sofa. RJ had poured a good amount of alcohol into the coffee nudge and she was beginning to relax.

Winter brewed its snowy magic outside. Something else was at work in this secluded cabin. Was it not but an hour ago that she thought the bear rug just wouldn't be fun for one? Now look who was here.

Although he sat at an appropriate distance from a houseguest, the lights were not so dimmed that she couldn't detect a look of kindled interest in his eyes.

The alcohol in her coffee drink liberated her imagination and the speculation wheels began to turn as she tried to figure out what RJ might be thinking. Her eyes widened as a thought came to her. If he couldn't have Brandy for Christmas, was he planning on working his way down the alphabet? What were the chances that the woman who'd made the needlepoint pillows had a name that started with an A? Allison. Yes, those pillows looked like they were made by an Allison. Or maybe a Yvonne or a Zena had made them and RJ was back to the top of the alphabet again. He was done with A and B and now ready for a C.

Claire jumped up. "Can I get you something from the kitchen?" Without meeting his eye, she cleared their dinner dishes and exited to the safety of the galley kitchen.

Snow flurries beat against the window over the stainless steel sink. The exterior Christmas lights surrounded the cabin in a holiday golden glow. She gripped the edge of the sink and tried to get her head together. Didn't work. She downed two full glasses of tinny-tasting water in an attempt to dilute the alcohol in her system and stop her wild imagination. Alphabet dating? Where'd she come up with that? That aside, although RJ had let his guard down a time or two in the past and sent her a wink or an admiring glance, tonight was different. Whether it was the secluded cabin, or something else, he wasn't showing any of the usual reserved nature of a man with a girlfriend. No. The vibes were a whole lot different tonight. She wished she could ignore these vibes and focus only on Brian. That would be the right thing to do until she'd official ended their relationship.

She washed the dishes in the sink and set them to dry in the dish drain. Outside, dark green pine trees were visible with their branches bending from the snow burden. So much snow had fallen that even the footprints up to the cabin were no longer visible.

"Did you walk up from the parking lot?" she called out to RJ.

"Yes," he said. She heard him moving around in the other room. "Typically I ride up on my snowmobile, but I let my neighbor borrow it when I'm not here. In return, he keeps me supplied with firewood. I'm assuming he's up here because the beast wasn't in its parking space."

Claire knew she was taking too long returning to the living room. She fussed with kitchen things that didn't need fussing with. She wiped down dry counters and invisible crumbs.

"Cabernet or a Merlot?" RJ appeared holding up two bottles of wine.

"Water."

"Water?" he laughed. "If you want water, check the pantry for bottled water. The tap water tastes lousy. While you're at it, grab two wine glasses."

Two cupboard doors later, she left the safety of the kitchen to return to dangerous territory. The room looked more inviting than ever with flames dancing joyfully to embrace the newly added log in the fireplace. White candles flickered on the mantle and only one lamp remained lit in a far corner, leaving the sofa and its soft pillows half in shadows yet still inviting. The flickering flames from the fireplace cast a pool of golden light across the bear skin rug.

RJ worked the wine opener into the top of the wine bottle. The wine bottle was not giving up the cork that easily. In fact, it appeared that the wine bottle was winning.

"Do you know what you're doing?" she asked, teasingly.

"This is not my first rodeo." He said in his self-assured manner, his attention fixed on the task at hand until he gave a final expert twist of the wine opener and the cork came out with a quiet pop. "Just takes a man good with his hands." He smiled.

Oh, dear, thought Claire, what was her boyfriend's name again?

RJ set the wine bottle on the side table while blindly pointing a remote control at the antique armoire, now with doors open.

"My dad's old stereo," RJ said, "and his music collection."

The softly rhythmic music of Boz Skaggs' *Look What You've Done to Me*' eased into the room from a sound system where blue lights twinkled like a small city existed in the blackness of the cabinet.

Candlelight, wine and sexy music, could this evening grow any more dangerous?

Chapter 3

She had seconds to decide whether to take another step into this romantic scene or find an excuse to escape to the guestroom until morning when she would return dutifully to spend the remainder of Christmas with the boyfriend she wanted to break up with.

If this were any other man, she would have faked a yawn and executed the "not interested" removing of her person from the scene.

The problem was, that this wasn't just any man. This was RJ, a man who both interested her and excited her, on all levels. Try stopping that train.

But she had to. Considering the number of times Brian had attempted to propose she was practically engaged, according to her mom. Even though she didn't want a lasting and sustainable relationship with Brian, she at least had to make a clean break from him. That was only fair.

As for RJ, just because he wasn't spending a holiday with his girlfriend, didn't give him license to light candles and play love songs in the company of another woman. What was up with that? And what about the needlepoint woman? In fact, what about all the other women who participated in one of his smoothly set in motion romantic scenes? And there had to be plenty. This man was no novice. Alphabet dating spun through her head again and with it came the thought that there was a benefit to all that experience. Well, if she was going to be honest, what woman didn't sometimes wonder what it would be like to be with a man who could expertly drive any model of car and know how to handle a stick shift? Seriously. What woman didn't have that thought a time, or two?

"I thought you wanted water?" RJ winked at her as he took the wine goblets from her hands.

A smart woman would return to the cooler temperature of the kitchen seeking escape from the magic of candlelight and a bear skin rug. And this man.

"I'll try the Merlot," she said.

It was getting warm in here. She removed her ski cap and down vest. To cool her neck, she swept her hair over her shoulder. After accepting the glass of wine from RJ, she made a point of sitting in the opposite club chair. RJ made no comment. Whether he was amused or put off, she couldn't tell. His face was half in shadow as he took a sip of wine and sat down again on the sofa. She took two gulps of wine to settle her nerves.

"Do you have any board games?" she asked.

"None." He took another sip of his wine. She could have sworn a smile played at the corner of his mouth.

"Deck of cards?" she tried again.

"Can't remember where I put them."

She drummed her fingers on the arm of the chair. She could play this game. Maybe not as expertly as he could, but she wouldn't make this easy for him.

"What did you get Brandy for Christmas?"

He shot her a look, took a sip of his wine then set the glass on the side table. "How did your mom take the news?"

She rolled her eyes. "I'm probably being disowned as I speak."

"And your boyfriend?" RJ took advantage of having the sofa to himself and stretched out his long legs and folded his arms behind his head. "Or are you going to need a few sessions on how to break up with your boyfriend?"

She sucked in a horrified breath.

The therapist look he sent her said he wasn't about to go easy on her. "Don't act so shocked. We both know the real reason you're not spending Christmas with your parents is because you're trying to avoid Brian and another proposal."

"You do not know that!"

"Is it the truth?"

"Up yours!"

He drained his wine glass and seemed not in the least bothered by her anger. "I do believe that answered my question."

Steam rolled out from her ears. She drained her wine glass and set it down. "Why don't you try giving yourself some therapy? You date a woman who is not in the least your type. And I think I know why that is. In fact, I bet Allison wasn't your type either and purposely so. You date women you wouldn't be compatible with long term because, again, you don't want to get too close to someone in case you lose them."

He sat up, swinging his legs to the floor. "What the hell are you talking about and who is Allison?"

She rolled her eyes. "The woman who made the needlepoint pillows."

RJ looked thunderously perplexed. His eyes swung to the pillows and he snatched one up. "My grandmother made these and her name was Barbara."

She sure could have used a reindeer landing on the roof about now. A tension-laced silence filled the space between them. What was he expecting, an apology for an insanely wild accusation that came from a woman who held only Sunday-therapy-friendship status?

She held up her empty wine glass. "Refill?"

RJ scowled as he took their wine glasses over to the bar for a refill. He shook his head back and forth as he emptied the bottle of wine equally into their glasses. "Allison? Did you just pull that name out of thin air? I've never dated a woman named Allison before. Maybe an Anna or an Alicia."

"All right, okay." Claire swung her foot in agitation. "I'm sorry."

He handed her a full wine glass. Then to her surprise, he tapped his glass against hers for the second time that evening, although it had more of a "round two" ring to it rather than a "Merry Christmas" ring.

He returned to his reclining position. She braced herself. Maybe she didn't know RJ as well as she wished she did, but by the look of his set jaw and the glint in his eye, he wasn't going to let her off the hook for her freely offered relationship advice.

"For your information," he began, "I'll admit to having a hard time getting over my dad passing so early. And, I miss my dog." He looked down at the floor for a moment. "You're right. I should spend more time with my brother, and my buddies - for that matter. I realize now that I isolated myself after my dad died. It was such a shock to lose him."

"I'm sorry."

"Thank you."

In her merlot-warmed mind, she knew that she had entered the hunter's den exactly as he'd intended with the lure of sexy music and the romantic, warm glow from the fireplace. Part of her didn't care. She glanced over to the bear skin rug and tried to recall the last time she'd removed her clothes for fun. Brian wasn't exactly an eager volunteer of that activity.

"Claire."

"Oh, yes. What?"

"Are you falling asleep on me?"

She sat up straight. "No. Honestly. I was just thinking—
"

"About what?"

About not making a fool of myself. "Go on," Claire said. "You were about to lecture me about not giving you advice."

RJ wore a crooked grin. "I was saying that you shouldn't *assume* that the reason a guy doesn't let a woman get close isn't because he doesn't want to be close to someone special. Maybe he's just not connecting with that particular woman."

He had her attention. "I'm listening."

"Brandy was good company at first. Until she stopped trying to be someone she wasn't."

"What wasn't she?"

"A nice person."

Claire snorted a laugh. "I could have told you that."

RJ shrugged. "She picked me up at a bar one night after dad died. She was something to do, a distraction."

"There's nothing wrong with a distraction." Claire didn't care to discuss his girlfriend but was doing her best to be a good listener, however unpleasant the topic.

"She had good qualities."

Okay, that was too much. "Where? In her breasts?"

"Claire," he admonished. "She supports her grandmother and younger brother. She's taking them with her to Brazil."

She had to give Brandy credit for providing financial support to her family. She suddenly sat up straight. "Brazil?"

"So you are paying attention."

"She's moving to Brazil?" she repeated.

"Yup. She was offered a very lucrative modeling contract. So she packed up and left."

She stared at RJ. Why could she not make sense of this? "She's in Brazil and you are here."

"Yup."

She didn't want to know, but the question was out before she was ready to hear the answer. "Are you moving down there with her?"

RJ suddenly turned his head toward the front door. "Did you hear that?"

"What?"

There was a solid thump on the ground outside. "That." He stood. "I'd better check it out."

Icy wind and a swirl of snow flurries swept into the foyer as RJ opened the door. Beyond the golden halo cast onto the ground from the Christmas lights, the dark night held an ominous feeling.

"I don't think you should go out there." She'd followed him to the door.

"It's probably just snow sliding off the roof," he said, sticking his feet into his hiking boots but not bothering to lace them. He zipped up his ski jacket. "Tell my mother I love her, if I'm not back in five."

"That's not funny."

He shut the door on the snowy cold and she was left in the sudden quiet of the cabin.

A horrible thought entered her mind, one that squeezed painfully at her heart. Did he find an excuse to go outside because he didn't want to tell her the truth? That he was moving to Brazil with Brandy? So why was he here? No. She was not going to visit the alphabet dating scenario again.

My God, he was a confusing man. Hadn't he just said that Brandy was only a distraction? That didn't sound like the qualities one looked for in a lasting relationship. Did he want to be with Brandy or not? She looked down into her wine glass and made a note to herself that, in the future, she would not try to figure out a man while slightly tipsy.

She returned to the armchair with the knit throw over her to wait for RJ's return. Even though she knew he was kidding, she kept her eyes on the clock.

She was wine sleepy and her eyes drooped but she wasn't about to doze off until RJ was safely back inside. Although that would mean he'd likely announce, then, that he was moving to Brazil. Maybe she should just march herself off to bed and let him freeze out there, would serve him right if he had plans to seduce her as a parting gift before joining Brandy in Brazil.

Claire knew right then, that, sure as Christmas, she would not be another one of RJ's women in his long list of alphabet women. She didn't want to be just a distraction.

Holy rum balls. She was in trouble.

RJ was taking too long, making Claire very concerned. When the next thump sounded outside, Claire was at the fireplace in two heartbeats taking up the fireplace poker. This was getting a bit scary. She hurried over to turn off the stereo system so that she could listen more intently. The cabin was uncomfortably quiet. She moved back to stand in front of the fireplace and to keep an eye on the front door.

A draft of cold air moved across her cheek and lifted a strand of her hair from her neck before extinguished one of the candles.

"RJ?" she called out.

The lights flickered.

And, flickered again.

"No," Claire whispered as the lights went out. "No. No. No."

Her pulse raced fearfully. She tightened her grip on the fireplace poker.

The only relief from the darkness of the room came from the remaining candles on the mantle, their dancing flames sending shadows along the wall, and the low flames from the dwindling fire in the fireplace. At least it was a friendly pool of light cast out to the edge of the seating area. But beyond that, the foyer and stairs, kitchen and hallway to the bedrooms lay in mysterious darkness.

"RJ, is that you?" she called out.

A log gave way in the fireplace and rolled against the grate. She jumped, dropping the fireplace poker. Another thump, this time from somewhere in the house, had her falling to all fours onto the bear skin rug, frantically feeling around for the poker. So intent was she in her desperate search that she didn't hear RJ come up behind her in stocking feet.

"What are you doing down there?"

She let out a scream.

RJ stood above her in the candle's glow, warming his hands by the fire and brushing snow from his hair.

"Oh my, God, you scared me half to death." She fell over onto the rug with a hand over her heart and her arm draped over her eyes.

RJ lowered down to sit with his long legs stretched out in front of him and his back to the oversized fireplace screen. He gave her legs a playful nudge. "You're jumpy."

"The lights went out and I kept hearing thumping noises. Do you know what it sounded like?"

"What?" He smiled.

"Like someone dragging a body down the stairs."

He laughed. "You have quite the imagination."

"Hey! I was worried about you." She sat up and smacked him on the shoulder.

"You were worried about me? That's sweet."

"Yeah." She smiled back at him. "I can be sweet."

He brushed her long fringe of bangs out of her eyes. "You're always sweet. It's part of your nature."

She was melting again, and nervous again. And low and behold, they were both now on the bear skin rug.

She kept perfectly still on the rug with her legs tucked beside her. Her knee was not but a few inches from his thigh. "What did you find outside?" She wanted to talk about anything but either one of them.

"Just like I suspected, snow is sliding off the roof and off the trees. That's the thumping we're hearing. It's not very safe outside, right now." He put a hand to the back of his neck and came away with small chunks of snow that he flicked off to the side.

"How did you get back inside?"

"I came in through the garage. I keep a key hidden outside."

Her heart slowed from the fright, yet her pulse continued in a steady beat sitting so close to RJ.

Firelight lit up his handsome profile. She could see the crow's feet at the corners of his eyes, lines that she guessed were from all his smiling and time spent outdoors.

Without the baseboard heater humming away, the temperature in the cabin began to dip. RJ added more logs to the fire. He collected her down vest and ski hat from the chair where she had tossed them, and dragged the two knit throws from the sofa. He spread one of the knit throws across her legs and then his own after reclining on the rug with his back to the fireplace.

Claire smiled her thanks and slipped on the down vest, settling the ski cap onto her head.

"As soon as I thaw out, I'll go back outside and get the generator started. Are you warm enough for now?" he asked.

"Yes, thank you." Beneath her hands, the luxurious silkiness of the rug added its own warm and comfort.

The fire snapped and crackled and cocooned them in its warmth and glow as the snow continued to fall on this Christmas Eve. RJ smiled at her in a way that made her feel so young at heart, like this was their adventure, something that only the two of them would share in a memory one day.

Her question as to whether he planned to move to Brazil was yet unanswered. But with that warm look in his eyes, she knew he wasn't thinking of anything else but here and now.

Maybe this wasn't going to end the way she wanted. Heck, maybe a woman just shouldn't ask questions or think about the order of things when she knew that a moment like this might never happen again, not with someone who made her feel as RJ did.

RJ leaned towards her. She knew what was about to happen, yet, he hesitated.

"Claire?" he said. His eyes locked on her lips.

"Yes?"

"In my younger days, I might have kissed another man's woman. I'm not so sure I should be doing that tonight."

"Probably not," she said, hoping that he would kiss her anyway, "but, in truth, I've been trying to break up with Brian for the last six months. We're just not right for the other."

"Mm. Sounds like you need to have a talk, the two of you."

"Yes," she replied. It was time for that.

There was warmth in his eyes, enough to know that this man liked her, but in addition, there was now a decisive set to his jaw. She knew then that RJ wasn't going to kiss her.

She was learning something new about him tonight. This boundary line man wasn't going to go into another man's territory.

"Are you moving to Brazil?" she asked softly.

"No," he said with the seriousness she needed to hear.

"You and Brandy are done?"

"Yes."

"So, I could kiss you and not get into trouble."

His eyes crinkled. "Oh, I think you'd find yourself in trouble. Just not from Brandy."

She leaned closer until her mouth was only a breath away from his.

"I wouldn't do that if I were you," he said, without taking his eyes off her lips.

Claire grabbed hold of his shirt and pulled him with her as she slowly eased back onto the rug. He didn't resist until she was on her back and he hovered a few inches above her. He braced his arms to either side of her, trapping her long hair under one of his hands.

"Let's stop this here," he said. "It wouldn't be fair to Brian."

She didn't release her grip on his shirt. She felt the warmth of his leg against hers and his breath across her cheekbone. No other part of him touched her. With Brian, she never held his gaze for long. With RJ, she couldn't look away.

"What if I don't care what Brian thinks?"

"You might think clearer in the morning when the wine wears off." This from the man who had set this romantic scene to begin with?

She released him. RJ wasted no time moving to sit on the arm of the chair. It worked like cold water.

Claire sat up. "*You* poured the wine. *You* turned on the sexy music and lit the candles."

He lifted his hands admitting his guilt, but said nothing.

"Why? If you were not planning on seducing me?"

RJ ran a hand through his hair. "All right. I'll admit to all of that. Being free of Brandy, the first thing I thought of was you. It was impulsive, but I just got in my car and drove up here.

She was stunned by this admission.

"I planned to put the moves on you. My way of convincing you to break up with Brian, I suppose. Not very nice of me, I'm afraid. But since we're talking truth tonight, finding alone time with you is all I've thought about since you moved next door to me."

She was on her feet. "RJ..."

He stood as well but only to put the armchair between them. "When the snow slid off the roof and onto my head, it was like my grandma boxing my ears all over again." He paused. "I'm not going to sleep with a woman I like as much as you only to find out later that you can't break up with Brian."

She'd never seen RJ so serious before.

"I couldn't take that, Claire." He removed a flashlight from the drawer of the side table. "I'll take the bedroom down here. You can have the upstairs bedroom. I'll help you get to your car in the morning."

RJ didn't make it two steps down the dark hallway when he suddenly stopped and backed up, holding his hands in the air.

Claire initially saw only the bottom half of a man stepping out of the shadows, wearing sopping wet red baggy pants and running shoes on his feet. As he slowly moved into the room she noticed he wore an equally wet army coat unbuttoned over the rest of his rumpled Santa costume. The dark-haired man had a five-o'clock shadow and red rimmed eyes. He wiped his bright red nose along the sleeve of his army jacket while holding a handgun steadily aimed at RJ.

"Appreciate you leaving the garage door unlocked for me," he said with a Southern accent. "Sugar-pie," he said to Claire. "Get over here with your boyfriend; makes it easier to shoot you both if I have to."

Chapter 4

The bad Santa dried out before the fire, eating RJ's crackers and tuna fish snack.

"Get me another beer," he said to Claire with his mouth full.

"She's not getting you a beer," RJ nearly growled. "I'll get it, asshole." RJ laid a comforting hand on Clair's knee before rising from the sofa where they'd both been ordered to sit.

"I'll come with you." Clair said.

"Hold it. Hold it." The bad Santa used his gun to direct the two of them to stay put. "I'm no dummy. The two of you are not leaving this room, together." With a smear of mayonnaise at the corner of his mouth, the bad Santa ordered RJ to remain in the living room. "Your girlfriend goes and gets me a beer and that's that. Unless you want me to put a hole in her head, *asshole*."

Claire made quick work of retrieving a beer from the refrigerator. She felt like a robot, walking over to the intruder, handing him the cold can without touching his hand. But the creep made sure his big, fat hand closed over her fingers and he squeezed hard. She had to forcefully pull her hand out from under his sweaty hand. He laughed, popped the beer open and guzzled it down.

He belched his *thank you.* A cloud smelling of beer and tuna fish floated back to the sofa.

RJ waited until Claire was back on the sofa beside him before saying again to the intruder, "What do you want?"

The rumpled red suit belched again. "Don't get antsy with me. I'm here to dry out and get a meal and then I'll be out of your hair. Oh, and if you have any cash on hand or expensive watches, I'll be taking those." He held the beer in one hand and pointed the handgun at Claire. "What kind of car are you driving?"

"Why?"

"'Cause the cheapskate owner of a snowmobile couldn't be bothered to leave a full tank for me. Now what kind of car are you driving?"

RJ stiffened beside her.

Could she lie and get away with it? "Subaru."

He snorted a laugh. "Can't see you in any of those older style granola wagons down there. There's a white BMW in the parking lot. Bet that's yours."

Claire tensed. This man was not going to steal her new car. "I said, I drove a Subaru."

"Sugar-pie, if I take your car keys and find they don't open any Subaru down there, I'm not going be too happy. And you'll know 'cause you're coming with me."

She swallowed the lump of fear in her throat. "The BMW is mine."

"Thought so."

"You said you wanted a meal and then you'd leave," RJ reminded their intruder.

"I can lie just like her." With his mouth full of saltine crackers, their uninvited houseguest said to Claire, "Bring me your handbag, liar, liar pants on fire."

"She's not going anywhere with you."

Claire recognized the steel set to RJ's jaw as she walked her handbag over to the bad Santa.

Keeping one eye on RJ, the Santa dumped her handbag upside down onto the bear skin rug. "Think you're a tough guy, don't ya?" he said. He put the BMW car keys in his pocket and proceeded to empty her pocketbook of her cash. "Jackpot!" He grinned as he held up a fistful of cash. He then instructed RJ to toss him his wallet. *"All I want for Christmas is other people's money,"* he sang as he claimed the large bills from RJ's wallet. "Won't get me far but it will get me somewhere." He looked about the cabin. "Now, what do we do 'till morning?"

Morning sun streamed in through the window in the front door. Claire's breath clouded in the chilled air. She was stiff from the long, uncomfortable night on the bear skin rug, with her wrists tied together in front of her and her ankles bound as well. Luckily, she had the warmth from RJ's long form stretched out beside her, tied up in a similar fashion.

The bad Santa snored away on the sofa beneath the down comforter from a guest room. Another down comforter lay over the top of Claire and RJ. Her shoulder and hip hurt from having to lie in one position all night.

"You okay?" RJ moved beside her.

"Yes," she whispered. "I'm freezing, sore and hungry. But I guess we should be glad that that's the worst of it, so far."

"Agreed." RJ had spent some of the night trying to work the ropes loose. He cursed behind her. "Damn crook is good with the ropes."

On the end table near the Santa's head, Claire's cell phone began to vibrate and the face lit up.

"I bet that's my mom calling," she whispered.

RJ lifted his head to look over her shoulder.

The bad Santa woke up, blinking his eyes as if not recognizing his surroundings. He sat up quickly, stretching his arms over his head and yawning loudly. All the while, Claire's phone vibrated and blinked on the end table.

The bad Santa looked at Claire and RJ. There was no cheerful Santa this morning. He scratched his chin and frowned. The phone vibrated again and caught his attention.

He picked up the cell phone and read the caller ID. "Mom," he said. "Isn't that cute." He looked over at his hostages. "Whose phone is this?"

"Mine," Claire said.

Bad Santa pressed a button and put the phone to his ear. "Hey, mom, Merry Christmas." He paused, as if listening to the response. "What do you mean, who is this? I'm your long lost son and I want a spanking." He laughed. "Do you want to speak to your daughter?" He listened for a moment then said, "Well you can't!" Bad Santa disconnected the call. He looked at the phone closer. "You got a data plan?" he said to Claire.

"Yes."

"Nice." He put the cell phone in the pocket of his army jacket.

"Creep," Claire said under her breath.

"Easy, there," RJ said near her ear. "He'll be out of our lives soon."

"Time to roll." Bad Santa was on his feet, yawning and scratching again at his beard. Claire stifled a gasp when he pulled a pocketknife from his pocket. The bad Santa deftly cut his prisoners loose.

RJ helped Claire to her feet, both of them working out the stiff kinks. The bad Santa glanced at an expensive watch on his wrist that Claire didn't believe for a minute was hard earned.

Both she and RJ were allowed to use the bathroom, one at a time. And then to Claire's disbelief, the Santa made the two of them stand in the hallway while he left the door open and used the facilities, all while keeping the handgun trained on them.

"Unbelievable," RJ muttered, both he and Claire trying to look everywhere but the open doorway to the restroom.

Claire and RJ donned their ski jackets, hats and boots and were ordered to stand near the front door while their captor peered through the window over the sink.

"Looks as quiet as a Christmas morn'," he said. His eyes fell on RJ's large backpack. Then on RJ's six foot, athletic frame. With his hand patting his own thick waistline, he sized up RJ. "Think we wear the same size jeans?"

"No," RJ's reply was curt.

"You boxers or briefs?"

"Are you shitting me?" RJ was losing patience.

"Answer the question, asshole."

"Boxers, asshole."

"What size socks?"

"For Christ sake! Take my backpack. I don't care."

Claire put a reassuring hand on RJ's arm. They didn't need a knock down drag out fight with a man holding a gun and a knife.

"What's the plan?" Claire asked.

The bad Santa first made quick work of emptying RJ's backpack of all but the socks and the toiletry bag. He inspected the bag's contents of razor, toothpaste, toothbrush, deodorant and a sleek black tube. As if a manhunt in place to search for this criminal was not a pressing concern for him, the bad Santa twisted off the top of the black tube and sniffed. "What's this for?" he asked RJ.

"Lotion."

"No wonder you got nice skin." Bad Santa squirted some of the white lotion into his hands, rubbed them together and then rubbed it all over his face, leaving white streaks on his forehead and cheeks. Satisfied with that, he proceeded to take from the refrigerator the remaining cans of beer, a package of cheddar cheese, a tube of refrigerator cinnamon rolls and a jar of green olives. He slung the backpack over his shoulder. "Ho. Ho. Ho." He grinned through his darkening beard and gestured with the handgun toward the door. "Let's go."

The glare of the snow blinded them as they stepped outside, RJ keeping a tight hold on Claire's hand and keeping himself between her and their captor. All was quiet in this winter wonderland. The pine trees stood with snow holding down their branches. Sunlight glistened off the ice crystals on the frozen snow.

Walking was difficult as they broke through the top frozen layer of knee-high snow and made their way to the road. It was hard to tell where RJ's property ended and the road began.

They passed several cabins with smoke curling from their chimneys. Claire could not remember which cabin belonged to Judy and Earl. Still, she silently wished for one of them to be looking out their window at this early hour. Their progress was slow down the steep road that twisted through the pine trees. RJ's firm grip on her hand kept her steady. The buckles on the backpack jingled behind them. Bad Santa sang under his breath as they walked.

"I saw mommy doing Santa Clause, again and again and again -"

RJ came to an abrupt stop. "Seriously?"

"Come on," Claire urged RJ. "Just keep walking."

Off in the distance, helicopter blades beat the air.

"What's that?" Bad Santa had at least stopped singing.

RJ exchanged a look with Claire. She saw the hope of rescue in his eyes but he kept his expression neutral as he said to their captor, "Maybe it's the real Santa coming to kick your ass."

"Hey, wise guy," Bad Santa said, "I'm getting real tired of your attitude. I'm thinking that your girlfriend is, too, and that she'd rather be with me. What do you think about that?" he said to Claire. "Want to do it with me in the backseat of your BMW?"

RJ dropped his shoulder and charged the Santa full bore, knocking him flat out on his back in the deep snow. The dark hair and army jacket disappeared into the deep snow with RJ's hands around his neck.

"Look out!" Claire called out a warning.

The nose of the handgun pressed into the side of RJ's neck. "Get - off."

With careful deliberation, RJ stood, doing his best to control his anger. He was forced to help the Santa to his feet when ordered to do so.

Breathing hard, and trying to regain his authority, bad Santa repositioned his backpack but he kept a careful distance from the taller man with more muscle.

The beating in the sky grew closer. Their captor sent a nervous glance toward the tall trees above them on the hillside.

"Hurry it up." He pointed his gun at them. "Keep moving and no talking."

They proceeded on; their boots making noise as they broke through the frozen snow, the bad Santa breathing heavy behind them. Alongside the road and deep into the pine forest, branches were breaking under the burden of the wet snow. The first time a branch snapped off, they all jumped.

Their captor's nervousness increased to the point where he was moving faster than Claire and RJ and kept having to slow in order to keep them in front of him so that he could keep his gun trained on them. They came around a corner where a cabin sat nestled against the trees with smoke curling from its chimney and a Christmas wreath and red bow on its front door. Further down the road, the parking lot was in view with its snow-covered vehicles.

Claire swallowed her disappointment at not seeing any sheriff vehicles or fresh tracks from any vehicle that might indicate that they were not alone. The cars in the parking lot looked like they were not going anywhere soon - including her own.

They walked around the road barricade where tall pine trees stood to each side. The snow was so deep around the perimeter of the trees and their overhang of branches that wells had formed around the base of the trees.

"Looks like you two are going to be busy, uncovering my new wheels," Bad Santa said.

There came another snap of a breaking branch from the tree line. Suddenly there was a blur of movement. A dark-haired man in a ski jacket charged out from behind a tree.

The bad Santa was caught off guard as he was tackled from the side. Staggering backwards with the heavy backpack acting as an anchor, bad Santa fell back into a tree well with his attacker on top of him. RJ spun around, and after his initial surprise, immediately dove in to assist. The struggle that ensued dumped snow from the branches above to completely cover the three men below.

"He has a gun!" Claire tried to warn the other man.

A helicopter suddenly appeared over the top of the parking lot, its blades beating the air and sending snow flying from the trees and whirling up from the parking lot. Two armed men jumped from the helicopter just as several more ran out from the trees. Someone grabbed Claire and pulled her to safety behind a snow-covered vehicle.

The helicopter landed in a nearby field and the snow began to settle.

A swarm of armed law enforcement officers dressed in black and dark green winter jackets and snow pants converged under the branches of the pine tree.

One by one, three snow-covered men were pulled out from the snow well and from under the overhanging branches. Claire breathed a sigh of relief to see RJ's familiar broad shoulders and also the dark-haired man she recognized as Earl.

Completely covered in snow and looking like a badly dressed snowman, bad Santa was pulled out from the tree well not looking so well with a red lump swelling over one eye and a bloody lip.

Claire rushed over to throw her arms around RJ. She buried her face into his ski jacket. RJ hugged her close and kissed the top of her head. "It's over," he said.

Judy came running down the hill with her ski jacket unzipped and her hair flying. She threw her arms around Earl, the man who'd first tackled the bad Santa. "I called 911 but they said someone had already called it in."

RJ's backpack was returned to him as well as Claire's car keys and her cell phone. The cash was now evidence along with other valuables and cash found in the Bad Santa's big pockets.

A sheriff's vehicle drove out of the parking lot with the apprehended Santa in the back seat. Two power company vehicles slowed on their way out of the neighborhood, the drivers looking curiously over at the gathering of law enforcement vehicles. A trail grooming vehicle operated by a sheriff's deputy lumbered slowly into the parking lot towing a snowmobile behind.

A vehicle pulled into the parking lot and two women climbed out and proceeded to set up a coffee and sandwich station for the volunteers and officers coming down the hill from their part in the manhunt.

"My poor mom," she said to RJ, thinking how alarming it must have been for her mom to have a stranger answer her daughter's phone. On cue, her cell phone vibrated. Claire quickly answered. "Mom? It's me. It's okay. We're safe."

"Oh, thank, God. Claire, honey, I was so worried. My instincts told me that you were in trouble. That's why I called the sheriff's office. I gave them your cell phone number and they said they might be able to track you by satellite. Who was that rude man on the phone?"

"It's a long story. But I promise to tell you everything as soon as I get home."

"Honey, if you want to spend Christmas somewhere else, we understand. We love you, sweetheart. We're just glad you're safe." The shake in her mom's voice was audible. Her mom took a deep breath. "Dear, there's something you need to know."

"What?"

"Sweetheart, I'm afraid it's bad news."

What news could be bad after an experience like this? Claire moved away from RJ, and Earl and Judy who had just joined them bringing with them hot coffee in paper cups. She stopped two snow-covered bumpers away from the group in order to have more privacy. "What is it?" she said, bracing herself.

"Well, dear, you don't have a boyfriend any more. Brian's been trying to call you but he finally just left me a message. He broke up with you, sweetie. I'm so sorry. He said he met someone else and had a plane to catch to the Bahamas." Her mother sounded put out. "What a louse. It would have been nice of him to tell us before I had your father hang fifty three dollars-worth of mistletoe all over this damn house."

Claire couldn't believe what she'd just heard. "Did you say that Brian broke up with *me*?"

RJ and Earl were exchanging details of the take-down when RJ suddenly stopped and locked eyes on Claire.

Aside from the little burn that comes from being dumped, Claire also felt some guilt at the relief she immediately felt.

"Don't worry, sweetheart," was her mom's advice, "there are other fish in the sea. Think of Brian as the little flounder. What you need to do, dear, is to go for the big tuna."

Her mom said goodbye, adding that as long as Claire had other plans for Christmas, they were going to accept their neighbor's invitation for eggnog and poker. Claire slipped the cellphone into her pocket. Here she was, suddenly unattached, although the news delivery was third-hand, she still took it as official. And yet, she wasn't quite sure what to do next. She was suddenly nervous in front of RJ like a shy freshman at a school dance.

RJ wasn't even listening to Earl and Judy. He took a sip of his hot coffee, never taking his eyes off Claire while she got her bearings as an 'available' woman.

"Everything all right?" RJ called over to her.

"Everything's good," she replied, keeping the distance between them.

Sheesh, what was wrong with her? She wasn't sixteen anymore but a grown woman who liked what she was looking at. Really liked. So why didn't she go get it and take her chances on where she'd end up?

"Maybe you should give your boyfriend a call, wish him Merry Christmas," RJ said with a spark of irritation in his eyes, drawing a startled look from Judy who was watching their exchange. "And tell him what it is you need to tell him."

"I would, but—"

"But what?" RJ challenged her.

Well, if he didn't look so darned sexy when he was demanding, Claire might have kicked snow at him. And if he was a bit more agreeable, she might ease his misery and tell him that she didn't need to tell Brian anything. Brian had kindly done the breaking up via her mother.

"He wasn't available." She shivered in her ski jacket and shoved her hands into her pockets. A parking lot of dirty snow and curious onlookers was not the place to tell RJ what she wanted to tell him. She might have fallen for this man, but she needed to look out for herself. Claire practiced in her head what she might say to RJ. "*I'm not the alphabet dating type and those are my boundaries.*"

As if he'd read her mind and was ready to tackle the fine details, RJ dumped his coffee in the snow and shoved the paper cup into his pocket. Her heart gave a leap of excitement as he moved toward her, but he stopped after covering only half the distance.

"He wasn't available, or you're having second thoughts?" he said.

It surprised her to see the shadow of uncertainty in this confident man's eyes.

They were interrupted when a sheriff's deputy jogged over, hailing them.

"We're ready to takes statements from the four of you," said the deputy. "If it's more comfortable for everyone, we can take the trail groomer up to your cabin where we can get warmed up. This could take a few minutes and the temperature's starting to dip with this new snow front moving in."

"Can you give us five minutes?" RJ said.

The deputy checked his wristwatch. "Wish I could. But I've got to finish up here and get home ASAP. Don't want to get snowed in at the station. My girl's waiting for me."

Earl and Judy ended up between RJ and Claire as the four followed the deputy across the snowy parking lot to their transportation.

Judy held Earl's hand as they walked. She looked curiously from RJ to Claire then spoke in a low voice so that only Claire could hear, "Are you two doing okay?"

Claire knew that Judy had heard RJ's sarcastic mention of a boyfriend. As for her and RJ's relationship status, it was far too soon to be even calling it a relationship. Judy waited in concern for an answer.

"RJ and I are not a couple," she told Judy. "It's a long story, but we did not intend to be up here together. At least I didn't plan it that way."

"Oh," Judy said, before a humorous grin spread across her face. "Well, that's how a lot of things get started. You may not have intended to, but there are other forces at work when it comes to what brings a man and a woman together." They were now several steps ahead of the men and had arrived at their transportation. Judy looked back toward the men. "Speaking of forces, RJ's certainly anxious to clear the area and get you alone."

At the cabin, the deputy worked efficiently taking their statements. Judy offered to make a pot of coffee.

Between the deputy's careful attention to his handwriting and the slow drip of the coffee maker, RJ paced back and forth on the hardwood floor.

The group had left their jackets on due to the chill in the cabin. Claire stood next to the baseboard heater that hummed as it worked to warm the area.

"Okay, that about wraps it up." The deputy pocketed his pen and shook each one of their hands.

RJ didn't close the door after the deputy but instead held it open for Earl and Judy who were sipping at their coffee. It was Judy who took the hint. She took the coffee mug out of Earl's hands. "Let's leave these two alone. Besides, we have presents to open."

"It's okay, there's no rush," said Claire, torn between wanting to be alone with RJ and not. The long night and the last few hours had taken a toll on her. She was tired and hungry and she couldn't think clearly. Had RJ said last night that he didn't want to kiss her if there was a chance she couldn't break up with Brian, or had he said that it had been a long time since he'd kissed another man's woman?

RJ closed the door and threw home the dead bolt. "God, it's about damn time." He turned immediately to face her. "In about two seconds I'm either going to grab my gear and go home or come over there and kiss you. It will all depend on what you're not telling me." His shoulders dropped a little. "Come on, Claire, put me out of my misery."

"Brian broke up with me and I don't want to just be a distraction for you," she said it all in one breath.

He didn't move for a moment. Then he closed the space between them with the most purposeful look upon his face. She backed up until her rear bumped against the kitchen counter. RJ placed his hands on her hips and stood so close that there was no room for uncertainty. It only seemed natural to stand on tiptoe as he slowly lowered his head to kiss her. A kiss long and slow as the snow began to fall.

Her blood surged as her heart pounded in her chest. By the time he lifted his head they were both breathless. "You'll be a distraction, all right." He tugged on the zipper of her ski jacket. "You'll be a distraction every damn day."

She smiled as he slid his hands inside her jacket. "Is that a good thing?"

"Oh, yeah," said RJ, lifting her onto the counter. "That's a very good thing."

ABOUT THE AUTHOR

Photo by Rachel Whitney

Award winning writer **CARMINE VALENTINE** resides in Washington State. When not working her day job, she's writing romantic suspense and paranormal. She's also an online student with Arizona State University, having returned to school after twenty-some years to finally complete her Bachelor's degree.

This is her second short story published with Cajunflair Publishing. You can find her short romantic suspense called "The Last Blind Date" in Book 3 of the Seasons of Love series, SWEET SUMMERTIME LOVE.
Please visit her website at
www.carminevalentine.com to keep abreast of what's coming next.

Coming Soon:
WINTER OF THE VAMPIRE (Paranormal Romance)
KILLER REGRETS: (Romantic Suspense)

DEDICATION

For my siblings Sue, Greg, Dee, Nola, Robin and Hilary.

Thank you for all your encouragement and the kick in the pants when I needed it. Please keep kicking and the books will keep coming. I love you.